BLOODS AND CRYPTS

Once again, America is under siege. A devastating terrorist attack has destroyed one of the nation's most treasured landmarks. With Mt. Rushmore now reduced to a pile of rubble, Major Josiah Key, commander of the secretive Cerberus Unit, is dispatched to hunt down the mastermind responsible: the most fanatically evil extremist the world has ever known. And he's hidden in the most isolate region of the Hindu Kush mountains of Afghanistan.

Climbing to the fiend's remote, mysterious caves, the four-person Cerberus team encounters bloodless corpses that lead them to confront one of the greatest evils in human history: *the Vetela*...unholy creatures who inhabit the bodies of the dead and the source of all vampire legends. Their sole purpose is to guard the terrorist, and with his help, the Vetela, are finally ready to come into the light and lay waste to all humanity.

Blood Demons

A Team Cerberus Thriller

Richard Jeffries

LYRICAL UNDERGROUND
Kensington Publishing Corp.
www.kensingtonbooks.com

Prologue

Craven knew his master was serious. He knew it in the most abhorrent way conceivable.

Craven had moved to Veranesi to become an acolyte, and had been serving the master for years. He had become this slum's *taaboot* in order to best perform this function. When someone died in this warren of fetid stones, it was Craven who came to take the corpse away—often leaving the site filthier than when he entered.

In truth, he could have only become a "caretaker of corpses" in these bowels of the village, since the rest of Veranesi would not have allowed him anywhere near their deceased. Veranesi was a place that studied, embraced, and even venerated death, and anyone who did not have to beg Craven's services prayed he did not exist.

His name was not Craven, but he did not remember, or even know, his birth name. Craven was his death name—the name his mother gave him as she died of dysentery in his arms, telling him feverish stories of his past and future lives on the Night of Demons.

Craven could not remember how old he had been then. He might have just become a teenager, but he doubted it. He could only judge by his memories of being strong enough to hold his mother on a muddy bank of the Ganges, keeping her torso above the water line as she clutched and screeched at him.

He could have been as young as five, he decided, since, by then, his mother was little more than a skeleton covered in parched, paper-thin flesh. As she contorted and writhed in his spasming arms—pumping blood, mucous, water, and feces into the blessedly dirty river from her submerged lower half—she vomited out her hysterical demands and dire warnings.

His father was *Mahasona*, she swore—the most feared demon, the one whose very name meant vileness.

"That is your fate, that is your destiny, that is your calling," she babbled at him. "You cannot escape it, you cannot avoid it, you cannot deny it."

When she had finally become very quiet, still clutching at him with claws that seemed sculpted by the gods upon him, he simply loosened his muscles until the Ganges's mighty current pulled her away. The scratches her broken nails left in his flesh festered for what seemed like months.

The woman had been right. For a pitifully short time, Craven had tried to find a way out of his doom, but each time it seemed as if he might make a human connection, the internal and external disease his parents had infected him with made him a source of revulsion at best, shame at worst. All too soon, he embraced his fate and went in search of his father.

To his surprise, and then quickly his fear, it did not take long. In the cramped recesses of every town and village he was forced to hide in, the name of the "Great Demon" could be heard. To Craven's addled mind, it was as if he was following whispers that floated in the fusty air like stinging nettles.

By the time he had reached Veranesi, their meeting seemed preordained. Even before then, Craven accepted that he was seeking his master, not his father. And his master was the first man he set eyes upon once he stepped onto the stones of the rocky graveyard on the outskirts of the city. As the legends said, his master was a fierce giant with the head of a bear and the eyes of a tiger. From deep within his cowled robe, Craven heard him say but a single instruction.

"Serve me well."

Then he walked away, deep into Veranesi, bringing the souls, skins, and skulls of his victims behind him like the folds of a draping cape.

Every year since then, Craven brought his master an offering on the Night of the Demon. At first it was the freshest corpse he had collected. Initially, he had tried sneaking into the hovels of the recently deceased and stealing the bodies, but the family members who caught him—rather than have him beaten or arrested—had begged him to complete his task, with their repulsed consent.

Eventually, emboldened by his master's acceptance of his offerings, Craven dared make one request: "Free me."

It seemed as if his master ignored him, but Craven knew he did not. Each year, on the Night of the Demon, he gave his offering and made his request. But, as the years wore on, his master grew bored.

"Fresher, stronger, younger," Craven had heard him say. Or maybe he heard the master *think* it—he was never sure.

Soon, Craven began experimenting in preservation, trying to keep the youngest bodies fresher longer, littering his abattoir with his experiments in different stages of decomposition.

The results satisfied his master for a time—too short a time—but then the demand for more potent offerings returned.

As horrified as the other slum-dwellers were, none dared approach Craven. Yet none rebuffed him when he appeared to take their deceased from them. Eventually, however, a young doctor dared visit, emboldened by the whispers that had reached him. Other doctors came later, amazed at the tales told by the first man.

All seemed impressed by Craven's skills, if not his appearance and rancid odor. There were no complaints about his demeanor, however. In stories told around café tables, Craven's manners were always described as unfailingly humble, soft-spoke, and polite. Soon, the doctors, too, were giving the man tasks they found too distasteful to complete.

So that year, on the Night of the Demon, Craven had brought his master a fresh fetus, taken from the corpse of a pregnant girl. For the first time his master had met his eyes, and, self-aware of his own accomplishment, Craven had taken that moment to elucidate his traditional request.

"Free me of my pain."

His master had not answered in thoughts or spoken words, but his eyes had glimmered with understanding, and his expression had set in acknowledgement.

That had been the year before this, and, as the seasons had passed, and the Night of the Demon had approached, Craven felt as if he were about to be truly born. He had no idea what year it was, or how old that made him. He knew from how the heat and rain was diminishing that the time was coming. Then, he knew from the full moon that it was the very night.

He stood in his worn, permanently stained, robes. His feet, as always, were unshod. He took a thin canvas sack and pulled it over his shoulder, its contents across his dark, sinewy back. He didn't bother looking around the long, thin, narrow, stone room that had seemingly been constructed around him by necessity—straw mats in one corner, stone tables in another, drains in the dirt floor that emptied fluid into the Ganges, and discolored buckets of steel and wood everywhere.

One way or another he knew he would not return to it.

When he stepped into the night, he did not see his neighbors, and they struggled not to see him. That was especially true on the Night of the

Demon, when forgotten souls are remembered and charity is done though prayer. Those who were not hiding would be at Mass or doing vigilance at family graves.

Craven trudged a path that was not well-worn, but one he knew well. It was a path that stank of offal, flowers, muslin, silk, and ivory. It was a trudge through excrement, food scraps, and rubbish. But the aromas and obstructions grew few and then gave way to nature. It took him out of the residences and into the hills.

At a place where three paths met he came to a mass of seemingly impassable rocks, but, as he had many times before, found a place that left just enough room for a human to twist themselves through a fissure. Inside was another path that seemed to grow in length and height as he stepped. There was a pulsating glow from around a corner that led him, as it always had.

As Craven stepped around the outcropping, his master's inner sanctum lay before him. The foul scent came first, long before he laid eyes on the place. In the triangular-shaped space, the walls were etched with images of an elephant, deer, goat, horse, and sheep. His master sat amid them, on a throne of stone, eating pig flesh and drinking buffalo blood with red hands painted upon his own hands, and red eyes painted above his own eyes.

He sat behind a bonfire that made the shadows of his inner circle dance. But Craven could only see the shadows. The inner circle was veiled from his still-human eyes. The only other human he could actually perceive was his master's companion for the evening.

Each year, there had been another—always the most vital, always the most lovely—stretched out at his feet, as if in a living coma. Craven was certain that others also presented his master an offering on this night—an offering that was far out of his ability to attain.

But this year, even Craven paused, his pained eyes widening in acknowledgement. The dark-haired girl who was curled between his master's feet and the fire was the most beautiful he had ever seen—as if her face, shape, and even her essence had been fashioned from his innermost desires.

"Yes."

Craven could not tell whether his master's voice appeared in his ear or in his mind. It made no difference. By causing him to form it, Craven may have cursed himself to many more years of abject servitude. He quickly and expressionlessly laid his burden down on the other side of the fire and pulled the sack from around it with no hesitation.

A thin, young, dead girl was revealed. A thin, young, dead, pregnant girl.

His master lurched in the seat, one hand reaching for her, but then he froze, his expression changing. It was not distaste, but it was clearly a memory of a flavor he had tasted from Craven's previous offerings.

"Fresh," Craven said softly. "No preservatives."

His master's eyes locked on his for the second time. "Tonight?"

Craven nodded. "Tonight," he echoed. "Her blood may still be—" But, by the time he said it, his master was already on his offering.

Craven looked away. He always had when his master fed, and since his master had never corrected him, he didn't dare change, no matter how impressive the offering. As he waited, however, he did dare something. He dared to dream.

He, and certainly his master, knew that he could hardly do better than this. Yes, he could bring live offerings, but his would never compare to those of the others, simply by nature of his environment. Certainly he could take younger and richer prey, and, while their terror might make them more exciting to his master, they also both knew that sort of prize would not be long in coming. As long as Craven remained in the bowels, any authority might look the other way. But once he set foot above his station, he risked exposure to everyone. And exposure was the one thing his master would not tolerate.

But now, tonight, his master might contemplate finally fulfilling his request. Tonight would be the perfect time, when Craven was certain all the circle knew that this was his crowning offering. From here it would only be repetition, or attempts to recapture previous tastes.

So Craven waited for acknowledgement, even long after the sounds of feeding had diminished—sounds that, to Craven's ears, included both the carrier and her unborn passenger. He waited, hoping and daring, until all that remained was the crackling of the fire and the moaning of the wind.

Finally he dared to look back toward the flames. He looked just in time to see his master feeding on his offering's bowels.

His mother's words returned to him. *Watch! Watch, for when they devour the still living offal, they devour the life essence!*

His master had never done that before—not in front of him. Now was truly the time to dare more than dream.

"Master, please," Craven pleaded in agony. "Fulfill my request. Fulfill it now!"

Craven found that his eyes had closed in supplication. When he opened them again, he was alone with a dying fire.

Craven did not know anything else until he found himself standing by the roaring Ganges, directly above the spot where his mother had died.

Here, the fifteen-hundred-mile-long river seemed to boil with its own angry life, like the pulsating back of a serpent coiling to strike. As he looked into the broiling current, it seemed to form the face of his mother—both mocking and entreating him.

He took a step to join her but stopped when he heard another voice in his mind's ear. A deep, soft, soothing, female voice—one that was nothing like his mother's, even before the disease gripped her.

"What did you want?"

Craven turned to see his master's companion—the one who had lain at his feet—standing a yard away from him. She wore a thin robe, belted at her waist—a robe that revealed both her shapely legs and astonishing cleavage.

"From your master," she continued as if the roar of the river were nonexistent. "What did you want?"

All he could do was stare. Her beauty was cathartic, even hormonal.

She smiled, making him feel even weaker. "Do you think I am a dream?" she asked. "Do you think all of this is a dream?" She motioned gracefully at the surroundings. "Do you think it has all been a dream since the moment you became aware?"

When she glanced away, it gave him the power to answer, despite the gasping weakness of his reply. "A nightmare."

Her smile widened and became more believable. "For you, I'm sure it was." She lowered, and shook, her head demurely. "But I can assure you it is not." When she raised her head again, her eyes locked on his. "When your master was beheaded eons ago, a deity took pity on him, for he was once a proud warrior. The deity quickly replaced it with the first head that could be found." She shrugged sadly. "But what do gods know, or care, of mortals? The result was grotesque, and people became ill and terrified at the sight. So he took refuge in graveyards—"

"Like me," Craven realized.

The woman's smile became tender and knowing. "Like you. So tell me. You have told him, so now tell me. What is it you want?"

Craven was not intimidated by her question. In fact, quite the opposite. He suddenly felt superior to her. *She must be Tajabana,* he realized. *Freshly made. Her awakening hunger must be enormous.* It had to be the only reason she would dally with him.

"Power," he answered, perhaps being truthful for the first time in his life. But not insightful.

She laughed. Although he reacted at first as if she were mocking him, he immediately realized that her laughter was honest.

"Oh, my dear fellow," she said sympathetically as she took her first step toward him. "You'll have to do better than that. Now really, what is it that you truly want?"

"Power," he repeated as her lovely, elegant hand reached for his scalp. "Over innocence."

The forefinger of her other hand caressed his cheek, turning his face from hers. "That's better," she assured him, her fragrant breath making his flesh crawl. "Although I cannot guarantee you that, there's one thing I can do—"

He was tempted to inquire further, but then her tongue was at the back of his head, at the exact spot where his skull met his spine. Then, there, on the banks of the Ganges River where his mother had died, Craven was set free.

Chapter 1

Mount Rushmore National Memorial Superintendent Bernard Gensler would never forget the little girl's face.

Normally he'd never remember it. He had seen so many faces, every day, since taking the job to manage the Black Hills of South Dakota tourist attraction—in fact, around three million faces a year. But it was the strangest thing. As this blond girl, who he judged to be about three years old, made her way through the crowds, flanked by her mother and father, no one seemed to notice her.

Instead, if anyone looked down from the awe-inspiring sight of the presidential faces carved into the mountain above them, their eyes seemed to glance off the twelve-ounce orange juice carton she held in both hands in front of her as if she were a flower girl at a citrus wedding. They seemed to focus on that, and not see the angelic face behind it at all.

But Gensler's eyes had become sharper in the eight months since he took over the job. His gaze now almost always went to any weak link in a pattern of movement. And while there were always many children at the park, even now when the weather was getting cooler, most were in strollers or their parents' arms. This little blond child was walking steadily and serenely, the juice carton like a shield.

Gensler fought the urge to approach the trio, because he also had learned it was never wise to make suggestions to parents on how to treat their offspring. That was one of the reasons he had gotten the job in the first place. The previous superintendent had always erred on the side of overcaution, until the pile of complaint emails and letters had toppled over onto her.

Instead, he paused in his own walk to study the trio's progress. Other sightseers seemed to flow around them, like drops of oil in water. Fairly certain that there were no impending collisions for the moment, Gensler's gaze shifted back to the child's beatific face.

It truly was amazing, as if fashioned from every movie, painting, cartoon, and picture he had ever admired. It was so striking and serene that it was only after he managed to move on that he realized he had not even bothered to look at her parents' faces. At the time, he had shrugged. It wasn't as if he didn't have things to do.

He was proud of the changes he had made that allowed this child to fully enjoy the stirring, even awe-inspiring, attraction he was now responsible for—from the Memorial Grounds, Information Center, Visitor Center, Sculptor's Studio, Evening Lighting Ceremony Amphitheater, and Rushmore Plaza Civic Center to the paths, trails, restrooms, parking spaces, exhibits, and even scenic roads that all came under the aegis of the National Park Service. He may not have been serving the Marine Corps in an official capacity any longer, but he was honored to be a part of the Department of the Interior—no matter how his old "few and proud" buddies kidded him about the "step down."

Gensler continued his unofficial rounds along the Avenue of Flags Walkway, as ever enjoying the fifty-six flags that represented the fifty states, one district, three territories, and two commonwealths of the United States—arranged in alphabetical order with the As near the concession building and the Ws near the Visitor Center and Museum. And they all seemed to be waving at the beautiful, grand sculptures of George Washington, Thomas Jefferson, Theodore Roosevelt, and Abraham Lincoln that artist Gutzon Borglum had begun in 1927, and his son Lincoln Borglum had finished in 1941.

Gensler truly enjoyed taking the long way 'round to the park café, rather than huddling in his office. To be among the people he had done this all for was his best reward. After 2001 and the World Trade Center attack, the security had tightened like disapproving lips all over the country. But here they focused on improving public buildings and viewing area safety rather than restricting access to the mountain itself.

But that wasn't as bad as the overreaction in 2009, when a group of Greenpeace protestors had managed to make it to the top of the presidential heads to drape an anti-global-warming banner there. Following that was years of limiting access and clamping down on the circulation of images of the top. National Park Service officials believed distribution of these images constituted an unjustifiable security threat.

Even then Gensler had come across the report from the U.S. Government Accountability Office that read "preventing individuals seeking to climb to the top of the monument for nefarious purposes is difficult." But he had found that the real problem was the lack of funds needed to man those surveillance feeds and police the summit.

The superintendents before him had struggled to balance the visitors' freedom with park security, but they had neglected to incorporate the human factor. Upon his hiring, he almost immediately realized the key was using their limited funds to their best advantage, as well as steward training.

These forest rangers were more comfortable with trees than they were with other people and had to have an attitude adjustment to change their preconceptions about "the annoying interlopers." Once he made it clear that every visitor should be treated like a possible nature lover, and led by example, the mood slowly but steadily changed.

They all worked to make any visit so enjoyable that few seemed to notice Gensler's steps to make sure the presidential sculptures themselves were well and truly off-limits. Nobody could get up there, but he did everything in his power to make sure they didn't even think about wanting to.

Gensler breathed deeply of the fresh, crisp, autumn air. They were in the weather sweet spot where the southern Chinook winds took on cold Canada air trying to permeate the area, leaving them in a pocket of peace. As he straightened at the crest of his breath, he unavoidably glanced upward. His eyes, sharpened by years of training, narrowed. His brain, sharpened by the same training, slammed down the sudden panic that filled it.

There were three specks in his vision, where they couldn't be, moving along the crest between the stone coiffures of Teddy Roosevelt and Abraham Lincoln. Two black specks and one blond one.

Not possible, Bernard Gensler thought. He blinked, praying they were shadows of soaring birds or clouds. But when he looked again, they were still there, and still moving—getting ever closer to the edge of the precipice.

Not possible. They couldn't get up there. There was no way they could've gotten past security.

Gensler's arms moved while his gaze didn't falter. Up came both his hands—in one his smartphone, in the other the Sunagor Super Zoom Compact Binoculars he always kept in his jacket pocket. Without looking, he thumbed the universal code on the cellphone's digital buttons, linking him with every ranger and staff member, and stuck it against his ear.

"Code green," he said quietly. "S, l, x, t and a." As he was giving the message meaning "scalp-line between Teddy Roosevelt and Abe Lincoln," he brought the most powerful compact, zoom binoculars available to his eyes as calmly as he could.

"Not possible," he heard someone gasp from the monitor room.

Not possible, Gensler heard echoed in his own mind as he thumbed the Sunagor up to its full hundred and ten times magnification. It was as he feared. Somehow, it was the little girl he had fixated on, or her twin. But even if she were a twin, the people who had flanked her before were flanking her now.

But his fear was not just because they had somehow gotten past all the security measures, but because he knew there was no conceivable way they could have gotten up there that fast—not unless they were all, somehow, twins. Another blond twin who was still holding a twin juice carton in front of her like an offering to the gods.

Above the buzzing in his head and the ambient sounds from the tourists all around him, Gensler became aware of other voices in his ear. Babbling coming from ranger stations all around the back and top of the mountain stridently maintaining that they had seen nothing and no one had passed, mingling with desperate questions and even accusations.

"R.S.," he said strongly as he watched the three figures stop at the lip of the cliff. *Radio silence.* It was an antiquated code, but still effective. "Move," he ordered the rangers nearest the spot. "Secure, safeguard." Those were meant for both the location and the trio.

All the while, he never took his eyes off the three specks. His breath caught in his throat as the blond girl seemed to lurch forward, but he breathed again when the man beside her suddenly gripped her shoulder. He watched as the man and woman leaned down. The girl looked up at them.

"What are they doing?" Gensler may have whispered. *Are they talking? What are they talking about?* "Move, move, move!" he snapped, the word becoming more urgent with each repetition.

As he did so, he started becoming aware of nearby tourist voices also becoming more urgent and strident. Others had binoculars too.

Gensler's head craned forward on his neck, desperately hoping that somehow might help. But as he did, the three atop the monument stopped talking, the girl turned back to face him, and the adults flanking her each gripped her elbows and ankles.

"No," the superintendent said, the word seemingly torn from him by talons. But his building dread prevented nothing. The two adults swung the girl back and forth as if they were aerialists about to launch their youngest member to the top of a circus tent.

"No," Gensler breathed with each swing. "No!"

As two park rangers appeared at the far side of both Washington's and Lincoln's heads, the two adults hurled the little girl off the cliff. Gensler watched as she swung out in a huge, diving arc, holding the juice carton out over her head.

He didn't even stop watching when a loud explosion—it sounded like a firecracker in a metal trash can—engulfed the carton and her. Everything after that seemed to be moving in extremely slow motion. The shock wave blew off massive, ugly chunks of Roosevelt and Lincoln—noses, slabs of Lincoln's beard, Roosevelt's cheek—while scarring the chins and mouths of Jefferson and Washington. The sound of the blast and the crack of the monument took a few moments to reach the onlookers, but after that the crumbling roar was constant. The biggest pieces struck outcroppings on the faces and on the mountainside itself, shattering the stone into smaller chunks, like an obscene asteroid entering Earth's atmosphere and shedding its rocky skin. More facial curves and details were ripped away, smaller fragments that were no longer identifiable as other than what they were: ancient granite and metamorphic rock. The *crack-crack-snap* of each strike announced new destruction that was obscured by the dust cloud, but invoked horrible ruin that no one wanted to see—yet could not turn from. The dust set up a haze in the air that was constantly thickening and expanding, like smoke blown slowly from a monster cigar. The pasty, off-white fog was like a scrim to mute the pain of the vignette being played out behind it.

But it didn't. It couldn't. Nothing could. And the distant sounds couldn't blot the nearby screams and shrieks and guttural roars and swearing and orders to *run, run, move!* that everyone seemed to be shouting at everyone else.

It was the longest and yet most viciously scarring few seconds Gensler could remember having lived through.

* * * *

"They threw her because she wouldn't have done as much damage if she had merely jumped," Bernard Gensler muttered.

"What?"

Gensler looked up as the harried, incredulous Pennington County sheriff tried to encompass all the activity of the Mount Rushmore security office, while local police, Highway Patrol, Park Police, rangers, emergency medical personnel, and even officers from the local Air Force base struggled to proceed.

"Nothing," Gensler told the sheriff. "Just trying to collect my thoughts. Christ, I'm just trying to *think* thoughts."

The minutes following the attack were chaos, as tourists screamed and ran in fear of further explosions. Thankfully there were none, and there was protocol to follow, which Gensler had his staff practice monthly. But others had protocol to follow as well, and the park was locked down within the half hour—state police interviewing every visitor while those injured in the panic were tended to.

CIA and FBI agents were on their way, but Larry Michaels from the National Security Agency's Q Directorate was already on scene. When Gensler had asked how he had arrived so quickly, he admitted to being on vacation with his family.

"Yeah, you'll have to have your thoughts collected," Michaels said. "These monsters not only used a child to carry a bomb but they stained this—what did Franklin Roosevelt call it?"

"The Shrine of Democracy," Gensler reminded him. "When he officially opened it." The man must've paid some attention during his vacationing tour.

"Yeah," Michaels drawled, trying, like everyone else, to get his head around it. "The same year the Second World War started, right?"

Gensler nodded absently.

"Well...no matter what your thoughts, you'll probably get shit-canned for this."

Gensler looked at the NSA man sharply, but his words belied his angry gaze. "I probably *should* get shit-canned for this," the former Marine snapped. "My watch, my fault."

"Bernie," Pamela Chinoa interrupted. She had been the one on duty at the surveillance screens when it happened. She had been the one who gasped. "We checked and rechecked the footage from every possible approach. No one got by. No one even appeared."

Gensler couldn't disagree. He had pored over the footage himself, as many times as he could once he felt certain his staff had the turmoil under control. "But still somehow they got up there," he said bitterly. "And two are still missing while two of our own are still dead."

Chinoa's mouth shut and grew tight, her eyes watering. The two rangers who had appeared at the last second were the victims, their fronts torn apart—seemingly from the explosion's shrapnel.

"How could they have gotten up there?" Gensler seethed. "Why weren't they killed by the explosion too? Worse, how could they get out again?"

"Worse?" Michaels snorted. "How is that worse?"

"Because," Gensler snarled at him, "this time we were on alert."

Michaels shrugged and sniffed. "They must've slipped out in the panic."
"We were locked down," Gensler said almost to himself. "No one was getting in, yet they somehow got out. And no one saw them either way."
"We sure as hell saw what they did," Michaels said, looking at his cellphone screen. "The visitors might not be able to get to their cars yet, but even with the Wi-Fi shut down, tourists' videos of the explosion are already all over the net."

Gensler looked up abruptly. If there was enough coverage that videos could get out, any call he needed to make might go out as well. It might be picked up by any manner of surveillance device, but that didn't bother the former Marine in the slightest.

"Pam," he said, all but snapping to attention, "I'll be in my office. Let me know if anyone needs me."

"Yes, sir," she said, but he was already on his way out of the security room, his thumb dancing on his phone screen.

As he strode down the hall, surveying the activity outside, he felt a swell of pride mingling with his misery. His staff and the local authorities were working together at prime efficiency. Something terrible, inexplicably terrible, had happened, but the response was more than he could have hoped, or asked, for. He prayed that it continued.

A good sign was that the person he was calling answered on the first ring.
"Chuck," Gensler said. "You've heard?"
"I've heard," retired General Charles Leonidas Lancaster replied. Unbeknownst to Gensler, he was replying from Tashkurgan, Kashgar, Xinjiang, China. "I'm watching the video now."

"Chuck," Gensler continued with immediate confidence born of long experience. "I've checked our surveillance footage closely and I can't tell if it was the juice carton or not."

Lancaster paused a microsecond longer than normal. "Well," he said evenly, "if the explosive wasn't in the juice carton—"

Gensler interrupted. "Didn't you tell me about a report you read where a soldier swore his superior officer wasn't shot, but exploded from the inside? It was in Syria, I think."

"Yemen," Lancaster corrected. "Yes, I did. And I know just the man to talk to about it."

"Good," Gensler replied, feeling more hopeful than he had since setting eyes on the angelic blond girl.

"I'll need a full report, Bernie."
"You'll get it," Gensler promised. "NSA be damned, you'll get it. But one more thing for now, before this place is overrun—"

"What?" Lancaster asked quickly, knowing how these things went. "Chuck," his fellow former Marine said, his voice tight and unbelieving. "There was no blood. A little girl blew up from the inside, and I saw flesh and bone, and even muscle, but no blood. I may be going mad, but I tell you. To my dying day, I'll swear on a tall stack on Bibles. There was no blood."

Chapter 2

Josiah Key learned all he needed to know about Sujanpur, Punjab, India, one smoggy afternoon. It was the afternoon when no one seemed surprised to see a naked man run through their festival market carrying a child's corpse.

The former Marine corporal had come to this village after being assigned to investigate reports of bloodless bodies. He and his Cerberus team had been following the rumors all along the India/Pakistan border—from Attari to Amritsar to Dera Baba Nanak, then finally, to this smallest, humblest, most northern town, which was also closest to the border.

The problem was that they just kept missing the corpses because all the previous cities were quick to get rid of their dead. It wasn't like Attari, which was the last Indian stop on the Trans-Asian Railway, or Amritsar, the spiritual center of the Sikh religion, or Dera Baba Nanak, which was one of the most sacred Sikh centers, would let any corpse, bloodless or blood-full, gather dust.

By the time Key and his team arrived, the possible evidence had already been cremated. India hardly had time, or room, for the living, let alone the dead. But the mortician at the last stop shared, as all the previous ones had, word of another such body. Thankfully, like many morticians everywhere, the ones in India prided themselves on their English proficiency.

Not surprisingly, a bloodless corpse was quite the conversation starter, especially among dealers in dead bodies. And the chance to talk to living people who weren't grieving was also something that loosened tongues, especially when the ones not-grieving were a placid, handsome man; his tall, muscular associate; and a lithe, green-eyed, redheaded young woman—all wearing slightly shimmering, thin, light, gray T-shirts, slacks, loafers, and open, zip-up jackets.

"You're in luck with this one," the Dera Baba Nanak mortician had said, obviously having a different standard for "luck" than the average citizen. "My Sujanpur colleague says it is a child's corpse."

"Not so lucky for the kid," Morton Daniels—Key's tall, muscular, shameless right-hand man—commented.

"No, no," said the mortician. "Traditionally all Hindus are cremated, except saints and children. The body should be washed in a mixture of milk, yogurt, butter, and honey while mantras are being—"

The team didn't hear the rest since they were already out the door and into the Ford Ecosport Ecoboost—the fastest sport-utility vehicle they could readily find in India. Terri Nichols, Key's lithe, redheaded, right-hand woman, had floored it and made the sixty-nine kilometers in record time, despite the habitual traffic on these Punjab roads. The vehicle's interactive map showed her exactly where the small local constabulary was, but they all studied the area as they neared.

It was a humble, unimpressive town that seemed to be stuck between the 1950s and 1970s, wedged between canals of the Ravi River. The air was heavy with moisture, with the colors of green and brown seemingly coated on everything from wood to marble to metal. Off in the distance they heard calliope music and saw what looked like cheap Christmas lights.

"Place is supposed to have a big garment market," Nichols murmured, having let the Ecosport's onboard computer feed her information along the way. "Probably means most townies are good with English too."

She, like Key, had wanted to get familiar with the local language, until they both quickly discovered that India had more than a hundred major languages, as well as nearly sixteen hundred minor ones.

Nichols pulled in front of the small police department, and Key and Daniels were out the door almost before she had stopped the vehicle. But they all reached the front desk at the same time.

The cooperative constable on duty, who was, indeed, conversant in English, directed them to a cement hut out back, where unclaimed, unidentified corpses were stored. All it took was one look at Key's impressive International Crime Investigation Department ID. It was so much more effective than any explanation Key could give about the Cerberus organization he ostensibly worked for. No matter how he tried to describe that, even to himself, it hardly sounded credible.

So, although the Sujanpur constable on duty had no way of knowing it, the Cerberus team's support unit had made sure the hunters were supplied with effective identification cards, and even badges, tailored to whatever location they were sent. Meanwhile, unbeknownst to the Cerberus support unit, *CID* was the name of India's most popular, longest-running TV series, with more than a thousand episodes to its credit—all of which had been seen by the Sujanpur constable on duty.

"Lucky for us there's only a couple of thousand people in this backwater," Nichols murmured as they walked out the rear door of the small station, crossed the worn, muddy, rectangular yard, and stepped into the bunker that housed the bodies.

"We spend way too much time in morgues," Daniels complained as they all surveyed the depressing enclosure. "Look familiar, Joe?"

There was a low, dirty ceiling with two strips of yellowing, flickering fluorescent lights, two stained metal tables with rusting legs, and a meat locker on the far wall. Naturally Key couldn't help but recall a similar one in Thumrait, Oman, where they had first seen the devastating effects of their previous, prehistoric, adversaries.

"What, we're supposed to just rummage around until we find the girl?" Nichols asked, staying close to the entrance.

"Better that than to have a suspicious chaperone," Key reminded her.

"Aw, just take a look." Daniels grinned as he ambled toward the meat locker's freezer door. "Smaller than a woman, bigger than a baby, not breathing—you can't miss her."

"Shut up, Morty," Key sighed as he moved beside Daniels.

"Okay," the big man snorted as he pulled open the heavy vault door. "Say we got here in time. Say the kid is in here and actually bloodless. So what? What are we looking for?"

"I think it's one of those 'we'll know it when we see it,' right?" Nichols offered from the door.

Key nodded, stepping into the meat locker. "First things first," he quoted his father as he surveyed the wooden shelves along the freezer walls. "We claim the body and bring it to Professor Rahal."

There were two body bags on one side and a naked man on the other. Key stepped toward the smaller of the body bags as Daniels eyed the unclad man across the aisle.

"Fresh meat," he said drily, then joined Key as the former corporal unzipped the smaller bag.

He looked down into the face of an angelic child who couldn't have been more than three years old when she died. He then nearly twitched when a voice popped into his ear.

"I guess they all look like that when they're at peace," he heard Nichols say gently before looking over his shoulder to see her at his side. The men had known the young lady long enough not to be surprised by her enhanced reflexes anymore. Not after what she, and they, had been through. But they were, constantly.

By then Daniels had checked the other bag, making sure it wasn't also a child. "Okay," he said. "We just take it and take off, or are we stopping to check with Barney Fife first?"

That was as far as the former sergeant got when the naked man suddenly appeared, grabbed the child, and ran.

To the agents' amazement and annoyance, the man had done it so quickly, powerfully, and silently that even Nichols was taken by surprise. Daniels was so startled he didn't even blurt profanity. They froze an unwanted moment, each chastising themselves in their own way, then took off after him.

Nichols was first out of the bunker, and probably would have been even if her reflexes hadn't been heightened by an *Idmonarchne Brasieri* infection and Professor Rahal's subsequent treatment. Daniels was next, just by dint of his size taking up the entire doorway as he lumbered after her. That was fine by Key, who knew it was best that he get the big picture, focusing in on what had been vague details before.

He was tempted to jump into the SUV, just to keep up with Nichols, but the first thing he realized was that the streets were too narrow and haphazard to make the Ecosport any advantage. The second thing he noted was how fast the naked man was going. He had looked every inch a corpse—haggard, emaciated, aged—but now he was running like a teenage shoplifter. Thankfully Nichols was going after him like a gazelle.

Key saw that Daniels was already drifting to the west. Smart cookie: he was automatically finding another path that would narrow the naked man's escape routes. So Key moved quickly to the east, to create a trident of pursuit. The naked man was sprinting south, directly toward the calliope music and Christmas lights.

They all ran into thickening crowds. It seemed that everyone in town was at, or going to, the garment market, which was either always like this or celebrating some special festival. Either way, to the Westerners' eyes, it still seemed like a minor flea market, transient street fair, and rinky-dink traveling amusement park in some lower-middle-class suburban town.

Nichols was just steps behind the naked man when he burst into a patchy, compact fairground between tent-like booths; bent, discolored, miniature, ancient rides; and a makeshift stage from which a local band played classic catchy, danceable, Indian pop music. None of that was a problem. In fact, it effectively hemmed in the naked man. The problem was were all the young men in out-of-fashion jeans and shirts acting like it was their own personal mosh pit.

They were jumping, kicking, and thrusting their arms in the air to the live music, while the few women present were off to the sides. The latter were the ones who started reacting to both the naked man and redhead first. Their little shrieks and cries acted like a wave, catching the attention of the dancers like a pond ripple. The result was the naked man turning toward Nichols on the far side of a human circle, while the path was closed off behind the redhead by curious, concerned festival-goers.

Nichols slowed, letting her peripheral vision take in all the confused faces. But she concentrated on the man, who was now holding the corpse like a sleeping child while babbling something in Punjabi, the local dialect.

"What is he saying?" she asked no one in particular. But her sharp tone elicited a reaction from a nearby co-ed.

"He says you are a demon, a redheaded demon, who attacked his family."

Nichols didn't look away from the man as she quickly responded. "Tell them he is a child molester who stole that girl. I'm trying to stop him!"

To the co-ed's credit, she tried translating for the crowd, but the naked man was louder, and already speaking in their language. Nichols tried taking a step forward, but suddenly she was confronted by several angry, suspicious young men advancing on her. She recognized the look of distrusting amazement. She had seen it wherever redheads were not the norm—which made up most of the world.

She heard the co-ed's shrill admonitions cut off, then found out why. Daniels was right beside her, his back bent, his fists clenched, and a ravenous grin on his otherwise mirthless face.

"What's Punjabi for 'bring it on'?" he growled.

Nichols didn't want a riot, but left that to Daniels. She took another step toward the naked man, who started shoving the nearest young men in front of him, all while still babbling in despair and fear. She could see exactly what he was doing but was nearly powerless to stop him. Even with her heightened speed, she saw no way to get to him without becoming entangled in the encroaching crowd.

As Daniels looked ready to take them all on, Nichols kept her gaze locked onto the child snatcher. To her angry despair she saw him take the final step toward the fairground's north-most exit, all while looking directly back at her with a triumphant, knowing grin on his face. That's when she saw Josiah Key appear behind him.

To her regret, she let her relief and pleasure infuse her own face, alerting the man. He ducked, crouched, and scrambled like a wet pig, shaking off Key's hands, and started running again. Infuriated at herself, Nichols stepped before Daniels while pulling her Sig Sauer P239 from its shoulder holster. As she saw Key go after the naked man, she pointed it straight up and fired.

"Make way for the redheaded demon with a gun," she cried, and used the crowd's momentary shock to race through them.

She heard Daniels following suit, accompanied by the exclamations of a foolhardy few who tried to stop him, but by then she was already out the fairground's other side—hardly noticing that it led to a stony, root-veined, vine-covered path. If the information she had gleaned on the drive here was to be trusted, this had to be the trail to the temple fort, which stood between the town and the river.

A second later she was past Key, wishing she also had the time to take a shot at the naked man, but knowing that she couldn't risk hitting the child. Dead or not, that was why they were here, and any further damage to her might negate the whole mission. Her speed was being turbo-charged by her anger and resentment, so she no longer had time to question anything because she was on the guy.

His surprise was almost gratifying as she grabbed his neck with one hand and brought the gun butt down on his head with the other. They both went down on mossy ground in front of three stories of crumbling brickwork surrounded by leafy shade trees. Nichols mirrored the man's triumphant, knowing grin as she landed across his back, but then also mirrored his surprised expression when, rather than stay down, rendered unconscious by her blow, he rolled, twisting, and came up in a crouch, still holding the child.

Nichols was so shocked she didn't take the moment to just shoot him in the face, and then lost her chance as Daniels cannoned by her and brought his fist directly toward the naked man's nose, point-blank, with all the force he had gathered from wanting to take on an entire festival crowd.

He missed.

Daniels was stunned when he found his target was no longer directly in front of him, and was aghast when his momentum and lack of balance sent him flying forward like a hurled javelin. Nichols, who was directly behind him, was so confused by the big man's collapse that, once again, her gun remained unused.

Finally, both Westerners managed to catch sight of the naked man, who was scrambling toward the main archway, which framed the sparkling, dirty, roiling river beyond. They hadn't even started to regain their footing to continue the chase when Key stepped out from a rocky wash to block the naked man's escape.

He didn't rush the man, try to tackle him, or even shoot him. He just stepped out, far enough in front to go in any direction the man might choose, but also essentially cornering him within the small hall of the archway, since Daniels and Nichols were still blocking any retreat. Key's expression was not antagonistic in the slightest. If anything, it was curiously interested.

"We must've caught you within seconds of your entry," he said mildly. "You probably just threw your robe under the shelves and lay there, right?" Key shrugged, appreciating the naked man's blank face. "Who would have thought that whoever followed you in there would be after the same thing you were? Bad luck, yes?"

Key continued to stand still, casually surveying the man, and waited. The naked man didn't move for several seconds, but then they all saw his back curve and heard a strange animal sound. Key's eyebrows rose and his head shifted back on his neck.

"Are you snarling at me?" he asked in mock incredulity, before making a tsking noise and shaking his head sadly. "You shouldn't be growling at me. Not when you're so close to fulfilling your assignment." Key jutted his chin at the man. "Are you the only one sent to collect these corpses? Or did you go, on your own, by yourself, to clean up your mess? I mean, why else would you do it? Why not just leave well enough alone?" Key let his expression change to one of realization; then he smiled sadly and nodded with sympathetic understanding. "Or did you hear about some people"—he motioned to the strongman and redhead behind them—"who were showing interest?"

The naked man's lips came off his teeth, and the growl snapped off as both he and Key charged.

But to the surprise of all the others, Key did not leap toward the naked man. He leaped to the left of the naked man. Nichols and Daniels had hardly started to react when the big man felt disappointment that his superior had so blatantly missed the mark. The child snatcher would clearly get away, having made them all look like fools.

The naked man seemed to think that too, if his renewed expression of cunning triumph was any evidence. He all but dove past Key, his eyes filling with the hills, woods, and water beyond.

But that expression winked off like a snuffed candle when the child snapped out of his grip. The naked man stumbled a few feet down the rocky path, then twisted to see Key standing placidly behind him, holding the corpse child like a crafty cornerback who had intercepted the game-winning touchdown pass. Key waited a second until Daniels and Nichols flanked him, their guns at the ready, before commenting.

"Keep your eye on the prize, asshole," he said.

That was all he got to say before the temple fort grounds were invaded by a screeching assault team in military gear. "Down, down! Hands up, get down! Now, now!"

Key did not get down. He watched the naked man scurry off toward the river even faster than he had before, then turned to pinpoint the commanding officer of this bunch of stupid interlopers. To Daniels's surprise, Nichols's chagrin, and Key's presumption, it was the man they had known as Captain Patrick Logan.

"You have *got* to be kidding me," Key complained as he raised his hands, holding the child corpse to the sky like an offering.

Chapter 3

"Your miscalculation was you wanted to beat him, to defeat him. But we weren't there for him. We were there for his victim."

Josiah Key was talking to his right-hand people in yet another interrogation room, which looked like almost every other interrogation room anywhere in the world. Four gray walls, one gray floor, one gray ceiling, one cheap table, five cheap chairs, one door, and one one-way window taking up most of one wall.

Nichols was going to argue the miscalculation, although Daniels knew better. "But if we could have captured him," she started, "that would have helped us figure—"

"But we weren't fighting him like we were trying to capture him." Daniels sighed, already having accepted, and learned, from his mistake. "Admit it. We were fighting him like we wanted to shove his sneering teeth down his throat."

Key smiled at the growing maturity of his associate. He was even kind enough to say "we," when everyone, including Nichols, knew it really meant her.

Everyone at Cerberus had been relieved when Daniels, who was known to go after anything in skirts, pants, shorts, skorts, panties, G-strings, thongs, or anything remotely vaginal, had immediately started treating Nichols like a sister-in-arms and fellow Marine.

"I don't shit where I sleep," he once told Key when explaining how he targeted his "romantic conquests."

Nichols exhaled strongly, laid her hands flat on the table, and slowly nodded. "Yeah, I get it. You're right."

"What do I tell you?" Key grinned, pleased she had taken responsibility, but he had to make sure she wasn't just doing it as way to forget about it. "What do I *always* tell you?"

"You want to know how smart I am, not how tough I am," she said in a mild singsong, but with an honest, comprehending smile.

"It's not about how bad-ass you are," Daniels chimed in like a five-year-old reciting his alphabet. "It's about how effective you are."

"It's also not about *proving* how bad-ass you are," Key stressed. "To anyone, especially yourself!"

The door finally banged open, as Key figured it would. It was the main reason they had started the lesson in the first place. Key knew it would drive Logan crazy.

Sure enough, in walked Patrick Logan—wearing, as was his custom, a full uniform, and carrying, as was also his custom, a thick file. He seemed to always want to have it at hand in case he needed something to hide behind.

Daniels looked behind him in anticipation, but to his obvious disappointment, there was no beautiful blond Second Lieutenant Barbara Strenkofski, who had been Logan's aide when last they met. He had wanted to at least attempt a reconciliation after Daniels had left her "Mickey-Finned" in an Omani medical college break-room bunk bed—where she had successfully attempted to "romantically conquest" him.

Instead, there was a statuesque, violet-eyed brunette in a tailored uniform, sporting first lieutenant insignia. Logan looked pointedly from her to Daniels as she sat down, her notepad at the ready.

"Ah," Logan snapped as he slapped the file onto the table and settled in. "The men from Cerebral."

Key didn't take the bait. Nor did Nichols, but she did check his chest and crotch in pointed silence. Key was certain Logan had purposely used the misogynist greeting, and fairly certain he had purposely mispronounced the organization's name, but you never know. Somebody like Logan might actually think that was the name, but it made little difference to Key. He had heard every variation, from Cerebrum to Short Bus, in such a short time that he went back to simply saying he was from the CID—which actually wasn't a lie. Logan had originally made both he and Daniels CID agents back in the day, and the question whether they were still CID, or even Marines, would probably have to be unraveled by the NCIS.

Instead, Key looked placidly at the florid, ambitious officer and said, as way of greeting, "Captain."

Because they all knew Logan was far more thin-skinned than Key, they all expected the result. Logan stiffened, then sharply pointed at his uniform's insignia. "Colonel," he stiffly corrected.

"Oh, we got you a promotion, did we?" Key said like a cat toying with a mouse who was already dead. Cerberus had allowed Logan to take the credit for destroying the *Idmonarchne Brasieri*, and everyone in this room, except for maybe the buxom brunette, knew it. Getting a certain one of them to admit it, however, was a different matter.

"*I* got me the pro—!" Logan started before he realized he was acting the way he had wanted Key to act. "Never mind, *Corporal* Key. Maybe you could utilize your time to better advantage by telling me why I shouldn't let the local Punjabi authorities do to you what they are threatening to do to you."

If he was expecting Key to react in agitation, he really should have known better. It wasn't like they hadn't faced each other across much the same table in much the same room before. Key didn't even respond to the "corporal" crack since, although he had since been promoted to major, once he threw in with Cerberus he decided to leave rank behind.

"Because they know as well as you that we all have a problem that won't be solved with a hammer," Key replied calmly, then continued by giving credit where credit was due. "No matter how strong and effective that hammer may be."

Logan leaned back as if he had sprung his own mousetrap. "What we have, Corporal, is a terrorist problem, and I think that hammer you so accurately referred to will do just fine."

Key exhaled through his nostrils and couldn't help shaking his head in a "t'was ever thus" manner. He also leaned back and spread his hands to encompass the file on the table between them.

"So that's the theory you're going with?" he sighed sadly. "Terrorists who use a child as a bomb to damage property. Terrorists who can get from the base to the top of a mountain in minutes. Terrorists who survive an explosion that kills two park rangers who were farther away from the detonation than they were. Terrorists who can disappear from a lockdown even a TSA agent couldn't avoid. You really want to walk into the teeth of this that way?"

Both Daniels and Nichols wondered whether Key had used the word "teeth" knowingly. They immediately decided he had.

Logan looked as if Key had repeatedly slapped him in the face with a fish, but he also looked as if he thought of himself as a prize fish fighter. "What I want," he said tightly, "is for you and your Cerberus bozos to be as far away from this as possible, and if that means I have to lock the door of a Punjabi jail cell myself, I will."

Key stared at him until Logan was impelled to continue, through gritted teeth. "The bomb," he said, "was in the juice container."

Key couldn't keep his brows from raising a bit. Logan could guess all he wanted about what happened at Mount Rushmore, but he already knew that people exploded. They both had been on that beachfront in Yemen. They had seen it with their own eyes. He continued to just stare, waiting to see if Logan's denial was so big it might swallow him.

The newly minted colonel took the moment to look to his new aide, who handed him a sheet of paper from the file. "Would it surprise you to know that Aarif Zaman has taken responsibility for the attack?" he asked, his eyes on the paper.

Key had to think about that bombshell, but didn't need to think about it long. "Yes," he said, "and no."

That comment returned the favor to Logan's eyebrows, which also raised. "Why yes," he started to ask, "and why—"

He got no further because retired General Charles Lancaster strode in. "What took you?" Daniels blurted.

"Making sure the colonel didn't bogart our evidence," Lancaster answered without hesitation.

"Bogart?" Logan blustered. "*Your* evidence?"

"Yes, *our* evidence," Lancaster almost spat, swinging a piece of paper at Logan's face as if it were a scythe. "Officially signed and authorized. When will you get it through your thick skull that we're on the same fucking team?"

Logan grabbed the paper and read it so intently Nichols thought it might burst into flame. "When you bozos stop getting in my way," he growled.

"We will when you stop making us," Lancaster immediately retorted. "I don't have to tell you that your interference resulted in the suspect getting away, but I want you to know that makes us all wonder if you wanted it that way."

"What?" Logan exploded, vaulting to his feet. "What the— How dare— I don't have to sit here and take that!"

The colonel's tantrum didn't faze Lancaster in the least. "There's the door," he said evenly, cocking his head toward the one exit. "Don't let it hit you on the way out."

After a chaotic moment when the colonel and his aide hastily gathered up their papers, Logan all but pushed the brunette into the hall, but stopped in the opening. He turned with his mouth open but froze when he saw everyone in the room patiently waiting and staring directly at him.

"I...I..." he stammered. "I am in charge of this operation, and I will tolerate no interference."

Before anyone could reply, Logan slammed the door after himself.

Key sighed again and scratched his forehead. "Our evidence secure?"

Lancaster nodded. "And on its way to HQ."

Nichols looked from them to Daniels. "What's 'bogart'?" she asked.

The retired general laughed. "A word to give away my age."

When he said nothing further, Nichols shifted her quizzical gaze to Daniels.

"Don't look at me," the bruiser said. "I know as much as you."

Key interrupted the direction the conversation was going. "Aarif Zaman?" he asked their leader.

Lancaster grew serious and nodded. "Yes. He took full responsibility, and, in not so many words, dared us to 'catch me if you can.'" The retired general looked each of his operatives in the eye. "What do you think?"

"It's a trap," Daniels sniffed dismissively. "Zaman is one of the top a-holes in Afghanistan. By copping this sort of attitude, he's mooning everybody from one of the shit-hole's network of caves and basically saying 'come kill yourself trying to kiss my ass.'"

Key nodded approvingly at his friend before returning his attention to Lancaster. "More specifically, it's a challenge to a duel."

Lancaster found this of interest. He put one hand on his chin and cupped his elbow with the other. "Elaborate."

Key gave his superior a look that said "you know damn well," but explained anyway. "Aarif, or whoever, could have easily set the explosive off in the middle of the biggest Mount Rushmore crowd they could find. Maybe even during the daily lighting ceremony where thousands are gathered in an amphitheater made specifically for the event. But if thousands, hundreds, or even dozens of innocent American tourists had been killed, it would have been an invitation for invasion. This was a slap in the face—just showing off—a come-on that states 'look what we can do. What are you going to do about it?'"

Lancaster folded his arms and nodded. "Looks like we got ourselves a quorum," he said.

"Yeah," Key said glumly, "but the question remains, as Colonel Custer runs into an Afghan buzz-saw, what *are* we going to do about it?"

"Wait a minute, wait a minute," Nichols finally exclaimed. "What is all this about? Our orders were approved. We made no secret of our assignment. Why did Colonel Logan even bring us in here?"

"Because," Key answered her, "he wanted to know how much we knew." He took a second to look directly into the one-way mirror. "And now he thinks he does."

"Come on," Lancaster commanded. "Time's a-wasting. We got things to do."

As the retired general led the way out of the interrogation room, Key told Nichols how the last name of legendary movie tough guy Humphrey Bogart came to be known as a term for holding on to something too long. Even afterward she still wasn't sure, but Daniels promised to show her *The Maltese Falcon* before turning to Key with his own inquiry.

"Okay Joe, if you're in a question-answering mood, finally, just tell me one thing. What does Cerberus mean anyway?"

Key laughed, truly enjoying the moment because he was certain it would be the last time he honestly laughed for quite a while. "I'll tell you on the way back to HQ, Morty," he promised.

Chapter 4

"Cerberus was, and I guess still is, the multi-headed dog who guards the gates of the underworld," Key told Daniels as they stepped off just one of Lancaster's private jets. In this case, a Gulfstream G650.

"To keep angels from invading?" Daniels asked with feigned innocence.

"No," Key answered with feigned patience. "That's Judeo-Christian beliefs. This was Greek mythology."

"Oh. And this watchdog did what?"

"Kept the dead from getting out."

"So it *is* hell," Daniels stubbornly replied.

"Not really, but that's all beside the point."

"So, we're in league with the devil?" Daniels continued, glancing back to see if Lancaster had left the cockpit yet.

Key was unfazed. "Remember what the devil does for a living, Morty."

"Tempt humans to do evil?" Nichols chimed in, bringing up the rear.

Key looked back at her knowingly. "Yes, maybe, but then punishes them in hellfire forever."

"Hey," Nichols realized, "that's right."

The trio did not bother looking for a limo to take them to Cerberus HQ. They had landed on Cerberus's private runway, with their headquarters being no farther than a regulation airport terminal.

It, and they, were in Tashkurgan, Kashgar, Xinjiang, China—on the borders of Afghanistan, Tajikistan, Kyrgyzstan, and Pakistan. That was why Lancaster had chosen it. Long situated on a caravan route for the historical Silk Road, it was a market town for sheep, and therefore wool. And all went well until a disastrous decision by the founding fathers to construct one of China's burgeoning "fake" cities—exacting replicas of romantic world capitals—as a tourist and real estate investor attraction. But just like all the others dotted throughout China, the "copycat countries "—which included "duplitecture" facades of Venice, Paris, London, and even Manhattan—served as neither, and remained eerily empty. Until, in this case, Charles Lancaster appeared and made the Tashkurgan town fathers an offer they didn't refuse.

So Key led his hunters into a scaled-down replica of the Palace of Versailles, tucked between mountain ranges, sheepherders, and carpet weavers. They stepped into the famed Hall of Mirrors, which looked to have the same walls, floors, and design as the original, but without the statuary, furniture, chandeliers, and decorations. But it was far from empty. The tools of Cerberus's trade were everywhere.

Daniels scowled, having still not gotten used to the incongruity of the new organization, or its new headquarters. "Nah," he decided. "I think we're the devil's Whac-A-Mole. The monsters pop their heads up and we knock 'em down again. Right?"

Key smiled. "Okay, okay," he surrendered. "But remember, we believe what Logan-types can't or won't."

"Won't?" Nichols echoed, coming up on Key's other side.

He nodded to her, appreciating her technique of gleaning more information. "At least to anyone else," he told her. "If he does, he might have to admit, at least to himself, that there's more to life than just selfish little him and his power-money games—games which humans invented, by the way, to distract themselves."

"Oh, I hate it when you get all hippy-dippy touchy-feely," Daniels moaned.

Key immediately responded with a knowing grin. "Uh huh. But you love it when second louies do, don't you?"

Daniels reacted to the Strenkofski reference as if Key had cut him to the quick. "Geez, Joe," he whined, "you really know how to hurt a guy, don't you?" He elbowed Nichols. "C'mon, Ter, I'll show you my *Maltese Falcon* if you show me yours."

Nichols shook her head like a confused puppy shaking off rainfall. "We're seeing *Star Wars*?"

"*Maltese* Falcon, not Millennium Falcon!' Daniels exclaimed. "Bogart, remember?"

Nichols sniffed. "I'd rather train." She looked at Key. "Gotta learn how to fight smart, right?"

"And effective," Daniels agreed. "Then come on, squirt, there's room for both Falcons and fighting." Especially when the gym and armory were set up in this mock Versailles's version of the *Galerie des Batailles.*

"Have fun, kids," Key said, heading west. But before they were completely out of earshot, Key remembered something. "Morty!" he called, waiting for the echo to reach Daniels's ears. "You still in touch with Lailani?"

At the mention of the Filipino escort Daniels had taken advantage of in Oman, his eyes narrowed but widened again when he remembered she had repaid the favor by saving his life. "Yeah, maybe," he admitted. "Why?"

"I want to talk to her about something."

"Okay. Like what?"

Key was willing to say, but more pressing issues prevented him from going into detail right then. "Let's just say it's about some hits and myths."

"Okay," Daniels huffed. "Be cryptic. I'll set up a chat. Say when."

"ASAP," Kay replied. "Thanks."

With that, Key trudged toward the *Chateau Neuf* section. On the way, he gave thanks that Tashkurgan hadn't enough money to build the entire palace, or he'd be walking all day. Even so, it was a bit of a hike until he stepped into a cavernous warehouse of fake red brick and fake white stone, with a fake black tile roof. Originally the space was to house the king's hunting lodge, but now it was home to "The Hispanic Mechanic's Workshop"—wholly brought in from the Thumrait Air Force Base, only with even more improvements.

"Speedy," Key called without affectation, using the nickname of Manuel Gonzales, the most remarkable engineer, inventor, and all around synthesizer of stuff he had ever met. Just as he had when first stepping into the original workshop, Key marveled at the constructions either in process or completed around him. The injection of Lancaster cash had done even more wonders to the man's practical imagination. Key wouldn't have been surprised to see both the Maltese and the Millennium Falcon come to life in there.

"Joe," he heard, then spotted Gonzales coming around the tail end of the F. B. Law, a cutting-edge helicopter he had fashioned back in the Middle East. With him, as always, was his assistant, Faisal Safar—one of Cerberus's first agents and a man who both recruited and saved their asses multiple times.

As the Hispanic-American and Arab-American approached, Key held his phone out to them. "The photo app has multiple pictures of both a wizened naked guy and the child corpse we collected. I'd like to know who they both are."

Gonzales didn't ask how soon. Unlike Daniels, he already knew everything was needed right now. Instead he took a quick look, and whistled. "The nude gentleman does not look happy," Safar commented. "And unfocused. I gather these were candids."

"About as candid as it gets," Key admitted. "The stuff I asked for ready?"

"Just about," Gonzales said, already heading for a wall of computers. "Think the others'll be happy about it?" He plugged the phone in, and his fingers started dancing on a keyboard.

"I think Morty, at least, will be ecstatic," Key estimated. "They'll be his license to thrill shamelessly and fearlessly."

"Like he didn't have that already," Safar cracked as he joined Gonzales by the monitors.

"You waiting for initial intel?" Gonzales asked without taking his eyes off the screen.

"Let me know if-and-when," Key said, already backing away. "Next stop, the queen's clinic."

Gonzales and Safar were already so intent on their work that neither bothered with a parting quip. So Key marched to the *appartement de la reine*, otherwise known as the Queen's Private Apartments. In reality, it was a suite of rooms that Cerberus had made into "The Rahal Clinic"— modeled after the wing where Eshe Rahal had served at the Oman Medical College. Only now it was a cutting-edge facility with patient wards, operating rooms, and laboratories that put Frankenstein's Castle to shame.

Key found the attractive young Arab woman in the medical examination room, staring down at the child corpse they had taken from the Sujanpur morgue. She was wearing her usual uniform of scrubs and a lab coat. As soon as she saw Key, she embraced him with relief. After sending him into the nest of a Queen Arachnosaur in Shabhut, Yemen, she was always delighted he made it back to her in one piece.

They took a moment; then, as was Key's wont, got back to business.

"I thought you'd be further along," he admitted, noting that the child was still wholly intact.

"I," Rahal began, obviously looking for a way to explain her delay. "I didn't want to dissect her until I exhausted every other means of examination." She blinked apologetically. "I mean, once they're open, there's really no closing them again, right?"

Key looked beyond her compassionate face to the little girl on the slab. Even from that distance she looked exactly the same as she had in Punjab: almost glowingly, preternaturally angelic. It stirred something in him, something that he found himself fighting against.

"Now don't go all maternal on us," he said slowly. "Whatever she was, she isn't anymore. Think of her as an encyclopedia we have to learn. And we can't without cracking the cover, right?" He found himself holding Rahal's shoulders, remembering her warmth and tenderness.

Rahal nodded, with just a hint of embarrassed shame.

Key should have left it at that, but, for some reason, felt like nailing a tack with a sledge hammer. "Don't get all moony about the pilot," he said, wondering why he was saying it even as he was saying it. "She's already left her ship, okay?"

"Understood," Rahal assured him in a far more certain way than he deserved. They took another moment to observe the little girl on the table, each trying to comprehend the monstrosity of her fate in their own ways. Key looked away to find Rahal looking up at him with big eyes. "What do you think?"

"Better question is what do I fear?" he sighed. "Bloodless corpses. Creatures who are impossibly fast and strong. Creatures who don't appear clearly on camera. Does that ring a bell?"

Rahal sniffed. "You aren't seriously considering that, are you?"

Key looked down at her. "You know about vampires?"

Rahal shrugged and shook her head slightly. "My mother told me of the *Ekimmu* as a child. They could be walking corpses, winged demons, evil shadows, or even malevolent winds. But what they all had in common was a lust for life force and blood." She looked back up at Key, her expression changing from childhood fear to adult reason. "But those were fables used to keep us safe and obedient."

"What if she told you about giant spiders whose webs made men explode?" Key asked pointedly.

That didn't faze the professor. "But at least prehistoric insects were real. We found fossils. They're part of the natural world. Vampires? Vampires are supernatural. They're not real."

Key resisted the urge to grip her by the shoulders again. "Eshe," he said reasonably. "I believe everything, *everything*, anyone believes has a basis in fact for some reason. Cerberus was created for those reasons."

Again he should have shut up. But there was something about this child corpse's energy that was unhinging his usual control. "I know you're a scientist," he heard himself almost pleading. "And for many so-called rational people, seeing is believing. But sometimes believing is seeing, too. We have to come at this with open minds. Fables might be science we don't understand yet."

Her look of almost pitiful sympathy finally stopped him. "Okay, okay," he sighed. "I get it. I'm sorry. I'll let you get back to work."

She was already turning to the exam table and putting on a pair of rubber gloves. Her actions seemed almost dismissive. "Do you want to observe?" she asked as a sort of consolation prize.

"I would," he confessed, "but I have to meet with great Caesar's ghost."

She nodded absently, turning further away, but he couldn't help noticing her relief when he left for the *appartement du roi*—the King's Quarters, which should have been adjoining, but given the reality of royal life just prior to the French Revolution, was all the way on the other side of the manor.

He also couldn't help noticing his own relief, and the way his mind seemed to click back into shape the farther he got from the clinic. That troubled him more than almost anything else that had happened since he got the assignment.

Naturally, the King's Quarters had become retired General Charles Lancaster's offices. How big his desk was, and what it was made of, was rendered irrelevant by all the communication, information, and surveillance equipment that was surrounding, encroaching, and covering it. As with everything that touched Key's life, which *was* everything, he had researched his new boss.

Lancaster's life after retirement from the military was the stuff of legend. Starting with a security company, he had built a conglomerate with pragmatic common sense that spread to all areas of business—rewarding the best minds and ignoring the worst. And one of his favorite pastimes was rooting out genius inventions that corporations sought to suppress to protect their antiquated bottom lines, then using them exclusively for Cerberus.

Since everyone outside these walls thought he was crazy, they let him get away with it—especially since a crazy man might even fight back. And nobody wanted Charles Leonidas "Lionheart" Lancaster fighting back. History dictated that was a fight the attacker would lose.

"You looked pissed," Lancaster commented, his eyes seemingly everywhere at once. "That's not like you."

Key stood in front of the desk, looking over a bank of three monitors. He was already used to the retired general's seemingly fragmented, but actually laser-intense, focus.

"Got any thoughts on Aafir's game? What's his deal?"

Lancaster chuckled. "Oh stop it, Josiah," he suggested. "Only I should be able to do the 'elaborate' trick. If I had the time I'd give you the same look you gave me back in Logan-ville when I used it on you for the others' benefit. You know, the one that said 'you know damn well.'"

Key nodded, lowering his head. He breathed deeply, then fessed up. "Eshe just read me the vampire riot act. I have to admit I'm not used to getting dressed down."

Lancaster sighed, choosing to ignore the possible sexually oriented "dress-down" joke. "'Love makes fools of us all,'" he quoted. "'Big and little.'"

"Shakespeare?" Key guessed.

"Thackeray," Lancaster corrected. "William Makepeace Thackeray. But close enough." He leaned over to a monitor on his left. "What she thinks is not as important as what she does, and it would be good for you to know that your little talk at least got her back on track." He motioned for Key—who was not at all surprised by, or resentful of, Lancaster's intimate knowledge—to come around the desk, then pointed at the video feed that was coming from the medical examining room.

Key got there in time to see Rahal preparing her autopsy tools—just as the child on the table behind her sat up.

Chapter 5

The event elicited a scream from Rahal that could be heard out in the gardens.

Before it even started, Key was charging for the *appartement du roi* doorway, while Lancaster was stabbing buttons to establish ear-comm contact with the others.

"The clinic, now, with whatever restraints you can find!"

The screams continued, changing from surprise to terror, as Key raced down the Hall of Mirrors, passing even Nichols as she came in from the south, and then Gonzales coming in from the east. They didn't call him Speedy for nothing.

Daniels and Safar soon joined the race, the straps the Arab was holding and the spear Daniels was carrying slowing them down.

"What, what?" the big man called from the back of the pack.

Key was too intent on speed to answer, but not Lancaster, who came running up from behind Daniels.

"You know that dead child?" he grunted between huffs.

"What about her?"

"She's not dead anymore," he gasped.

The information hit Daniels like a water balloon, straightening his posture and doubling his speed.

Nichols was just a few steps ahead of Key as they reached the examination room, and what the redhead saw caused her to slide across the floor, waving her arms to maintain balance.

Key grabbed the side of the door to make sure he wouldn't make things worse—giving him just enough time to register the image of Rahal whirling around the room, waving her arms as if she were being attacked by wasps, while the angelic, naked child was tearing at her hair and face with her little claws.

"Fuckaduck!" Daniels bellowed as he all but inadvertently launched Gonzales into the room. The mechanic used the momentum to try grabbing at the child's tiny waist to pull her off Rahal, but as soon as his fingers touched the flesh, the child launched itself onto him instead.

"*Hijo de puta!*" he all but screamed as the tiny fingernails clawed at his eyes. He staggered back, clutching at the thing scrabbling around his shoulders—scraping down his neck and chest with her curled toes.

Rahal had dropped to the floor, clearly in shock, but she was still not so far gone that she couldn't turn to look at the others in astonishment. A part of her mind had wanted Key to catch her, or at least comfort her, but he was too busy yanking the others inside.

"Close the door, close the door," he seethed. "Don't let the thing out!"

Lancaster, who didn't think of protecting himself for a second, yanked the door closed behind him. "Fan out," he barked. "Surround it. Surround him!"

Nichols was on the other side of the area before Lancaster had even stopped speaking. Safar looked helplessly at the straps in his hands, but he didn't drop them. Key scoured the room for anything that could effectively help, as Daniels jumped forward, dropped the spear, and clamped onto the child atop the lurching Gonzales with both meaty paws.

But in the moment between the time his hands slapped and his fingers constricted, the child let out an unearthly yowl, squirmed and spun at the same moment, then whirled away from them—smacking into the floor and sliding under a Multix Digital Radiology Imager. They all heard her hit the wall with a solid thud.

Daniels yanked the disoriented Gonzales behind him protectively. Nichols skidded backward, bending down to see if she could spot the child. Lancaster stood tall, with his back to the door, his phone to his ear, his thumb ready to dial. Safar looked from the machine to Key and back again. Key stood in the center of the room, equidistant from the door to the machine, his back bent, his hands out in an "everyone chill" position.

The only sound in the room was Rahal's repeated gasping breaths.

Then Key pointed at Safar, and when Safar nodded, Key pointed at the scrubs bin—the laundry receptacle Rahal used to put her dirty clothes in—then held up a forefinger in a "wait" position.

"Maybe she's unconscious," Rahal started to whisper, but stopped when Key made a sharp "quiet" motion.

He then tapped Daniels on the back. When Daniels looked at him, he made a slow "follow my lead" motion as he started edging toward the digital imaging machine. A moment later, Daniels moved unerringly behind Key, like a baseball umpire behind a catcher, while Safar started edging along the far wall toward the scrubs bin.

Lancaster saw what Key was planning, and didn't like it. But because he could think of no better alternative, he stayed silent.

Key, Daniels, and Safar took another step—Nichols watching their progress carefully, ready for anything.

"She's just frightened," Rahal started to suggest, but then hushed when Gonzales urgently gripped her shoulder as he kneeled painfully behind her.

Key paused, so the others did as well. They held their breaths as he breathed deeply, then quickly dropped to his stomach and shoved his right arm under the machine.

For a second, nothing happened, then Key's face tightened as he swept his arm back and forth under the machine as if he were trying to scrub the floor clean. Then they all heard an enraged, trapped hyena squeal, and saw Key convulse on the floor before he yanked his arm back.

The child was the barracuda, Key's hand was the worm. Key hurled the child back with such force that it flew off his fingers, leaving a spurt of flying blood, directly into Daniels's arms. But the big man didn't try to run with it. Instead he immediately hurled it back the way it had come—only this time directly at the maw of the laundry bin that Safar was holding up toward him like an expert lacrosse player.

By then Key was there, grabbing the top of the bag, twisting it closed, and knotting it.

"Hold it, hold it!" he barked at Safar as the bag started twirling and scrambling around the floor.

"It's not holding!" Nichols yelled. "She's tearing through it like rice paper!"

It was true. The child was hardly in the trap before her little fingers started shredding the cloth like razors.

But then Nichols was there again, shoving the straps Safar had dropped back into his hands. Safar started frantically wrapping the tearing bag with the leather bands. But as fast as he could buckle them, the child was starting to rip them with both her hands and her teeth.

By then Rahal was scrambling through the closest medicine cabinet, her trembling fingers trying to prepare a sedative injection. "Hold her," she cried. "Just a few seconds more—!"

Key slapped Daniels toward the child's feet as he dropped to his knees by her head. Both grabbed at the thrashing child's ankles and wrists, but they were just too small, slippery, and surprisingly strong. The thing was snarling like an animal that was not even close to being trapped, and Key could see why. Despite their size, age, intelligence, experience, and all their efforts, they were losing. It was only a matter of seconds before the child would be free again.

Like a slippery eel, it was just about to clear their hands, straps, and cloth when a large, lattice cross-hatched, metal can slammed down over it like a cage, trapping it on the floor.

Charles Lancaster sat heavily on top of it, keeping it tight over the squealing child. It was the wrought-iron garbage can from his office. He had had it made extra large and extra heavy because of the sheer amount of refuse he created. As the child managed to slide it, and Lancaster, an inch back and forth, Gonzales and Daniels jumped forward to hold the edges down with all their might.

Key fell back, Rahal crouching by him, holding the prepped sedative raised in her right hand. Nichols helped a shaken Safar off the floor. Then they all stayed where they were, trying to comprehend what had just happened. They looked to Daniels for a wisecrack that would relieve the tension, but even the big man seemed at a loss.

But then the room filled with the last sound any of them expected. It was the most plaintive, mournful, gut-wrenching, heart-breaking sobbing they had ever heard. They looked down, incredulously, to within the wrought-iron cross-hatching where the naked, angelic girl was curled into a fetal position, crying like a lost child.

* * * *

"Shit."

Morty Daniels said it like it was a three-syllable word from where he lay in the intensive care unit of the clinic. They were all in there—in, or on, separate beds. The Chinese doctor Lancaster had on call—an amazing woman who insisted they call her Helen—had marveled at the equipment on hand, tended to Rahal, and was waiting in the cafeteria.

Now Rahal was testing each of them thoroughly, whether the child had broken their skin or not. And, given what they had just experienced, they all sat still for it. But several of them would swear that they could hear Key's brain whirring. Lancaster apparently had a better muffler.

The anesthetized child was in the quarantine unit—"wrapped up and strapped down," as Daniels put it. Lancaster had the Q.U. built to exacting specifications—ones he had personally double-checked, given the reputation of certain Chinese construction engineers.

"Don't worry," he had assured Key. "The bad ones are executed."

"The bad ones who are *caught* are executed," Key had reminded him. Even he knew about the train bridges and elevated highways that had collapsed from rampant under-bidding, inferior materials, and bribery in the recent construction boom.

But the Cerberus Q.U. was designed to contain everything from germs to any other prehistoric predators they might encounter. Key couldn't help feeling that this child might be a bit of both. "Shit indeed," he echoed Daniels. "What's the protocol?" he asked Lancaster.

Rahal answered. "I'll be checking your vitals every hour. Dr. Helen will be checking mine."

"How long?" Daniels asked, unable to keep a slight whine out of his voice.

"As long as I can," she told him. "As long as you'll let me."

"As long as necessary," Lancaster informed him with no uncertainty. Daniels nodded with equal certainty, and not even a hint of pouting.

"What should we be looking for?" Nichols asked, unable to keep a slight fear and doubt out of her voice.

"To paraphrase you," Key responded, "you'll know it when you see it. Or, in this case, feel it. Anything out of the ordinary, but especially visions, hallucinations, even unusual dreams. Nothing is too small to mention. Do not, whatever you do, try to slough it off, downplay it, or tough it out."

"Who, me?" Daniels challenged with a grin.

"Especially you," Key replied.

Lancaster sat up, realized what he was about to blurt, then slowly leaned back. "Elaborate," he suggested carefully.

"As soon as I got near the child," Key informed him, "it was as if the cement wall I had made to cover my emotions started to crack." He looked over at Rahal, who was taking Gonzales's vitals. "I'm thinking you felt it too, didn't you?"

Rahal stiffened. "What do you mean?"

"The way I was acting."

"Oh," she said, seemingly distracted by trying to read Gonzales's blood pressure. "Yes." She sought the right words before continuing. "You were uncharacteristically intense, even repetitive. You usually choose your words more carefully and only make your point once."

Key nodded. "I was agitated, unfocused, even confused. For absolutely no reason that I could see, the child's proximity had"—now he searched for the right word—"it had *unnerved* me."

"Could it have been the situation?" Lancaster asked. "Just that, nothing more?" It was clear that he didn't want his team leader to be vulnerable.

"Joe has spent a lifetime separating what goes on inside his head from what's going on outside his head," Daniels contended flatly. "This guy could win a chess game in a carpet bombing."

Key nodded in appreciation of the compliment. "I've told you," he said to Lancaster, then glanced at the rest. "I've told you all, the mental is not separate from the physical. If the body can be attacked, so can the mind."

Daniels smiled grimly at Nichols. "Like *I* told you, it's all a muscle, baby, the whole human shootin' match."

"So that's what we're dealing with here?" Gonzales asked.

"That's what we may be dealing with here," Key countered. "But it's more important than ever to keep reading your own mind, and keep it wide open until we're more certain." He sat up on the diagnostic bed. "You got the accessories I asked for now?" he asked Gonzales.

Gonzales sucked in his breath. "Just in time," he answered. "I was preparing to bring them over when the alarm sounded." He nodded at Safar, who brought a case over to the center bed, laid it on the padding, and opened it.

Inside were fourteen fingerless gloves, seven dickies, and seven bike shorts. The gloves reached up to mid-forearm, the dickey down to below the sternum, the bike short to the knee, and all were made of a lighter gray, nearly copper material. They were obviously designed to cover the human body's major arteries.

"Under armor?" Daniels suggested.

"Righter than you may know," Key commented, stepping over to the other side of the bed.

"Glad you added the 'may,'" Daniels muttered while twisting over for a closer look.

"*Batal hazar*," Rahal said under her breath as she joined the others.

Key purposely didn't look at her with narrowed eyes, but his self-control had no effect on Safar, who did. He knew she had said the Arabic phrase that could be translated as "stop joking, you have got to be kidding me."

"It's the truth. Not a single photo of the man in Sujanpur was in focus," he said quietly, and directly, to her. "Not one." She did not react to, or look at, him, but her expression shifted as if she were thinking they had all lost their reason.

Lancaster picked up on the undercurrent. "You will all wear these from now on, twenty-four-seven. No exceptions, no excuses."

"They're made from a special material," Gonzales assured them. "Slim, pliant, and comfortable as silk but hard as steel."

"Made by the same company who created Cali-brake," Lancaster informed them, referring to the revolutionary bulletproof material their uniforms were made of—which was one of the many patents Lancaster had rescued from repression by corporations more interested in status quo than progress.

"Even in the shower?" Daniels inquired disingenuously.

"Even in the shower," Gonzales said proudly. "Wash and wear. They dry even faster than skin. And, believe it or not, they make Cali-brake's wicking capabilities even more effective."

Daniels grinned. "Better living through science," he commented while reaching for the biggest size—the ones obviously made for him.

"I only wish that were true," Rahal said worriedly, stepping back.

Key looked over to her, but said nothing. Lancaster knew that was his responsibility. "Elaborate," he said knowingly.

"That girl in there is the victim," Rahal announced with certainty. "She may be infected with whatever the man who stole her was infected with. There are cases on record of sleeping sicknesses that were mistaken for death, and of infections that cause extra strength and speed." She stabbed a finger at Nichols, who looked on with concern. "But these are all natural. These are all real. They are not the result of some fairy tale *ekimmu* or blood-sucking vampire!"

"And no one said they are, Professor Rahal," Lancaster replied in a voice that was as calm as still water and as hard as graphene. "But until we know what happened to that child, and that man, we live with the motto 'better safe than sorry.'" He pointed directly as her, but not unkindly. "It is your job to find out what has happened, and what is happening, to that poor girl." He motioned to the others. "It is their job to stop it from happening to anyone else."

The seven core members of Cerberus stood silently, looking at each other. Then Eshe Rahal fell to one knee and, in a long-delayed release, started to sob.

Chapter 6

"Is she okay?" Nichols asked as Key entered the sleek, ergonomic cabin of Lancaster's latest acquisition to his air fleet—a gray and white HondaJet.

"Define 'okay,'" Key replied with a combination of resignation and irritation as he took one of the four plush seats bracketing the compact cabin. He was facing the cockpit, where Gonzales and Safar sat. Nichols sat opposite Key, who was to the right of Daniels—giving the big guy the most leg room. They were all wearing their Cali-brake outfits, complete with the new "Chain-silk" accessories.

"She's resting comfortably," Daniels advised, adding, "If that's any consolation."

"I'm not sure it is to her," Nichols answered.

"Agreed."

As soon as he was belted in, Key pulled out, and held up, an iPad Pro so all three in the hunter team, and the two pilots, if they turned around, could see it. It seemed perfectly at home in the HondaJet's clean, smooth interior. With the press of a forefinger, Lancaster's face appeared on the high-definition screen.

"Professor Rahal is under the care and observation of Dr. Helen," he immediately announced. Nichols wanted to ask if that was enough, but had too much respect for Lancaster to verbalize it. The retired general seemed to read her mind, however, and not for the first time. "That will have to do for now," he continued, "since I'm still vetting the security clearance of any specialists who could be of service. But I can assure you, from personal experience, that Dr. Helen is probably the best possible person for this unique set of circumstances."

Before any of them could inquire, Lancaster immediately went on to other pressing matters. "The child is being treated as if she is radioactive. All tests will be performed from as far distant, and as far protected, as possible, with redundant safeguards and security."

He paused to allow for any comments, but none were forthcoming. Key had too much faith in the retired general's intelligence, Nichols had too much respect, and Daniels couldn't care less. Any cock-up would just give him more opportunities to go ballistic on someone—or something.

"Faisal?" Lancaster finally asked.

They heard Safar's voice from the copilot's seat. "As I mentioned to Professor Rahal," he said, "not a single photo of the body snatcher—"

"Just call him the 'nude dude,'" Daniels piped up, "so we all know who you're talking about."

"Let's not," Lancaster said to the accompaniment of a general "*Grow up, Morty*" sigh.

"By any name," Safar said with gracious patience, "not a single image was in focus. In fact, it was almost as if someone had used a digital distortion device on the images—rendering the face indistinguishable. There was no way we could use facial recognition software to track him."

"The same could not be said of the girl, however," Gonzales chimed in. "You'd think a child that pretty who disappeared would be the source of an intense investigation, but we could find no evidence of it."

"Fingerprints?" Nichols asked, both hopefully and doubtfully.

"Nothing on record," Safar replied.

"I'll keep looking on this end," Lancaster assured them, "but, for now, you may not have positive identifications, but you have a definite trail of bodies. Time to retrace them, and find the source of this abomination. Best of luck and skill, team. Good hunting."

Lancaster's face disappeared from the screen, and, as the pilots readied for takeoff and Key stowed the iPad Pro, Daniels stretched like a bear waking from hibernation.

"So," he commented casually to Key as the jet prepared for liftoff, "we're on India serial killer watch while Logan is on Afghan terrorist trail, huh? Something sound screwy about that to you, Joe?"

Key looked sardonically over at his friend as if he were a forgetful grandpa. "So, you'd rather blunder into an Afghan bear-trap buzz-saw than get a rematch with our India phenomenon? You know, the child-snatcher who looks twice your age, doesn't show up on camera, and can run rings around you? Something sound screwy about *that* to you, Morty?"

Gonzales and Safar made a quick taxi down the Cerberus runway and took off toward Punjab—the HondaJet doing it all in less than three thousand feet. Once they were at their cruising altitude of thirty-five thousand feet, Nichols finally said what was on her mind.

"Joe, I'm sure the body snatcher stole the child from the morgue, but I'm not sure he killed her."

Daniels snorted. "Hell, I'm not even sure she's dead!"

"I'm not sure any of them were," Key informed them. "Before or after their alleged cremations."

Daniels shifted in his seat so he could look directly at Key with cynical skepticism. "So, you're definitely using the 'V' word?"

Nichols sat up, a variety of "V" words running through her mind. "Vagrant? Vagabond?" she finally guessed.

Daniels barked a laugh. "No," he told her with appreciation. "Vampire."

The redhead looked from the former sergeant to the former corporal, her own expression incredulous. "Really?"

Key was unabashed. "Not ruling it out," he said flatly. "Not ruling *anything* out. But one thing I'm fairly certain of, Morty. Your precious Afghan bear trap and our ghoul may be on a collision course." Key let them consider that, before he stood to start checking the on-board equipment they had loaded. "And already too close for comfort."

* * * *

Aarif Zaman looked out over his "kingdom." The kingdom that stretched from Urgon—a craggy, mountainous range of devastated villages—to the thick forests of Waziristan. He smiled upon his mostly unseen subjects; the chameleon-like Pashtun tribes who appeared when they were called and disappeared back into the countryside when their violence was finished.

He breathed deeply of the air of the Paktika Province, fragrant with the subtle scents of coal, sulfur, gas, and gunpowder that drifted on the wind from mines and bombings. He had his system of cave dwellings, his subjects, his soldiers, his concubines, and his slaves. He could want for nothing more. But he did.

"I want my identity," he told his visitor—the one who had silently taken in this grand tour, listening to all the terrorist's tales of conquest and destruction. The one who had, once it had come time to declare respect and allegiance to his plans and goals had, instead, asked one simple question.

"*What* do you want?"

The visitor had asked it before, on his very first visit, appearing unbidden and undetected months ago, bringing Zaman the most beautiful young woman he had ever seen. Although Zaman was ready to order the visitor destroyed, simply because he appeared by surprise, the order went unspoken. Now Zaman was certain his mercy had been his decision. But then, if he were truthful, he was not so sure.

It hardly mattered, since, when Zaman had told the visitor then what he wanted, the visitor had arranged for it to be so.

"I want to be singled out by the most powerful country in the world," he had answered that first time. "I want to be seen, acknowledged, and feared."

But now, that having happened, he wanted something different, something no less ambitious but somewhat more refined. "I want the respect and adoration stolen from me by all the many other warlords," Zaman told his guest. "Am I not also a child of wealth? Did I not renounce my family and that wealth for my people? Did I not leave university to fight with my people against the forces that seek to destroy them? Did I not supply my people with the weapons they needed in this fight? Is not all this true?"

"You have said it is so, *Effendi*," said his visitor, "therefore it is so."

Zaman felt a rush of pride, but also insult, which was an emotion he often felt in his visitor's presence. "So why am I not given the same respect and notoriety of those who have done the same before me? Why is not my name on the lips of every person?"

"If that is what you want, *Effendi*," his visitor said, "that is what will be."

"So let it be written, so let it be done," he wistfully repeated the phrase of the ancient pharaohs.

"Yes, *Effendi*. Yes."

Aafir Zaman looked down upon the bowing visitor, yet, somehow, also found himself looking up at him. The Afghan did not know how this could be, so he took a step back, and then another, so he could better observe his visitor as he straightened from his bow.

As always, Zaman thought he was seeing his visitor's face from within his hooded robe, but he was concerned that this time, as had happened before, all he would remember would be the red hands painted on his visitor's own hands, and the red eyes painted above his visitor's own eyes. He would, strain as he might, not be able to describe his visitor to anyone—except for those painted reflections, and the uncomfortable memory of black pits flecked with fire.

"Good," Zaman said with a sharp nod. Normally he would state his intentions and willingness to cooperate in any way, but he never had with his visitor. He just turned and looked back over his kingdom, praying that if he turned back, the visitor would be gone.

The visitor turned to his extraordinarily beautiful, dark-haired companion—the one he had brought for Zaman, and, as always, moved away with her. Zaman always remembered her coming to him, but always forgot that she never remained with him. And he never remembered to be insulted or upset by that.

When he turned back, his visitor and his companion—the one that Zaman had not been aware of this time—were, indeed, gone, and he couldn't quite comprehend how long it had been since his visitor had been there.

But they had not gone for everyone. Mahasona and Tajabana appeared before Craven, as they alerted him they would. The always pathetic, but now powerful, corpse collector crouched in his Veranesi hovel, awaiting their arrival, and bowed before them upon their appearance.

A moment later he was writhing on the ground, something having clamped upon every cell and pore in his body. It was a pain beyond pain—an indescribable, personality-eradicating sensation that he had felt often, but yet could never get accustomed to. It invaded and occupied his entire mind and body, but only for a second. Any longer and he would not be able to appreciate his release from it.

He did not beg, plead, or question. He already knew why it had happened. In fact, he was expecting, even welcoming, it. No one could keep secrets from his master long.

"The question I must answer," his master said, "is why you have kept this from me. I know why you have done it. I know your appetite better than you know it. But shame? Why hoard shame from the lord of shame?"

"Obvious," said Tajabana calmly. "He knows your plan, and his place in it, so he was afraid." She enunciated the last word as if it was the most distasteful thing she could say.

Mahasona saw the truth in her estimation, just as Craven thrashed on the ground again. "Shall I keep this grip on you for eternity?" he asked. "Is it, or your fear and appetite, more powerful?"

"Master, master, please!" Craven managed to sputter. But then the clamp was gone and Tajabana was kneeling down to him, his chin in her cold, warm hand.

"Yes," she cooed at him, "please. How could he, your master, of all things, deny you your feeding? But all he asks, all we both ask, is that you organize it in such a way that it does not jeopardize his plan for you, me, and this world. Do you think you can do that? We—*I* could help you. Can you do that?"

Craven scrambled over to his master's feet, slamming his forehead to the floor and babbling. "Yes, master, yes, I can do that, I swear I can do that. I will, you'll see, I will!"

"Your 'will' is tomorrow." Mahasona's words were glass shards in his brain. "Your problem is today. You will stop 'trying' to clean up your problem. You will eliminate your problem, now, or you will become part of it."

Craven felt his gut lurch and the shards in his brain turn to lightning.

"Yes!" he screeched. Then his bowels emptied, and the lightning was no more.

When he could see again, his master and his companion were gone. But still, a few of his master's words lingered.

"Your mess must be cleaned. Whatever—whoever, wherever—the cost."

Chapter 7

Nichols tried getting the fifty kilometers from Dera Baba Nanak to Amritsar even faster than she had before.

Their first stop had been to the friendly, talkative, eager, English-speaking Dera Baba Nanak mortician who had sent them to Sujanpur in the first place. Their second stop was at the nearby home of the couple who had brought their supposedly bloodless child to the mortician, also in the first place.

Now they were racing to the spiritual and cultural center of the Sikh religion because that was where the "special school" the couple's daughter had been recruited to was located. It was a staggering story that, in retrospect, was so obvious that Nichols wondered why no one had investigated it before.

"No one investigated it," Key had told her, "because no one saw reason to."

All three were shaken by their visit to the small apartment at the end of Dera Baba Nanak Road, where an all-too-calm young mother, wearing a blue *kurta* tunic over cream canvas pants, had welcomed them into her plain but clean living room—using careful, but fluent, English.

Although Key had made it clear that they were CID agents investigating her daughter's death—and all three were tense to say the least—the woman insisted on offering them cups of chai tea. And a very slow offer at that.

Both Daniels and Nichols had given Key a raised eyebrow—the former with *'what's* this *about'*? sarcasm and the latter with concern—as the woman had unhurriedly moved into the tiny adjoining kitchenette, but Key could only shrug at them with a certain amount of helplessness.

"What can I do?" he had mouthed at the others. "Snap my fingers and hope she comes out of it? Study her. We may need detailed descriptions soon."

The more cautiously the mother went, the more agitated most of her visitors became. Even before she reappeared, carrying a tray of small cups that gave off a soothing aroma of cardamom, ginger, and cinnamon, Key had already asked her another question.

"Were you the one who found your daughter?"

"I smoothed the chai with milk and sweetened it with honey," had been her reply. "I hope that is all right."

"Fine," Key snapped as she dreamily presented the tray to Daniels, then Nichols. Both had taken a cup as to not risk another delay. Finally she had turned back to Key. "Did you find your daughter?" he had asked her.

"No," she had said slowly, as if she was having some trouble recalling the fact. Key had been about to ask her another question but tightened his jaw when he saw that, once the memory was found, it flowed from the woman's brain to her mouth like a undammed brook. "I-I was called by the school. They said she had an accident."

"What school?" Daniels had blurted, then winced at his interruption. But, thankfully, the babbling brook of the mother's mind was picking up speed.

"A-a woman," she had stammered as if truly seeing her memory for the first time. "There was a beautiful woman who came here." She pointed at the door as if it was appearing from mist. "She said my daughter was special and had been chosen."

Nichols had leaned forward as if to ask for details, but Key had sharply made a stopping motion out of the mother's sight.

"Chosen," the mother had continued, her eyes getting clearer and her voice thicker. "For a scholarship, a full scholarship, to a special school. A private school—in Amritsar." The woman had said the name of the city with reverence. "Amritsar," she had repeated, threatening to go back into her reverie, but Key had seen that the vision of that golden city had been quickly usurped by renewed memories of her daughter. "So I let her go. I trusted them to love her as I love—loved—her."

Large, clear teardrops had started to fall out of the woman's widening eyes, like diamonds dropping out of a vault. She turned her slowly collapsing face to Key. "I didn't see her again—until they called about the—the..."

Key had been certain that the woman would not remember the school's name and address, but he was pleasantly surprised—at first, then justifiably concerned. He had expressed his concern to the others—then Lancaster, with Gonzales and Safar listening in—after they all returned the teacups to the tray, unsampled.

"I'm not touching that," Daniels had whispered to Nichols on the way back to the SUV. "Whatever that woman's on might be in there." The big man and the redhead had also been incredulous of the woman's credulousness, but not Key.

"Can you imagine what the mind-coating power of that naked vampire and the angel kid would be like in the form of a beautiful woman?" he had asked before requesting Lancaster find some hypnotism specialist to visit the poor woman. Then he had demanded that Daniels get in touch with Lailani, as Nichols gunned the Ford toward "The Golden City."

The SUV's comm-link was on speakerphone so everyone in the vehicle could hear, and speak to, the former escort Daniels had "met" in Oman.

"There are many 'first' vampires," Lailani said.

"'First' vampires?" Nichols asked Lailani, intent on the traffic, but also wanting to glean as much information as they could in the short amount of time they had.

"The ones that are supposedly the original creature that inspired the legend that became Dracula," Lailani answered, sounding as if she were discussing the weather.

Daniels looked at Key with a *"who would've thought?"* expression, which Key returned with an *"I did, which is why I wanted to talk to her in the first place"* look. The Filipinos he had known had all been well-versed in their mythology, which they seemed to think of as reality.

"We would talk about them during our off hours," she continued, referring to her fellow escorts at the club in Qurum, Oman, where Daniels had met her. "And every single story came from our families. But we kind of stopped after what happened to the—*pinays*."

Key could understand that. Those transgender lady-boys had been infected with the blood-detonating disease transmitted by the *Idmonarachne Brasieri* that Cerberus had managed to destroy. It seemed like years ago, but it had actually been only a few weeks.

"What are the top ones?" he asked her.

"*Aswang*," she said immediately, which made Daniels snigger—eliciting a look of warning from Key, but Lailani had already heard him. "It means 'demon' in your language, not 'ass' and 'wang,' you big ape," she continued. "Most famous in Philippines, Joe. Most famous everywhere in east. Shapeshifter—could be vampire, witchwarlock, or even werecreature."

"Witchwarlock?" Nichols interrupted again.

"Yes, good catch," Lailani encouraged. *"Aswang tik-tik, wak-wak, sok-sok, kling-kling."* Key looked nonplussed until Lailani explained. "Means both boy and girl, Joe."

"Christ!" Daniels exclaimed. "Werecreature? Are monsters getting politically correct now, too?"

"You imperceptive ape," Lailani said affectionately. "Not 'p.c.' It means what it says. A werewolf is wolf. *Aswang* could be many beast—bat, bird, boar, cat, dog, others."

Key jutted his chin at the comm microphone/speaker. "How do you kill them, Lailani?" Key asked.

"Same as Dracula sometimes," she unhesitatingly answered. "Cross, church water, garlic, head-chopping. But best with a whip made from stingray's tail."

Daniels' mouth twisted. "Well, *that's* pretty specific."

"Probably with good reason," Key retorted.

"Buntot pagi," Lailani said, translating the weapon's name. *"Aswang* not so much scared by whip, but by whip's noise. Also *agimats* amulet."

"My vocabulary is growing by animal leaps and bounds," Daniels remarked.

Although Key didn't appreciate Daniels's interruptions, he recognized the difficulty of taking all this in, and fully comprehending it. Giant prehistoric spiders might be frightening, but they were certainly more tangible than hypnosis, brain-washing, or whatever else their new adversaries were using. He checked the Ecosport's navigation screen and saw they were running out of time.

"Give me the top five, Lailani, name, powers, weaknesses."

"Top five?" she complained. "But there are so many, Joe."

"Try." He looked at Nichols, who held up five fingers. They were five minutes from arrival.

"Okay, for you, Joe, I try. Also for you, big ape." Daniels smiled as they heard Lailani take a big breath, then launch into her list. *"Aswang,* number one. Two, *Ekimmu*—drink blood, take soul, control minds. Need Spirit Bowl for protection. Three, *Penanggalan*—beautiful woman who suck blood of pregnant women and children, need thorny leaves for protection. Four, *Gyonshi*—drink blood, decapitate. Spell paper stop them, fire destroy them. Five, *Riri Yaka,* Blood Demon—can change into nine forms, eats flesh and drinks blood, killed by fire or brass knife."

Lailani took a breath as Nichols held up her forefinger to let Key know they were almost at their destination. He looked out the windshield to see a huge, beautiful city, anchored by the *Harmandir Sahib,* which translated to "the abode of God," and was more commonly known as The Golden Temple. It was the most popular destination for non-residents in all of India, and was always mobbed by thousands. Thankfully, the address of the special school, was, not surprisingly, on the outskirts of the city.

"So many more, Joe," Lailani complained. "So *much* more. Details, details."

"*Salamat*, Lailani," Key said, using the Filipino word for thank you. "I wish we had more time."

"I send you links, Joe," she promised. "More information. Much, much more information."

"*Salamat*, babydoll," Daniels interjected, punching Key's shoulder and beginning to pull himself toward the SUV's storage section. "We got to go."

"And *pakingshet pakyu*, foolish gorilla-man," she replied pleasantly, telling him "fuck you."

"Not the time and place," he immediately retorted, before breaking the connection. "She's a sweetheart, ain't she?" he commented honestly. "Married some businessman in Dubai, I heard. Maybe even an Indian guy."

Daniels's words seemed to bounce off Key's ears, so the former Marine doubled down. "All this vampire stuff is for shit," he emphasized, yanking up the dart guns from their cases. "These human monsters're just making little suicide bombers."

When Key still didn't respond, it was Nichols who picked up the gauntlet, steering the SUV into Dhaul Kalan village in the southwest of Amritsar. "It's not the 'what' that concerns me as much as the 'how,'" she said distractedly, placing most of her attention on the stone and cement walls of the colorfully accented blockhouses that made up the tree- and field-lined suburb.

"Let me know when we're a block away," Key instructed. "Probably best to park a few doors down."

Nichols nodded as Daniels handed Key the automatic dart gun Gonzales had specially fashioned for him. Normally dart guns are for shit; inaccurate and ultimately ineffective, but, according to the Hispanic mechanic, not this one. Nor the dart submachine gun Daniels was hefting.

The handgun was modified from the famed 1962 Walther LP53 air pistol, which sold at auction for half a million dollars. The machine gun looked like the rare Japanese Masudaya Thunderbolt target rifle, complete with its wicked shark-like shape, futuristic rocketship-style stock, and interlocking, dovetailing double barrel. And inside each were new darts, designed in the tradition of wax bullets, and packing an enhanced venom that Gonzales promised could take down an elephant in a heartbeat.

"We're getting close," Nichols announced.

They studied the narrow block. On one side was the white brick wall of an estate. On the other were three buildings, each behind a different gate. The first was a bronze fence made up of spears, topped with a fleur-de-lis trident. The second was a series of moon walls, with round, decorative inlays. The third was the charm.

They driveway entry was flanked by two square-shaped, multi-colored brick columns, separated by a black and red wooden gate. On either side was a twelve-foot marbleized cement wall with atrium-like decorations. Behind it was a three-story, marbleized cement building that gave the impression of a chopped-off pagoda.

Each floor was wider than the one before, each sporting a balcony that encircled the building. The second floor's balcony had an inlaid brick balustrade, while the third had a wrought-iron one. None of them could see the first story through the wall, but Daniels already had a small camera drone in his palm. It looked like a cocktail-umbrella-topped ball, only the cocktail umbrella was black and made of space-age polymer.

Key handed Nichols a dart gun, and both slipped on the double shoulder holsters—their Sig Sauer in one sheath, and what they were now calling the "Gonz-gun" in the other.

"Ready?" he asked everyone. Daniels and Nichols nodded. "Let 'er fly."

Daniels put his arm out the window and raised his hand. The little thing took off like a caged bird getting its freedom—sounding, to anyone's ears, like a hummingbird. Too bad the hummingbird was not native to India, but the local sunbird made a similar enough sound not to raise alarms.

Daniels thumbed what looked like a slide projector's control stick, while Nichols and Key watched a dashboard screen as the tiny, powerful lens inside the mini-drone started sending back video images. The "school" was quiet and seemingly deserted. The patchy grass did not seem particularly overgrown, but that could have been native to the species. The grounds had no evidence of educational tools, or even a playground, but it did feature some red flowering ashoka trees.

"Look in a window," Key suggested, knowing that Daniels would let the drone do something he'd never do: be subtle about it. He watched as the screen image neared the small, dirty, caged window of the top floor. It showed nothing but an old, dirty, empty room.

Daniels brought the view down to the second floor. They heard Nichols try not to gasp. They looked into a plain, but clearly once-occupied, room, with just a mat on the dusty floor. Lying on the mat was a *Nahji* doll— India's version of Barbie.

"Shit," she said. "We're too late. Looks like they cleared out."

"Good," said Daniels, shifting in his seat. "That means we can search the place without interference."

"Wait," Key warned. "Check the first floor."

Daniels did as he was told, although emboldened because he figured it would be as empty as the rest. The drone hummed around the entire circumference of the building, showing them four empty rooms, but also a trapdoor, complete with a big iron ring handle, on the far side.

"Too bad there's no basement windows to look in," Daniels grumbled.

"Morty," Key barked. "Houses in India don't have basements. Close-up on that trapdoor!"

Daniels responded immediately, and all six eyes peered at the dashboard screen. Naturally Nichols saw it first.

"Joe, those are wires. There are wires coming out of that thing!"

Fuse wires.

Chapter 8

The Ford Ecosport smashed into, through, and over the driveway gate and then flew straight into the front door. The two thousand, eight hundred, and fifty pound vehicle turned the front entry into a pile of crumbled brick and kindling that it then crushed flat, as Nichols brought the skidding SUV right beside the trap door.

Both Daniels and Key were out before the vehicle even fully stopped—Cali-brake hoods and infrared goggles on—the former sergeant swinging open the heavy wooden obstruction as if it were made of cardboard, and the former corporal grabbing the end of the wires at the same moment he thrust his top half down through the opening.

There was no time for subtlety. If they knew where the secret school was, the bare player might very well know they knew it—especially if the victim's mind-fogged mother had managed to retain the address. Key had put himself in their adversaries' place. If he had been them, he would have taken steps to leave no evidence. And if there were fuse wires involved, that meant those steps were explosive.

As he had hoped and dreaded, there the bastard-monster was. The creature was no longer unclad. He wore a robe but was standing in the square pool of light the open trapdoor made, amid four heavy-looking, rectangular, low-to-the-floor cages. The man's eyes glowed dully hateful in the greenish hue of the infrared goggles' vision.

Key thrust the Gonz-gun forward, wishing it was the less unwieldy Sig Sauer, as he pulled the wires back. His wire arm stopped abruptly. The wires were attached to something on the floor, ceiling, and walls. The robed man lurched toward the nearest cage, and Key shot him four times without hesitation—twice in the reaching arm, once in the chest, and once in the forehead.

Key felt empty satisfaction as the first two darts made the man's arm jerk away from what he was reaching for, and the next two made him lurch away while jerking his skull back. But Key didn't wait an elephant-dropping second before he yelled.

"Morty, Sig, perforate him!"

As he was afraid, the tranquilizer darts, even enhanced by Gonzales, seemed to have no effect on the robed man. He didn't seem to be even slowed down. Fully expecting the boom of Daniels's gun to accompany him, Key held on to the wires as he let his body flip down through the opening in order to give the Sig Sauer a clear shot.

There were no stairs, or even a ladder. Key dropped a full fifteen feet, landing on raw ground—amidst a space that looked to have been dug by hand to the size of a standard mausoleum. Key dropped, rolled, and came up in a ready crouch, processing his impressions of shackled chains in the walls, just before he returned his full focus to the robed man, who, to his annoyance, was still standing.

Key didn't want to risk releasing the wires so he could pull out his Sig. He just kept pointing the dart gun and firing until the robed man wrenched up a heavy iron cage like it was made of chicken wire and hurled it at him.

He heard Nichols screech, because her enhanced vision, added to the infrared, let her see what the men couldn't see yet. Children were in the cages. Key couldn't help that, certainly not at the moment. He dodged the thing, feeling its weight and stench as it flew by, and felt a tug in his hand as one of the wires twitched. If not for the Cali-brake and the Chain-silk, his hand would have been deeply sliced. As it was, the cage slammed into the floor with a vibrating, bouncing, clang—clueing Key that the enclosures had to be at least seventy-five pounds. The robed man had tossed it like a pinecone.

"Morty! Kill the bastard!"

"Can't get a clear shot," Daniels hissed in his ear-comm.

He started to explain but Key stopped listening for two reasons. One, he saw packs of explosives everywhere—on the floor by the cages, on each wall, and every few feet on the ceiling. Two, the robed man came at him as if the two men were attached at the sternums by retracting springs.

He saw the same feral face he had seen in the Sujanpur fort, then only the wall and floor, as he spun his body away from the attack. He pivoted on the balls of his feet just as the robed man came back, clawing at him as Key predicted he would.

Key did not just stand there and let the man's jagged fingernails tear at him. As each claw swung, he moved in rhythm with it, letting them move him without touching. He was close enough to see the remains of the darts he had fired into the man, splattered like pin-filled paintballs across his flesh.

But as much as Key tried to counter the attack, the man was too fast and he knew the space too well. Key tripped on another cage and, because he was loathe to let go of either the wires or the gun, he let himself go down.

By the look of vengeful triumph on the face of the robed man, the bastard-monster was sure he had Key at his mercy. Key emptied the darts into the man as he came to tear the team leader apart. But just before he touched him, a shape fell from above them, clamping onto the robed man's back like a pouncing puma.

Nichols had jumped the man, and, as Key watched, she nailed the barrel of her Sig Sauer to the middle of his back, and convulsively squeezed the trigger.

Neither Key nor Daniels, let alone Nichols, would have believed it had they not been there. Later, Lancaster would watch their uniforms' automatic video feed in super slow motion, seeing that, at the split second Nichols's trigger finger tightened, the shriveled, withered, robed man twisted his torso so fast that the bullets only creased his spine skin and tore the robe cloth.

But, in real time, all Key and Daniels saw was Nichols go down hard and the man twist away. But her bullets splattered, sparked, and ricocheted all over the space.

As Key vaulted to his feet, he heard Nichols screech in frustration for herself, and in fear for the children. Then he heard Daniels roar like a wounded lion. Key looked up just in time to see the big man let his torso swing into the trapdoor opening, bringing his Sig Sauer to bear.

"Morty," Key barked, "hold your position!"

But it was too late. Daniels tried to hurl his bulk onto the robed man, firing as he went. The man didn't dodge. Instead, he leapt at Daniels, then, incredibly, used the big man's dropping body as a stepping stone.

His kicking leg, so seemingly scrawny, not only vaulted him upward but also propelled Daniels to the ground like a slingshot. The big man smashed into the dirt, his infrared goggles cracking, his weapons flying. Key was already up and grabbing the Thunderbolt in mid-air, swinging it around as the robed man's claws sank into the trapdoor frame.

Key emptied the dart magazine all over the opening, all but perforating the man's back, ass, and legs. But even so, the next second the robed man was out and gone. Key and Nichols heard his bare feet crunching the splintered wood, asphalt, and glass of the front entrance. But the team leader and the driver saw two different things and had two different reactions.

Nichols saw their quarry escaping, so she looked to where Daniels was just coming around.

"Sorry, Morty!" she said as she used his back like a step stool. Nichols shot up fifteen feet like a gymnastic aerialist as the big man went down groaning again.

Key, meanwhile, had noticed the small, red, flashing lights that suddenly appeared on every pack of explosives. The light was tiny, but the infrared goggles helped him see a small logo next to the light on every pack.

Nichols was about to spring out of the trapdoor and give chase when Key's cry stopped her.

"No," he said sharply. "Let him go! He's primed the place with timed Octabane!"

Nichols froze in a crouch just beyond the trapdoor lip. Octabane, short for octanitrocubane, was the most powerful non-nuclear explosive known.

It, in itself, was not enough to keep her from going after the robed man. Octobane was insensitive to shock and wouldn't go off on its own. But that was why Key had included the word "timed." The bastard-monster had the explosive on clocks, and there was no way for her to know how many seconds were left.

Key did. They had started at sixty. That was how powerful the Octabane was. Even the bastard-monster had given himself a minute to get clear.

"Attach the towing chains to the trailer hitch," Key immediately shouted, "and throw the other ends down here!"

"Goddamn it, Joe," Daniels growled as he lurched alongside, his eyes darting from one flashing red light to the next. "They're not long enough to reach down here!"

Key didn't bother to say "I know." Instead he stabbed one hand at the chains in the wall, and filled his other hand with his Sig Sauer. "Yeah, but they are!"

The cellar was full of the sound of gunfire as the two men blasted the walls where the chains were bolted. Within fifteen seconds, their hands were full, and their hearing was clearing just in time for them to hear new noises—the Ecosport backing up, and its chains clanking over the trapdoor lip. Key used the chain's shackles to lock them to the cages—not missing the irony that using things that kept the children prisoner might also help free them—as Daniels grabbed the chain ends and hooked them together.

Forty seconds remained.

"Ter," Key shouted as he clutched one cage and signaled Daniels to do the same. "Gun it! Gun it! Get us out of here!"

Nichols didn't have to be told twice. She rammed the fifteen hundred cubic centimeter, four-cylinder engine up to its full turbo-charged ecoboost of ninety-nine brake horsepower at thirty-eight hundred rpm, shifted it into full four-wheel drive, and slammed down on the accelerator.

The vehicle lurched forward, yanking the cages off the ground. Key and Daniels grabbed on with all twenty fingers and four legs—prepared to survive this motorized version of being keelhauled. Only the car stopped in the middle of the entrance, the cages hanging like wrecking balls over the floor. The tires spun and smoked.

Thirty seconds...

"Ter!" Daniels boomed. "Speedy added a super charger! Hit the super charger!"

Nichols had wondered what the recessed red button under the dashboard was. She punched it, and it was as if retro-rockets had ignited. The SUV heaved forward like it had been shot from a cannon, and even Daniels had a hard time holding on as the cages leaped up into the air, nearly smashing the two men into the ceiling of the first floor.

It was even worse when they came down, both men wrenching their bodies so the heavy cages didn't land on top of them. Even so, the rear ends of the cages hit the lumpy yard like hatchets. They felt like plows being dragged by runaway chariot horses as Nichols sent the SUV down the street.

Both men were ready for the cages to swing like clappers, but no amount of preparation could help them when the they all swung into the estate wall opposite the school. Key grunted as Daniels howled. Although the Cali-brake saved their skin from shredding, each bump and swing was like getting pummeled by a heavyweight champ.

Twenty seconds...

Both men, clamped to the cages like ticks, thanked anything they could think of that the cages were as heavy as they were, or else they would have been crushed, lost, or scrambled at every turn. As it was, it was like being thrown into an industrial drying machine full of rocks.

Finally the vehicle straightened out and tore down the street, giving Key a second to look up. There was a turn up ahead. As the SUV picked up speed, Key knew the odds of even Daniels holding on at the turn were slim. He refused to even imagine what it was like for the children inside the cages.

Ten seconds...

Nichols knew that any turn would send the cages and men flying, so, as she had for the entire trip, she made the least damaging decision she could—driving directly at the fence and yard on the corner while all but standing on the accelerator.

The SUV smashed open the fence, tore up the yard, and rammed through to the other side. It sent the cages flying upwards and, for a second, Daniels felt as if he were back on a boogie board in the Hawaiian surf. He was wrenched to reality by the sound of Key's quiet voice in his ear-comm.

"Let go, drop, roll, duck, and cover."

Daniels did as he was ordered without the customary quip or question. The pain of hitting the ground was swallowed by the explosion and shockwave.

The school was instantly turned into matchsticks and the detonation broke windows for miles. The fireball could be seen as far away as The Golden Temple, sending countless *haji* pilgrims into paroxysms of prayer.

Chapter 9

When Daniels opened his eyes he saw a ceiling that looked familiar. He took only a moment, glancing side to side to see Key and Nichols in the Rahal Clinic recovery room beds on either side of him—none with any sheet pulled over the head—before he spoke.

"Fuck a duck," he sighed incredulously. "Either tell me I've died and gone to purgatory, or tell me how you pulled off this particular magic trick."

Gonzales and Safar let Lancaster do the honors. "Well, you're obviously not dead, master sergeant," said the billionaire as he hooked thumbs toward the Hispanic and Arab flanking him. "And these gentlemen were already on their way the moment Terri saw the fuse wires."

"And given that Speedy is his nickname," Safar said with a grin infused with the memories of the trip, "it wasn't a leisurely jaunt."

"No," Gonzales agreed. "It was actually one of the fastest, and hairiest, I've ever taken."

Later the entire team would get the details: a hasty F. B. Law hop to a waiting, specially equipped, four-hundred-and-twenty horsepower, four-wheel-drive, eight-speed, six-ton GMC Yukon Denali on the outskirts of town, then one of the nastiest races to Dhaul Kalan—all with Gonzales and Lancaster in constant communication with officials, sleeper agents, and contacts all over the Middle and Far East.

"Fast, nothing," Daniels marveled. "You could be faster than a speeding ticket, but how the hell did you get us out of Punjab?"

"In good, old-fashioned terms," Key said thickly. "I'm guessing you just smuggled us out, right?"

Daniels looked over to see Key struggling to sit up, as Rahal stepped forward to discourage him with a tender touch of her hand on his shoulder.

"How long you been awake, Joe?" Daniels asked.

"Just long enough to hear you emerge from your oblivion, Morty," he replied, his voice getting stronger. "Must mean that maybe you joined Terri's and my concussion club, huh?"

"No," Rahal reported. "Although the explosion was at least as powerful as the fifty-caliber, point-blank bullet Nichols took to the head in Yemen, you managed to get far enough away that you could be saved by the same thing that saved her: the Cali-brake suits and headgear."

"Even the Denali was nearly sent into a ditch by the shockwave," Safar reported, recalling his struggle to keep the rescue vehicle on the road. "But we thoroughly tested Cali-brake for months in Cerberus labs, even before you people were recruited. Not only is it bulletproof, but it has some of the same characteristics as exoskeletons. So I was pretty sure you were still all in one piece."

"Especially since your ear-comms were still sending and receiving even after the explosion," Gonzales added. "The place was matchsticks, and your Ecosport was toasted front to back, but we were able to collect you all and get out of Dodge before the local bulls froze the village."

Both Daniels and Key shifted quizzical expressions to the boss man, who was ready with the explanation.

"The local 'bulls,' as Speedy so quaintly puts it, quickly concluded it was not a terrorist attack," Lancaster explained. "Not in an abandoned school on the outskirts of town—"

"No matter how big the boom," Gonzales interjected.

Lancaster gave him a sardonically appreciative nod before continuing. "They're still not sure what it actually was, exactly, but the flight paths were only shut down for about an hour."

"Giving us just enough time to secure your coffins aboard the HondaJet," Gonzales concluded.

"You using 'coffins' the way you used 'bulls' and 'Dodge'?" Daniels asked, then lowered his chin to his chest after Gonzales and Safar slowly shook their heads no. "I don't suppose the authorities were pleased," he finally surmised.

Lancaster shrugged. "What they don't know won't hurt them."

Key had finally made it to a sitting position. "You said you got us all."

The jokey pleasure the team's awakenings had elicited in the clinic were subdued by Key's comment. Gonzales and Safar lowered their heads, then looked to Rahal and Lancaster.

"Yes, Joe," Rahal finally said quietly.

"So tell me," he said when she grew silent.

Daniels looked about to say "tell him what" when Lancaster cut him off. "I'm truly sorry to say that three of the four children were DOA."

A pall settled on the team, which was quickly made worse as they considered the circumstances.

"What they must have suffered was truly horrible," Rahal choked out. "They looked like stillborn fetuses rather than children."

Nichols, who had awakened first, finally spoke up. "Will they come back from the dead the way the other child did?"

"I pray not," Rahal told her, clutching the patient charts even tighter to her chest. "I did thorough examinations on them all."

They knew that meant autopsies, so if the children came back to life, it would be an even more nightmarish occasion. Daniels looked disgusted and Nichols looked tragic at the thought, but Key looked thoroughly pensive.

"That's three," he said to Lancaster. "What about the fourth?"

Rahal looked surprised, thinking that Key would have immediately asked for the findings of her examinations first. The Cerberus chief looked from her to the team leader.

"In a coma," he informed him. "But alive."

Key nodded, seemingly satisfied, but not happy. "Okay," he told Rahal. "*Now* findings."

It was Rahal's turn to look at Lancaster, who nodded with approval—his expression communicating that she need not have even inquired. But Key didn't mind. He assumed she had done it simply to give her extra time to gather mental strength. She could dissect an adult with hardly a second thought. But working with these obviously tortured children had clearly unnerved her.

"They had been undoubtedly fed on," she said. "And not just their blood."

"He ate *pieces* of them?" Daniels asked angrily.

"Hold on, Morty," Key said quietly, not taking his eyes off Rahal. "She'll get to it."

Even so, Rahal seemed grateful for the interruption. "No, Morty. Pieces of them were not missing, but—" She paused, seemingly struggling to figure out a way to say it accurately.

"All their limbs, bones, muscles, and organs were intact," Lancaster elaborated. "But somehow they were shriveled."

"Actually, not precisely shriveled," Rahal corrected. "Depleted. As if somehow, something had taken from their bodies the ability to replenish and regenerate themselves."

Key remembered what Lailani and Rahal had said about the *Ekimmu*. "Like something was feeding on their life force," he said almost to himself.

Nichols looked worriedly at the scientist, but this time Rahal stood straighter and nodded.

"Yes," she said. "Souls are still up for question, but not life force. Whether it's called the *mitochondria*, hydrogen pump, *qi*, like here in China, or even 'the force' in movies, there is energy inside us that allows us to talk, walk, think, move, live. That is scientific fact. And, although we have come across many creatures who drink blood, we haven't come across anything that can drink this life force."

"Yet—" Key added.

"Yet," Rahal agreed, her face troubled, remembering his telling her that he believed everything, no matter how outlandish, had some basis in fact.

The entire team reacted to that bombshell according to their own upbringing. It was Gonzales who ultimately broke the silence.

"How is that even possible?" he marveled.

"According to around five thousand years of human science," Rahal said flatly, "it's not." She looked from one to the other. "But every other test supports the supposition that these four were, and are, normal children."

"Did they have blood?" Key immediately asked.

"Yes," Rahal assured him. "A little less than they should have, but yes."

"That's why the fucker had four," Daniels snarled. "Let one recover while feeding on another."

Key controlled his own anger in order to, as he had suggested to the fucker, keep his eye on the prize. "Does that correspond with the first child we found?"

Rahal paused, conflicting emotions infusing her expression. She seemed to be internally arguing with herself, and even reprimanding herself for pausing in the first place.

"No," she finally answered. "The first child is different. She is not depleted in any way. In fact, her biological functions seem enhanced in somewhat the same way as Terri's. Her EEG is off the charts."

"EEG?" Nichols asked. Although the redhead had been extensively tested after her rescue from terrorists who were trying to turn her into a human *Idmonarachne Brasieri* weapon, she never asked about what tests those were until now.

"Electroencephalogram," Rahal informed her. "Measures the electrical activity of your brain."

"But does the first child have blood?" Key pressed.

For the first time since meeting her, they all saw the scientist look ashamed.

"Her vital signs are very weak," she said, seemingly just as weakly. "I'm afraid any intrusive test will kill her."

Daniels didn't even take a moment before snorting. "Hey, *death* didn't kill her. I doubt any test you could give her will!"

His words, rather than make her retreat even further, heightened her defenses. "You're assuming a great deal!" she retorted. "We have no scientific proof she actually returned from the dead!"

Lancaster looked ready to start barking orders, but Key's quiet, sharp words beat him to it.

"Stand down, Morty," he said before turning an understanding, even considerate face toward Rahal. "But he's got a point, Eshe. This is already ugly and promises to get uglier. We need to know their biology, how they tick."

"I know, Joe," she answered with apology, but also resolution. "I'll take care of it. Now."

He stopped her before she could leave. "What about the fifth child? The one in the coma."

Rahal stopped near the exit, looking helpless. "She's alive, but just barely. She needs time to recover before we can even begin to truly treat her. I'm sorry, truly sorry, but we just have to wait."

She turned, then stopped when she discovered that her way was blocked. Dr. Helen stood in the doorway, looking humble but pleasantly resolute.

"I am so sorry to interrupt," she said. "But the child—the one you call the fifth child? The one in the coma?"

"Yes?" Lancaster said, coming forward. "What of her?"

The old Chinese woman looked placidly up into the retired general's face. "I believe I can reach her."

Chapter 10

"Needles?" Daniels whispered incredulously.

"Acupuncture," Gonzales explained quietly, reassuringly.

When Dr. Helen said she could "reach" the comatose girl, it soon became apparent that what she meant was that she could wake her. The woman, still wearing a lab coat over a simple, hemp-cotton, Chinese-style shirt and pants, laid out her worn leather kit, which was full of individually wrapped, short, medium-length, and long needles—each starting with a tiny top designed for tapping, a thinly wrapped shaft top designed for finger-rolling, and a pin end that was so sharp and fine it nearly disappeared from sight.

The team stood in the adjoining observation room of the intensive care unit, which was equipped with multiple-angle video feeds as well as a surveillance window. It reminded Nichols of the time her father, a prison guard, had taken her to an execution. It was also the field team trio's first good look at the second child they had rescued—which Daniels, being Daniels, quickly noted was not nearly as angelic-looking as the first.

"This is just a kid," he sarcastically observed. "Just a normal kid." He looked back at her, his face threatening to express a sadness he always sought to repress. "Poor thing." Daniels dodged that emotional bullet by shifting his attention to Lancaster, who stood between him and Key. "I suppose she knows what she's doing, right?" he commented-critiqued of Dr. Helen. "She comes highly recommended, I suppose?"

"Yes," said Lancaster, with a grim smile. "By me." He took the moment to look directly back at Daniels. "I don't think it's possible to do what I did, either before or after my military service, without damage. Damage that became seemingly impossible for Western medicine to effectively treat."

"Correct," Rahal mused with concern. "English-speaking doctors all too often seek to treat symptoms with corporate-backed drugs, rather than help the body to heal the source of the illness."

"Nothing wrong with a good drug," Daniels said in an attempt to lighten the mood and break the building tension. It worked to a degree. A very small degree.

"That may be," Rahal conceded. "But there is something wrong with a bad drug."

"Dr. Helen agrees with both of you," Lancaster interrupted. "She told me an informed balance of the best from every culture's medicine is the wisest course of treatment." He looked back over at the older woman as she tenderly laid the child on her back.

"I suppose her course of treatment worked for you," Daniels commented.

"In spades," Lancaster replied. "Still does."

All conversation stopped as Dr. Helen picked a medium-length needle and brought it up over the child's body.

"I seek to stimulate, then activate, the posterior right cerebellum," came the older Chinese woman's voice from the observation room speaker.

They all heard Rahal's breathing deepen. "The brain's center for sleep, consciousness, *and* happiness," she murmured. "Oh, smart. Very smart." She looked up at Key. "By engaging both the happiness and consciousness centers of the brain, she'll make the girl want to wake up."

They all watched as Dr. Helen brought the needle down to the girl's calf.

"So—if this is about the brain, shouldn't she be sticking it in her head?" Daniels wondered.

"Effective acupuncture points are located throughout the body," Rahal told him quietly while keeping her gaze on the Chinese woman and the Punjabi child. "They are as complex as the human nervous system itself."

Silence descended on the observation room again as the needle touched the girl's skin, and Dr. Helen inserted it by rubbing the pin's shaft between her thumb and forefinger. Daniels, especially, was disappointed when no lights flashed, no gong sounded, and the girl didn't instantly awake.

"Now I seek to actuate the left and middle frontal gyrus," Dr. Helen said, seemingly to herself.

"This could take some time," Lancaster informed them. "No treatment works with a single needle alone."

In fact, Dr. Helen was already inserting a second needle into an acupuncture point in the girl's fibula.

Gonzales distracted himself from Dr. Helen's preparations by repeatedly going over Key's report in his mind. "I just don't get it," he muttered. "There was enough sedative in each dart to put an entire 'hood to sleep. But you say this fucker took a fistful of them in the face like they were candy."

"Several fistfuls," Key corrected quietly. "All over." Key then looked meaningfully at the mechanic. "But sedatives can't work if there's no blood for them to travel in."

Gonzales looked at him doubtfully, but couldn't argue the point. He looked down, deep in his own thoughts, as Rahal appeared beside Key, her hand on his shoulder.

"Might as well use the time productively," she told him. "I'll test the first girl's blood." She bit her lower lip. "Or lack of it. Finally."

Key placed his hand over hers, giving her an encouraging nod. "Save your punishment for the monsters who did this," he suggested.

She gave him a weak, but honest, smile, and was two steps toward the exit when Dr. Helen stopped her again.

"Eyes open," she said, apparently having not heard what Lancaster mentioned about possible delays. The team's heads snapped back to the window as if all on the same string. Sure enough, the fifth child, the one who had been in a coma, lay there serenely, her dark eyes open. Key remembered what Rahal had said about the brain's happiness center and was grateful for Dr. Helen's experience, knowledge, and skill.

"You ready?" Lancaster snapped at Safar.

The Arab-American, who had been at the surveillance camera control board the entire time, gave him a thumbs-up. "Translator programmed from the second we came in here," he reported.

The latest software was equipped to interpret all twenty-two major Indian languages, as well as more than five hundred dialects. Because of where they thought the girl was stolen from, Safar had concentrated the sub-programming on Punjabi and its fifteen primary dialects but was ready to adapt the software to interpret any variation.

"Ask her who kidnapped her," Lancaster instructed him.

Safar's fingers danced on the keyboard; then they all heard a calm, soothing, female voice say something in Hindi, Urdu, and then Punjabi. They watched the girl blink slowly, and then, unbidden, Safar's fingers moved, and the words were repeated, only this time in Doabi, Majhi, Malwi, and Pwadhi.

The girl had a small, twitchy reaction of recognition, so Safar repeated the question again in Pwadhi, the fourth most common dialect of the Punjabi language. He then looked up at Lancaster for any suggestions or instructions, but the retired general held up a pausing finger, recognizing the girl's facial movements. As far as he was concerned, the girl was thinking.

Dr. Helen carefully and painlessly added a short needle on either side of the girl's fibula to stimulate her right inferior parietal lobe, as well as her dorsal anterior cingulate, which would hopefully further awaken her memory, body-facial recognition, and even her reward-based decision-making process.

It seemed to work, because the girl's lower lip drooped, her eyes grew dreamy, and childlikewords began to emerge. The same soothing female voice that had spoken to the girl started speaking to the people in the recovery room.

"Beautiful woman..." she whispered. "Said...come. So beautiful. Be with her. Forever."

Key realized he wasn't breathing, even though his mouth was open. He corrected the situation and, like the others, leaned toward the window just in time to see the girl's eyes start to sparkle, and her lips stretch into a heartbreaking smile. Sounds continued to emerge from her, but the soothing voice didn't match them.

"Fa. Teh. Puh—"

Lancaster looked sharply at Safar, as the techie shook his head helplessly while his fingers stabbed. Thankfully for them both, Dr. Helen solved the mystery.

"She is singing," the Chinese woman said with barely contained pleasure.

Safar's eyebrows went up, and he adjusted the programming accordingly. Suddenly the soothing female voice was uttering recognizable words.

"What he...took from...my eyes."

Once again Lancaster looked accusingly at Safar. Once again, Safar could only hold his hands up helplessly.

"Ask her what happened to the woman," the retired general instructed.

Safar did as he was told, and the team watched as the new words, although just as soothing as the others, seemed to hit the girl's face like refreshing rain turning to painful sleet. Her little face twisted up and her eyes grew dark.

"No woman. Monster man. Monster man! No. No!" The poor child's little body began to tremble, then spasm.

"Stop," Key said. Lancaster didn't countermand the order, but Key wouldn't have cared if he had. His eyes fixed on the doctor. "Can you help her rest?"

But Dr. Helen was already removing some needles, and adding others all over the girl's body. As they watched, the girl's obvious pain and fear subsided, and she soon achieved a restful sleep.

Key turned to the others with a deep exhalation to see each team member dealing with the situation.

"What now, Major?" Lancaster asked evenly, figuring that if Key was going to shut the questioning down, he had damn good reason.

"What else?" Key said calmly. "We nail this fucker."

"How?" Daniels asked, though it was more like a complaint.

"Like this," Key snapped at his friend before looking over at Safar. "Scour the lyric databases, Faisal. Give us everything with 'what he took from my eyes' in them. Start with Hindi movie musicals."

Daniels's jaw dropped, but Gonzales grinned, hitting the big man in the arm. "Indian movies," he told him. "Some of the best in the world. All three hours long, all filled with at least six songs. Even though they are almost exclusively shown in India, it's the third-largest movie audience in the world after America and China." Gonzales reacted to Daniels's flabbergasted face with a sniff. "Everybody knows that, man."

But Key wasn't done. "Fa. Teh. Puh," he repeated to them, enunciating carefully. "Mean anything to you?"

Daniels reacted as if his superior officer had to be kidding. "Just baby talk, man!" he grumbled.

"Exactly," Key retorted as if the big man was a prize student. "She *is* practically a baby, man. So what is that in baby talk?"

Lancaster took a moment to look at Safar with an expression wondering if the translation software was sophisticated enough to translate Punjabi baby talk into useable English. But all Safar did was smile and nod.

"Fa," they heard, and turned to the young woman with the fiery hair. "Fire," Nichols guessed, looking at each person to gauge their reaction. "That's all I could think of. Fire."

Daniels threw his hands up and turned around as if everyone in the room had gone nuts.

"Teh," Rahal mused. "Tent?" It was difficult for her not to remember the tent where her mentor, Professor Basheer Davi, had hidden from the forces who wanted to turn the *Idmonarchne Brasieri* into weapons—the tent where he ultimately committed suicide before her very eyes. "Puh," she continued. "Pole? Tent pole?"

Key considered it, then shook his head. "You're thinking like you. Think like her." He pointed at the girl through the glass, gratified that she seemed to be resting peacefully, not sunk back into a torture-driven coma. The last thing he saw before turning back to the others was Dr. Helen's pleased face. "I don't think this girl was imprisoned in a tent when the monster man took her from the beautiful woman. So where would she be kept? In a region that's the spiritual center of the Sikh?"

Lancaster got it first. "Not tent pole," he said firmly. "Temple."

Key nodded in agreement. "Faisal," he called. "See if 'fire temple' rings any database bells."

"We were already in the bastard's fire temple, Joe," Daniels complained. "It's matchsticks, remember?"

"I don't need to know where the fucker *was*, Morty," Key came back at him. "I want to know where he is. Last time we saw him, he was literally on the run. I want to know where he's running to. And I'll use any clue to find out—even one from a poor tortured girl."

"Already got some hits you ought to look at, Joe," Safar announced.

"Ah," Key responded with relief. "Better living through science." He started moving toward the control board while getting Lancaster's attention. "How are the headgear enhancements coming?"

"Lancaster Labs is testing several prototypes even as we speak," the retired general informed him. "Want it battle-ready even more than you do."

"Doubt that," Key commented as he passed a still dumbfounded Daniels.

"Enhancements? What enhancements?" he demanded. "What are we going to do, wear tinfoil hats?"

"Well, as a matter of fact—" Key drawled as he came around the control board desk.

"No, no," Daniels mock-complained, throwing up his hands again. "Don't tell me. I'll find out when I find out."

Key nodded as he reached Safar, knowing all too well that this banter was everyone's release from the sad and frightening place they were in and planning to attack. But now it was time to get back to serious business.

"Eshe," he called to the still somewhat shell-shocked scientist. He waited until she snapped out of her reverie, then spoke kindly. "We need your findings, and this time, I promise, Dr. Helen won't interrupt."

"Of course, of course," Rahal answered, giving him a wan "don't worry, I got this" smile. "Right away, Joe."

She left the rest of the team and moved toward the intensive care unit as they moved out of the queen's quarters and into their control room, lab, workshop, and armory. She made it all the way to the radiation containment lockdown observation room before she stopped.

She stared at the tiny, wrapped, strapped, yet still angelic-looking little girl swathed inside polymer bubbles, feeling as paralyzed as she always did in the kid's vicinity. By all rights, the mind muddying this child seemed capable of was not possible in these circumstances. The most sophisticated security devices available, even to Lancaster, should have been effective. But in five thousand years of human science humans had never come across life-force eaters before. Or had they?

Rahal shook her head, as if the thoughts would come out her ears. *He had to be wrong*, she found herself thinking. *I have to prove him wrong.*

She went to her desk, unlocked the top right drawer, and rummaged around in the back until she pulled out the small, bubble-wrapped package she had taped there. Inside was a prepaid ghost phone that her students had presented to her upon her retirement from the Oman Medical College.

"Just in case you ever need it," her top student had said with a sunny, innocent, smile. "Or us."

Rahal looked skyward, praying that what she was doing was right, at the same moment she accepted the ever-growing feeling that she needed help that none of these warriors could supply. Then she looked at the anonymous, disposable phone number app, got the dummy email address and password, and tapped out what she hoped would be her only private, anonymous, untraceable message.

Need help, it read. *Top expert infectious diseases.*

Chapter 11

Craven hated going into the caves.

But making the pilgrimage from his prisons to the lairs of Aarif Zaman felt positively freeing after his fetid life. The dusty ground beneath his bare feet, and the expanse of sky above him, made him feel more elated than nearly anything else he had ever experienced. Nearly.

So, as he approached the entrance to the network of caves, he felt it all being slowly taken from him. Even his Veranasi crypt felt expansive and welcoming compared to the labyrinthine maze of this Paktika Province network of caves. Within moments of his entering, he felt submerged in a long, winding coffin.

But, despite the mounting feeling of claustrophobia, Craven was amused by the wavering of his power in close proximity. Some of Zaman's soldiers didn't appear to see him at all, while others would wonder, ponder, or even do a double-take when he appeared in their vision—a ragged, haggard, ancient man in a thin, stained robe. But not a single person raised an alarm or even spoke to, or of, him.

So Craven was free to observe their preparations. Much had been accomplished since his previous visit. Now he could see the cunning of the battlements, and how they had dug, fashioned, and erected a series of blocks and junctures that impelled any interloper to continue deeper into the stone and rock warren.

The gaunt man continued toward the entrance of the camouflaged cavern. It was a relatively wide aperture, where at least a dozen of Zaman's men could take a stubborn stand, only to twist and turn around a seemingly simple outcropping. Craven approached the spot, a rare smile widening on his face. He imagined himself as one of those interlopers, shifting his weight from left to right to follow their adversary around the outcropping.

And then came the surprising expanse—a yawning, multi-tiered grotto, from which entire mezzanines full of Zaman's soldiers could fire upon, or threaten to fire upon, them. Or something even worse.

As he passed the entry spot to start his descent into the grotto, Craven looked down upon several of Zaman's soldiers preparing a further surprise—a cunningly installed explosive designed not to destroy, but to trap, anyone foolish enough to pursue a quarry into the area. Craven let the cunning intelligence of the groundwork fill him. He combined it with the sensations of freedom the expansive landscape had instilled in him.

He wanted to be filled with euphoria. He felt he needed to be filled with it if his deception was to work. He continued to trudge, unacknowledged and perhaps unseen, across the grotto until he reached what Zaman called his vantage point—a small military headquarters from which he could survey the entire grotto without the risk of being reached by anyone trapped there. As Craven got ever closer, navigating the steep inclines like a mountain goat, he saw many more soldiers installing disguised booby traps to prevent an attack or escape. He gauged the effectiveness of his mental disguise as he felt the energy of his master grow. As long as none of Zaman's soldiers became aware of him, he knew his strength was potent.

As he stepped into Zaman's cavern headquarters, one soldier widened his eyes, seemingly repulsed by Craven's appearance and smell. It was little wonder, since that was the moment the man saw his master and his master's companion.

It was as if Zaman was of no importance or consequence, despite the fact that he stood directly next to Mahasona and Tajabana. They all wore their traditional garb—the terrorist chief in a turban, *khet* upper tunic, *partug* pants, and boots, while his master was in his hooded robe, and his companion in her open one. Although Zaman had been speaking expansively and excitedly when Craven had entered, he also did not acknowledge the appearance of the wizened man. In fact, he kept speaking as he slowly drifted away from the others, seemingly unaware he was still talking and moving.

By the time Craven reached his master, Zaman was all the way across the room, although speaking as if he were not.

"It is done," Craven lied.

His master did not even look at him. "Of course it is," he replied. "You would not have come if it had not been done."

Craven felt compelled to drop to his knees, prostrating himself at his master's feet. "Command me," he gasped, his clawed hands shaking. "What more can I do to serve you?"

"Await," Mahasona said. "Await the start of the renewed era. Be prepared to assist as necessary."

Craven started to move away, half-crawling and half-scrambling. He mentally demanded that he remain silent, but his mouth would not obey.

"Yes, master," he babbled faintly. "Yes—"

His power to obscure his presence returned as soon as he dragged himself out of the enclosure. Still, as he scrabbled down one grotto wall, he found he could not rise. He kept crawling like an insect until the unseen pressure on his back started to relent. He dragged himself to the outcropping at the start of the pit, and there he was finally able to get to his feet.

As he started to retrace his steps, he longed to return to the sprawling landscape where he could breathe again. Only then, when his master was completely distracted by his plans with Zaman, and Craven was deep in the Waziristan woods, would he start to plan what he had to do next. But he had not taken another full step before he heard the soft feminine voice deep in his mind's ear.

"What have you done?"

He turned to see his master's companion standing calmly amongst the soldiers and workers, who continued to toil without acknowledging them in any way, despite the extensive swashes of her shapely flesh exposed in the deep openings of her robe's front. Had they been able to perceive her she would have certainly been beaten or burned to death for such a blatant, almost satirical, transgression of their gender policies.

Women had been banned from appearing without a head-to-toe *burqa* anywhere the Taliban ruled or being heard at any time—not even the sound of their footsteps. And here this Tajabana stood, her achingly beautiful head, neck, cleavage and legs all but exposed in a silky robe that belted tightly around her curvaceous shape.

Craven managed to raise his head and gaze into her unearthly eyes, but the power of speech failed him as he noticed the splash of freckles that adorned her forehead and nose in a way that reminded him of an inspiring constellation. As with everything she said and did, it only added even more to her allure.

"I—" he finally managed to stammer. "I have done as I was bidden."

"What were you bidden?" she immediately responded, her tone nearly innocent and inquisitive.

Perhaps she had not heard, Craven thought. Yes, she had been right beside them at the time, but perhaps his master had prevented her hearing, as he just had for Zaman. But hadn't she foretold of his master's order, just before his master had uttered it?

"I—I cleaned the—my—mess." He forced his head to remain unbowed. He forced himself to look directly at her astonishing face.

"Did you?" she asked, seemingly in a hopeful tone.

He felt his head make a single, jerking, nod. "Whatever, or whoever the cost."

She was Tajabana, he told himself. *She must still hunger, but now for power. The master's continued deference must have emboldened her.*

"Whatever," she nodded. "But whoever?"

Now her tone had shifted slightly to ingenuous incredulity. Craven felt his stomach lurch, which he reacted to with fearful defiance.

"Who are you to doubt me?" he hissed as if his skin had sprung a slow leak. "Does the master know what you did to me? Should the master know that you bestow empowerment without his presence?"

The woman reacted with widened eyes and a sudden, beaming, smile. "Would you tell him?" she urged happily. "It would be so much better if it came from you. Please, would you tell him now?"

Craven felt his back bending, his head twisting to the side. "No, no," he nearly begged. "He is much too busy now. I mustn't."

"Yes, yes," she said agreeably. "Much too busy preparing for the renewed age—the renewed age that might be threatened if *gweilo* were to discover the plan before its time."

She had used their word for hominid devil. He felt his guts twisting and his mind throbbing. She knew. As always, she somehow knew.

"Yes!" he yelled in her face, as if in exultation, but, at the same moment, he lunged at her—his fingers claws, his curved, skeletal member erupting from his robe, and his slavering, pointed tongue whipping out of his mouth.

It was what he had done to his victims—his extended hands clamping onto their skulls, his inflating, stabbing tongue filling their throats, and his scimitar-like male member skewering and locking inside them for a frozen second before the feeding started.

But not this time. This time, when his flesh was a hair's width from hers, she erupted off the ground like a sun going nova. Her arms were wide and encompassing, her fingers were splayed, and her legs were open as if she were being drawn and quartered. He could have sworn she was levitating off the ground. But her mouth was also open and screaming.

The scream seemed to smash into the walls, floor, and ceiling of the cave, roaring through it like a tsunami of sound. Her eyes blazed, and her hair roiled around her irradiating face, as Craven was thrown back by the force of her defense. He smashed into the ground and slid back into a wall.

But as soon as he landed, she was there, her left thumb deep in one nostril and that hand's first two fingers deep in his eyes. He felt her nails threaten to pop them like grapes, but then slide off to clamp down into the muscles and fatty tissue between the orbs and his skull's sockets.

"Yes," she echoed his last word, her voice soft, even loving, in his ear. He felt her drawing his head forward by his nose and skull. Her other hand rested on the base of his spine. "It *is* time for feeding. But not yours—."

He remembered the first time she had done this to him. He remembered her freeing him from his pain on the banks of the Ganges two hundred and fifty-three years before—only to replace it with an aching, agonizing appetite. He remembered the feel of her—not her teeth, but her tongue—at the base of his skull. Her tongue, and then, somehow from within it, its needle.

This time he knew he would never be free. This time, the suffering would be worse, and eternal. This time he would pay for his lie with damnation. But this time he also remembered the traps Zaman's soldiers had been setting in the walls. This time he remembered the detonators they were carefully secreting so the explosives could be set off by signal or strike.

"Ah, so sad," he heard his master's companion coo as her firm, full breasts pressed against his back. "You will be so much better without a mind of your own."

Craven lurched, attacking the cave wall the way he attacked the children—fingers clawing, teeth clamping, tongue and loins pumping, legs pressing, feet scratching.

His pinky nail found one detonator. That was all it took to set off a chain reaction. The continuing and concussive explosion was so powerful it left a permanent scar on the Urgon countryside, and could be seen from passing Ariana Afghan Airline planes.

Chapter 12

"We've got him!"

Colonel Patrick Logan spun around at the cry. "Zaman?"

Stupid question, thought the shapely brunette he had chosen as his aide. *Who else would it be?* But what she said aloud was an entirely different matter. "Yes, sir, they have a location. It's—"

But he cut her off, grabbing the phone from her hand. "What have you got?" he barked. "Talk to me."

Of course, she thought, knowing him all too well even in the short time she had been under his command. *He'd want to feel that he found the location himself.* She had little doubt that would be the way it sounded to everyone he spoke to from now on. She watched his face as he got the news from the ground intel as well as the spy satellites. It looked as if he were about to have the greatest orgasm ever.

Would he finish the call with a "good work"? she thought. *Of course he wouldn't.* And he didn't.

"Alert my units," he snapped. "Wait a minute, never mind, I'll do it myself." He disconnected the call while muttering "If you want something done right—" and immediately made another.

His brunette aide waited for the inevitable, and easily predictable. She saw his mind working on everything but the military strategy, then witnessed his face brighten as his call was quickly answered.

"Mount up, boys!" Logan cried. "I found him!"

* * * *

Retired General Charles L. Lancaster arrived at Bagram Airfield, one of the three main U.S.-friendly bases left in Afghanistan, feeling pissed and elated. He would have preferred Camp Leatherneck in Helmand Province or Forward Operating Base Delaram in the province of the same name, but Bagram was closer—a mere three hundred and fifty miles from Cerberus HQ—and more elaborately equipped.

The "elated" came from landing at a well-oiled military machine in the throes of doing what it did best. The "pissed" came from why he was here at all. Lancaster was in full uniform and respectfully returned each salute he received. His personal pilots once agreed that he'd probably get almost as many even in civvies. As he marched into the thick of the preparations, he kept a sharp lookout for his quarry, who he knew would be wherever he looked the best.

Sure enough, Logan was right at the juncture where the Combined Task Force 1st Cavalry Division, the 82nd Combat Aviation "Task Force Pale Horse" Brigade, and the 3-10 Task Force Phoenix linked. There, the 455th Air Expeditionary Wing of the U.S. Air Force was working with Logan's U.S. Marine Corps unit to expedite a surgical strike on the last known whereabouts of Aarif Zaman and his forces. As he neared, Lancaster could clearly see "taking down Bin Laden" visions dancing in Logan's head.

Letting Logan take credit for stopping the Arachnosaurs had been an honest, but stupid, mistake. Lancaster had underestimated the brown-noser's self-worth issues. The retired general had hoped to create an eager-to-please ally and front, who'd toe the line in exchange for more acclaim. But, sadly, the more credit Logan got, the more power he wanted, and the greater his self-delusion of his own intelligence. He didn't want to owe anybody, even secretly.

"Using a sledgehammer on a carpet tack?" Lancaster asked from directly behind Logan's left earlobe. A normal person might have to shout over the noise of the engines and equipment, but Lancaster had learned how to properly use his larynx.

Logan glanced over his shoulder, and his expression turned sour. "Don't have time for you now, Chuck," he snapped. "Going to collect a wanted terrorist."

He purposely marched toward the command aircraft—one of the newer MV-22 Osprey tiltrotor helicopters—as Lancaster looked sympathetically at the staff sergeant who had suffered Logan's empty orders. Lancaster returned the sergeant's salute, then fell into step with Logan.

"We saw the same intel, Pat," Lancaster said evenly in his ear as he watched the dozens of fully equipped assault soldiers piling into CH-53E Super Stallion choppers. "Apparently, we interpreted it differently."

Logan stopped short and whirled on the retired general. "How else could it have been interpreted? One second the hills of Paktika Urgon are as they've always been. The next second almost an entire chain of them erupts, leaving a scar that could be seen from space, for Christ's sake. What does that say to you, oh glorious interpreter?"

"A coal, copper, crude oil, or even natural gas mine could have exploded," Lancaster replied. "It happens. Or any number of other things."

"Or," Logan fumed, getting to within an inch of Lancaster's face—having to twist his head up at the much taller man. "Or Aarif Zaman, who was last reported in that very area, was preparing another heinous attack on an American landmark, and one of his Pashtun flunkies mistook a red wire for a green wire. That happens, too!"

"Okay," Lancaster said reasonably. "Let's say that did happen." He motioned at all the high-impact, ultimate-intensity activity around them. "Why use the cavalry for a glorified mop-up operation? Send in the drones."

Logan reacted as if Lancaster had presented him a daffodil. He shifted his head back on his neck, then his expression became suspicious. "Oh, you'd like that, wouldn't you, Chuck? What, while we're tooth-picking every inch, your Cerebellus boys try an end run to get all the glory?"

Lancaster had a hard time not rolling his eyes at the man's transparency. He just told Lancaster what he would have done—something the general would never do. But before he could disagree and offer assurances, Logan's look of disbelief turned to shrewdness.

"Why come all this way just to undermine me?" he wondered. "That's not like you, Chuck. There's got to be more to it than that. What are you not telling me, you crafty bastard?"

Lancaster inwardly sighed, remembering what his grandfather used to say. "You can lead a horse to water, but you can't teach him to fish." He figured Logan would never take an honest warning, but maybe now that he had "gotten it out of him," he would.

"There's more to this than meets the eye, Pat," Lancaster said as evenly and clearly as he could. "We're still working on it, but I can guarantee you we're not dealing with just a terrorist here. I am treating you as I would treat any of my people. This is not the time to go in blind, hopeful, or certain. I couldn't just sit back and not let you know."

Logan stared at him. Lancaster waited, hoping that, by some miracle, Logan would get beyond his ambition, and filter this through something other than his own innate distrust. And, much to his credit, he did. But much to his discredit, he replaced it with hurt pride.

"Oookay, Chuck," Logan finally said, already turning away. "Message received. Now, if you don't mind, I have a terrorist mess to clean up, which I will attempt to do without tripping over my own feet or ignoring the USMC rules and regulations that have served us well for the past two hundred and forty years!"

Lancaster watched him go double time to his Osprey tiltrotor command center with a certain resignation. *Well*, he thought, *I tried.*

When he turned back to his own jet, he found Logan's new aide standing beside him, in a full pencil skirt, black heels, tailored shirt uniform, clutching a clipboard to her majestic chest. He hoped, for her sake, she wasn't as buttoned-up as she looked.

"You going?" Lancaster asked. She shook her head, gratefully. He put out his hand. "General Charles Lancaster, retired."

She shook his hand in her strong, but not too strong, elegant, one. "First Lieutenant Rita Jayson," she said in a firm voice—one, like Lancaster, she didn't have to strain to use on the noisy runway. She looked up at him with striking violet eyes. "He'll be using wavelength zero niner two, by the way." Then she turned and headed back to the control tower.

As Lancaster went in the opposite direction, he murmured, "Got that, Speedy?"

"Roger, sir," Gonzales answered from Cerberus Versailles, then looked at Safar playing his keyboards like Elton John. "Hacking invisibly into their feeds now."

They all watched and listened—Lancaster on his jet's screen, and the Cerberus team in the Hispanic Mechanic's Workshop—as the Logan-led Assault Team Zebra sped toward the Urgon hill range. As the unit neared, Lancaster was willing to consider that maybe both he and Logan had made the right call. From the copters' vantage point, the area looked every inch like a devastated mining town. What was obviously a chain of caves had been torn open from the inside.

"Wow," said Daniels.

"My sentiments precisely," Safar breathed.

They all fell silent as the attack force descended ever closer. The advanced video lenses zoomed in to show the details of the devastation. Each witness picked out body parts, but only body parts. And even those body parts were torn, snapped, flayed, and burnt almost beyond recognition.

"They must have been using Octabane too," Nichols guessed.

"Makes sense," Lancaster said approvingly. "Another link in the chain of evidence that our mission is related to theirs."

To Lancaster's satisfaction, Logan made two observational passes over the devastated area, the second being even more detailed than the first.

"No one could have survived the intensity of this blast," Rahal mused. That garnered a look from Key, but only for a moment. Then his gaze returned to the screens as the choppers started their final descents.

"How many helmet cams can you tap into?" he asked Safar.

The tech was about to answer, but snapped his mouth shut as he studied his monitor arrays. "I was about to answer 'how many do you want,' but that would result in all the screens being taken up by postage stamp-size squares," he explained. "Let me break it up into forty-eight quarter-screen images from the soldiers in front, in the middle, and bringing up the rear. Okay?'

"Works for me," Daniels piped up. "Joe, you want to watch the front? Ter, willing to take the middle?"

"And you?" Nichols asked.

"I, of course, will watch the rear."

"To each their own," Nichols chirped.

Key remained silent but realized that even his team was treating the exercise like a done deal. But that only made his attention all the sharper.

Logan's unit hit the ground. Logan himself, of course, was nowhere to be seen. He "had" to remain in his command center chopper, which, according to its video feed, was still hovering above the location. Both Lancaster and Key knew it would only land once they got the word that the site was secured and the "coast was clear."

That was not long in coming. The head team of the unit made a circuit through the open-top tunnels the explosion had made the caves into—first all the way forward, then all the way back. The center units broke off as needed to check that every tributary off the center paths was well and truly sealed, while the rear teams scoured the area for any other openings or escape routes.

Lancaster and Key found themselves leaning ever closer to their screens to try catching glimpses of anything else that was moving, be it birds or burros. Key spotted a Kashmir nuthatch and red-fronted serin—both indigenous to Afghanistan—but nothing else.

The soldiers seemed to think the same. The chatter on their comm-links was all in the affirmative, with a chorus of "all-clears" stretching from Key through Nichols to Daniels. They all watched Logan's tiltrotor begin to descend via its video feed, as well as from a few witnessing ground troops.

All but Gonzales, who was leaning in to a monitor screen on the far, bottom, right. *"Espera un minuto,"* he breathed, tapping the upper left corner. "What is that? A carpenter bee? A bush cricket?"

"What?" Key immediately asked, but Gonzales was shifting toward Safar.

"Can you close-up on this?" he asked, pointing at the screen.

"What?" Daniels complained. "He can't control a soldier's helmet—! Never mind," he quickly corrected himself as Safar did just that.

"Can't control the cam," Safar explained to Daniels as everyone else, including Lancaster, practically pressed their noses to the glass. "But can control this screen."

They all watched as a one-inch section of the chalky white dirt of the excavated cave wall began to crumble.

"Shhh—" Lancaster began to hiss, not as a method of quieting anyone, but as a preamble to a short, sharp curse word.

Key's eyes pin-balled to every vid-feed on every screen, looking for what he had been looking for before. Any non-U.S. military movement. Any at all.

He saw the trunk of a Deodar cedar tree shift.

That was the only way he could describe it. The dark brown bark of the coarse, strong, thick, bone-shaped tree did not chip, fleck, or break. It seemed to waver in his vision, as if he had been crossing his eyes. But he hadn't been crossing his eyes.

"Shit!" Key snarled. "Can we reach them? Can we tap into their comm lines?"

But then it was too late. As they watched, the inch-sized piece of the crumbling wall turned into a foot-sized patch, then a yard, and then the wall itself collapsed around a surging human figure. A surging human figure thrusting an AK-47 in front of him.

And once that first man appeared, many more appeared, each and every one coming out from the walls surrounding the soldiers as if they were being hatched from eggs.

The chaos that resulted was almost too much for any of them to decipher. The audio-comms were full of Logan's screechings of escape and retreat, and the images from his tiltrotor vid screen was full of fuzzy, lurching images as his command center all but clawed back into the sky.

For a moment, they all could see what the MV-22 Osprey cam could see: the long open-aired tunnels filled with U.S. Marines being surprised and surrounded by what appeared to be an ant-farm's worth of insects overwhelming them. But then, even that image began to get fuzzy, as if the lens was being smudged by Satan's thumb.

"Fuck, a—" Daniels gagged. *"How?"*

But then Key was at Nichols's side, his encouraging voice in the ear of the girl with the enhanced reflexes. "What do you see, Terri?" he asked quietly. "Focus, concentrate. Tell me what you see."

She did as she was told. "Each helmet-cam got fuzzy," she said. "First they were clear, picking up the images of the ambushers, then, each began to unfocus, then wink out. One by one, one after another, until—"

She didn't finish the sentence. She didn't have to. Instead she pointed. Safar immediately fed the single remaining image onto all the screens.

Coming out from the cedar tree, wearing a perfectly Deodar-camouflaged robe, was a man. As he approached the last remaining working helmet cam, he pushed back the hood, revealing his identity.

"Yes," said Aarif Zaman in perfect English. "Yes, you see your folly now, stupid soldiers? Send as many as you want. I'll just keep going until you stop me."

Then that camera too became unfocused, before flashing out.

Chapter 13

"Logan's getting torn a new one."

Key wasn't surprised by Lancaster's information. As much as Daniels, and even Nichols, would have loved to savor the repercussions of Logan's thirst for personal glory, the field team had more pressing matters to attend to.

They had quickly discovered that "what he took from my eyes" was, most likely, a lyric from one of the many songs in a 2014 Punjabi movie titled *Kashi*, which was another historical name for the city of Veranesi which, to no one's surprise, had been described as "The City of Temples."

Almost as soon as they witnessed the last helmet-cam in Paktika winking out, they didn't have time to mourn. They were on their way to. Veranesi. Meanwhile, things were happening almost as fast in Afghanistan.

"Wonder where the colonel's tail is right about now," Daniels drawled. "I figure it was so far up between his legs it would be crowding his tongue, but with his foot so far down his mouth I'm not sure everything would fit."

He and the others were stretched out in Gonzales's latest creation—a cargo jet synthesized from parts of an Airbus Beluga, an Aero Spaceline Guppy, and a Boeing Dreamlifter—which the mechanic had dubbed the B. D. G. Lawgiver.

"Well, his mouth is still working, Master Sergeant," Lancaster assured him from a video-conference link in Cerberus's Chinese Versailles HQ. "He calls it 'demanding,' but I call it begging—begging his superiors to give him a crack at making this clusterfuck right. He even called me for help pleading his case."

"You going to give him any?" Key inquired.

"Still deciding," Lancaster replied. "If I did, he promised never to doubt, or cross, me again."

"You believe that?" Daniels snorted.

"Of course not," Lancaster retorted, "but he might still be useful in the short run, while it lasts."

"Sterling praise," Key muttered drily.

There was an uncharacteristic pause coming from the other end, as if Lancaster was deciding whether to elaborate. Finally, he did. "By the way, Joe, he asked me to pass on a personal message to you."

"Oh dear," Daniels interrupted. "This should be a doozy. What do you think, Joe? Go for it or leave well enough alone?"

Key sighed. "Let's have it, sir."

Lancaster quoted it verbatim without further preamble. "'Now I knows how it feels getting your whole unit killed.' For what it's worth, Joe, I honestly think that's his idea of empathy."

Daniels was, remarkably, at a loss for words. Not Nichols. "Class act," she said, shaking her head. "Class act all the way."

When Key remained silent, Gonzales filled the void. "But whatever you, or his superiors, decide," he called from the cockpit, "they're going to have to find Zaman first. No doubt he's gone to ground, either moving to, or creating, a new hideout."

"That shouldn't be difficult," Daniels sniffed, "considering all the crooks and nannies in the shit-hole he slinks around in."

"Let's see what we can do about that," Key suggested, pleased to get back to business. "I may not be a big fan of Colonel Logan, but I'm less a fan of Aarif Zaman."

"Good point, Major," Lancaster acknowledged. "The sooner you can track down and bring in this particular—" the retired general paused, unhappy with all the slightly sick nicknames Daniels had come up with for their quarry. "Monster," he finally decided, "the better chance we'll have."

"Toward that end," Key said, "any more information from C5?"

He was referring to the fifth child, who they had rescued, and who Dr. Helen had awoken.

"She has remained aware," Rahal interjected from the Chinese Versailles clinic, "but still requires more recovery time. I can tell you, however, that she does not recognize C1."

"She visited the quarantine unit?" Nichols asked incredulously.

"Yes," Rahal reported. "We still can't get a clear photo of C1, so Dr. Helen thought it was important enough to bring C5 over on a gurney."

"Can you get a clear picture of C5?" Key immediately wondered.

"As a matter of fact," Rahal mused, "yes."

Before anyone could dwell on that interesting tidbit, Key continued as if it had no particular importance. "You got an ID on any of them yet?"

"None," Safar informed them from the copilot's seat.

"They're virtually unrecognizable from what they were," Rahal explained, "and their fingerprints and dental impressions were compromised by their—" She paused, like Lancaster, looking for an appropriate word.

"How do you describe that anyway?" Daniels wondered. "Shrinkage?"

"No, Master Sergeant," Lancaster instructed in no uncertain terms. "That is not how we are going to describe it. But I'm sure we'll come up with an appropriate word, if necessary, prior to your return. In the meantime, I have arranged a contact to meet you at Lal Bahadur Shastri Airport. I'm certain he will be extremely helpful in your hunt."

"Or, considering the more than twenty thousand temples in town," Safar called out, "your *haj*."

"Twenty thousand?" Daniels repeated. "Don't you mean two thousand?"

"No, he does not," Key told his brawny associate. "Get ready for anything."

Daniels, and the others, did just that in the remaining time of the nearly nine-hundred-mile flight. But once the BDG Lawgiver taxied to a stop in a remote cargo area of the tarmac, the field team trio found a tall, aristocratic man with high cheekbones and ice-blue eyes awaiting them at the bottom of the aircraft's stairs. He took a moment to admire the somewhat unusual cargo craft, then offered his hand.

"Christopher Peters," he said with a light accent that combined British and Hindi tones. He wore a *dhoti* tunic and a *dastar pagri* turban.

"Gone full native," Daniels whispered to Key as they approached.

"Ah, good," Peters commented as he shook hands with each one. "Traveling light, I see. From what Charles told me, I was afraid you'd be fairly bristling with bips and bobs."

"Uh, no," Key told him after a momentary pause. They were wearing their most basic Cerberus Cali-brake and Chain-silk uniforms—with only a light, zip-up, collarless jacket. "Thought it best to bring only what was necessary, since time is of the essence. Besides, we didn't want to attract undue attention."

"No worries there," Peters assured him as he led them toward the nearest parking area. "Although you've arrived between the *Nag Nathaiya* and *Ganga Mahotsav* festivals, our not-so-fair city is never at a lack for rabble—most of whom are either consecrating their dead or seeking gurus."

The man led them to a vehicle that seemed just odd enough to make Key wonder whether Gonzales had a hand in creating it. It was a small, narrow, four-door, white sedan that looked like a combination of a classic London taxi and a classic Volkswagen Bug.

"That's why I was admiring your air conveyance," he said with a proud smile. "It reminded me of my little 'artful dodger' here." He opened the back door for Nichols while motioning Key to the front passenger seat. "Designed specifically to go where other cars can't, or won't."

Once they were all in, and Peters started what sounded like a putt-putt combination of a golf-cart and lawn-mower engine, he glanced in the rearview mirror. "It's fifteen miles to town," he informed them. "What do you need to know?"

"I was just about to ask you the same thing." Key smiled.

Peters chortled, prompting raised eyebrows from Daniels. He had never heard an authentic Indian-English chortle before. "Yes, your commander is not exactly 'Jack the lad,' now is he? Best to hear it from the horse's mouth at any rate."

As he pulled the vehicle onto Highway 31, he gave them the lowdown with no shame or disclaimer. He was the great-grandson of Corporal Terence Peters, a soldier involved in the infamous 1857 massacre of innocent Indian bystanders.

"My family has been atoning for it ever since," he told them, "and I am proud to continue the tradition in this"—he motioned out the front windshield—"city of silk and soon-to-be stiffs."

Daniels laughed. "I like this guy!"

"I'm honored," Peters said with a modest smile.

"'Soon-to-be'?" Nichols echoed. "I thought everybody came to burn their dead on the Ganges River."

"Good catch," Peters commended her. "I see why Charles has so much faith in you." He caught Nichols's green eyes in the rearview mirror for a moment. "No, my dear. While the daily ritual ablutions along the stone *ghats* fronting the river, in this most holy of all crossing places, are the most obvious to the eye, the most prominent is what is not seen." He took a moment to glance at Key. "If you are dead here, you are dead, and no amount of unhygienic river water and funeral pyres will change that. But if you die here, you attain instant *moksha*."

Key knew what was coming. In fact, he was already turning his head toward the master sergeant when he said it.

"Milkshake? You get an instant milkshake?"

Peters laughed—whether out of honest appreciation or politeness, none of them were able to decide. "No, you pillock," he replied with sardonic affection. "Enlightenment. You get instant enlightenment. Something every pilgrim, guru and monk spend their entire life seeking. But all any given *banma* and *banpa* have to do is time it right so they die here."

He swung his arm along the windshield as Varanasi proper began to appear on the horizon. Even though they were prepared, the Cerberus agents had a tough time taking it all in.

"It looks like spoiled kids tried to out-do each other with multi-colored religious Lego sets," Nichols marveled, "and didn't stop."

"Do they have cement docks and forts in Lego sets?" Daniels asked her without taking his eyes off the visual chaos out the windshield. "Add boats and bikes, and a rainbow mob of people, and I think we're just about there."

"Your Mark Twain," Peters told them, "once wrote that this city is 'older than history, older than tradition, older even than legend, and looks twice as old as all of them put together.' And that was in 1897."

"Joe," Daniels complained. "How the living milkshake are we going to be able to find the bastard in this mess? Talk about a needle in a haystack—"

Key didn't bother answering. Instead he simply looked over to the driver, who sported a grim grin. Peters took a moment to knowingly return Key's gaze, then answered the master sergeant.

"It's a lot easier to find the pin if it's painted bright red," he said. He glanced back at the others as he took an exit far away from the center of the city. "Charles told me you're looking for a body snatcher, a corpse stealer, yes?"

"Yes," said Key.

"Well, you were sent to the right chauffeur," he continued as the car began to wind through increasingly restricted streets, hemmed in by structures that looked even older, and uglier, than what Mark Twain was referring to. "Over the decades I've become something of an expert in what you might call 'corpsploitation.'"

That elicited raised eyebrows from virtually everyone in the vehicle as it began to crawl into a part of town that always seemed in shadow.

"Charles described your monster to me as you described it to him." Peters continued as the car grew ever slower on the dusty bricks and dirt of the narrowing roads. "No way he's hanging out with the holies—not someone like that."

Peters pulled onto a small cement platform that was wedged between a grove of gnarled trees and a crumbling maze of rundown buildings. "We'll have to walk from here," he advised them. He glanced down at layers of cracked slate. "The roads have been covered by squatters' shanty towns."

They followed where he led them. None had to ask, nor did he feel compelled to explain, that more than a hundred thousand citizens lived in slums spread throughout Varanasi. The interloper and his guests were all pragmatic people who were not prone to figurative bleeding hearts—or even literal ones, if they could help it.

As they walked, the cracked cement gave way to broken bricks and pulverized plastic, separated by strings of tattered clothing. Anything that could be fashioned into makeshift walls and roofs was—all using ancient stone and rotting wood as skeletons. The only people brave enough to stare back at them were the aged *banmas* and *banpas* Peters had referred to before. They were not angry or resentful. They seemed too hungry and resigned for that.

"Where are the children?" Nichols whispered. "Has our guy been stealing them all?"

Peters shook his head curtly. "Other monsters are giving him a literal run for the money," he explained acerbically. "You remember the silk I mentioned in the same breath as the stiffs?" Nichols nodded. "Each piece," Peters continued, "can cost up to a thousand pounds, because of the tightness of the weave." He looked directly at the redhead with a slightly sickened smile. "Guess who does that—for slave wages?" He took a moment to scour the area for what he was looking for. "Some say this is the world capital for that sort of thing," he murmured absently. "One more missing, exploited child, more or less?" He shrugged, seemingly diffidently. "Who notices that sort of thing anymore? Ah."

He had spotted the person he wanted. Key looked in the same direction, and immediately picked up on the energy coming from an old woman— seemingly the oldest woman in the immediate area, who squatted on an unseen seat or rock or wall—both hands atop a knobby branch. She practically screamed "village elder."

Once again Key was impressed by Lancaster's contacts and reach, as Peters approached the old woman, waving the others closer.

She obviously recognized the Englishman—either because or despite his local clothing. He said something urgent to her in one of the many Indian languages. Then she looked at the others, one by one, and started babbling through toothless gums.

"She says she's been waiting for you," Peters translated. "She's been waiting to tell what she knows, what her family knows, what everyone in this slum knows, what everyone in every slum knows, but no one outside the slums will listen."

Key locked eyes with her. Hers looked like sharp pieces of flint sank in watery aspic. She kept talking.

"If anyone had come looking, or asking, they would have told," Peters continued translating, "but no one did, and no one here would go out to find someone who would listen, because we need him to take the bodies away. Every day we die. Every morning and every night we die. We cannot eat them, and if we burned them, everything would burn. We would all burn. So we let him take them away. And, if now and again, more than just the dead are taken, who are we to say? Who are we to know? Who are we to count?"

Key asked Peters, but kept staring at the woman. "Does she know where he is? Does she know where he lives?"

He watched the Englishman ask, and saw the woman nod. Peters straightened and looked meaningfully at the others. "It is not far," he informed them. "They even have a sobriquet for his abattoir."

Key looked up at Daniels, expecting and receiving his puzzled expression. "Nickname," he defined.

"Then why didn't he just say that?" Daniels asked Key before looking back at Peters. "What is it?"

"Fire Temple," Peters told them.

Chapter 14

"I don't like it."

Daniels's hushed comment was an understatement. The sight of it was bad enough, and it had also been difficult to find. At first glance it looked like a combination junkyard and latrine that was just far enough away from the outskirts of the slum to protect what was left of the residents' olfactory nerves. Upon closer inspection, what initially seemed to be a crumbling part of the refuse's foundation turned out to be an overgrown, overwhelmed block house.

Peters had to look especially carefully to find even its entrance—a small, squat opening covered only with what appeared to be a tattered, stained burial shroud, with the words *Aag Mandir* scratched and scrawled above it.

"Fire Temple," the elder Englishman softly translated for the others.

"Fire temple my third eye," Daniels muttered as he neared. "It's a graveyard for garbage." He glanced at Nichols to see how her enhanced senses were holding up. "This is the last place crap goes before it dies."

"I believe everything here is already dead," Nichols commented.

"Okay," Key quietly interrupted, holding up what looked like a little, conical piece of wax between his thumb and forefinger. "Use the new tech."

Daniels and Nichols followed suit. They all placed it in their other ears, opposite their ear-comms. Peters was too polite and circumspect to ask the question he obviously wanted to, but the three Cerberus agents noted his expression.

"We're guinea pigs today, old boy," Daniels whispered to him. "Something our tech wiz concocted."

Peters's expression changed to sardonic skepticism.

"Wish they had been working on 'nasal-filters' too." Nichols gagged.

"Not a bad idea," Key murmured. "A little late, but good." He looked to Peters. "Best to stay here. We know what this guy is capable of."

"Oh no, dear boy," Peters quietly protested. "What if your earplugs malfunction? Or you need an important translation?" Seeing Key's resolute expression waver, he offered a compromise. "Tell you what. I'll stay back, phone at the ready. First sign of trouble, I'll scamper. I assure you."

Now it was Key's turn to "not like it." But he had unavoidable visions of the new tech somehow making them dizzy or off-balance. The tech was supposed to counter whatever these creatures threw at their mind's chemistry, but he knew damn well that the brain was so complex it really couldn't even understand itself. And Lancaster Labs got these prototypes to them faster than it took to create a new Ben & Jerry's ice cream flavor. And if the worst happened, being in constant touch with HQ and the airport Lawgiver via their ear-comms wouldn't be good enough.

So Key nodded curtly at Peters, then looked to the others, who were both holding what looked like black and silver fountain pens in one hand. With the other, they slipped on what looked to Peters like head-adhering sunglasses that all but sealed their eyes behind concave half-eggs. Key didn't need to tell him they were equipped with the most advanced night vision Lancaster could acquire. Night-vision that made infrared look like blindfolds. Now even the darkest cave would appear lit by the summer sun.

With a nod from Key, the three stepped inside.

None of them thought that a thin, frayed shroud could contain the worst of the stench, but they were wrong. Key forged ahead as Daniels almost covered up his stunned stumble, but Nichols had to take a second to nearly retch before controlling her gag reflex.

Definitely, Key thought. *Definitely going to requisition enhanced nose-plugs.* In fact, he hoped Lancaster had already ordered his labs to start creating them. He forced his mind to ignore the foul smells and concentrated on the sights and sounds.

The abattoir was exactly like a morgue combined with a slaughterhouse that was never cleaned. The "floor" was much like the ground outside— dirt and rock and garbage all packed together, but in here it was also long soaked in skin, organ tissue, bone, muscle, cartilage, blood, excrement, urine, semen, mucous, saliva, and spinal fluid. Both Daniels and Nichols caught nauseating whiffs of even vaginal lubrication. For a moment, the master sergeant was blinded by rage, but he blinked himself out of it.

Key tried to ignore what he was stepping in to concentrate on the things atop various platforms on the ground. Two were stone slabs, a few were wooden planks, one was sheet metal, and the one in the center was a marble wedge. On most were various pieces of dissected bodies, as if ravaged by starving cannibals. Daniels found himself flashing back to his family dinner table after Thanksgiving, simply as a way of staying sane. But on three platforms, in three different sections of the area, were more recent, less devastated, forms.

Each agent gravitated to the one nearest them. Key stared down at an old man who appeared to be the corpse taker's most recent "favor" for the nearby slum—in that the wretched cadaver only seemed a week old. Nichols stared at what initially looked like a child's doll that had been left out in the sun too long, but she quickly realized it was the child itself—even more shriveled than the ones they had failed to save. Her only solace was that her shades didn't fog up or dampen. If she was going to stay with Cerberus, it was no time to start tearing up.

Daniels looked down at the one on the marble slab, wondering if the naked creature was taking up cannibalistic barbecue. This body was the most ravaged. It was so horribly burnt, most of its foot bones were exposed through ashen, flaking skin, and its lips were gone, as was most of its right arm. Daniels only looked away when they all heard Key's voice.

"Yeah," he said to Lancaster more than anyone else. "Seems like he's definitely still on the run. This place looks like it hasn't been used for days, if not weeks."

"All right," the retired general sighed, his tone obviously disappointed. "Ascertain what you can and get back here. Be thorough, but things are progressing more rapidly than I would like."

Key did not like the sound of that. Lancaster was not one for curbed complaints or pregnant proclamations. "Yes, sir," he nodded, and turned to start scouring the place for any clues of the bastard's present whereabouts.

"I say," he heard. He turned his head to see Peters in the doorway, daintily holding the shroud curtain wide. "May I?"

"Might as well, if you can take it," Key told him. "Anything you can find or figure out that'll help us would be greatly appreciated."

"I know this is most unusual," Peters replied as he stepped in, "but my sincere thanks. I've never seen a more extreme example of 'corpsploitation' in all my years of study." He looked apologetically at Daniels, who had taken a moment to look at him with distasteful disbelief. "It started when my father's own body was stolen from his grave," Peters explained as he went from one set of remains to the other. "That was for political reasons, I suppose, but then I heard more stories of necrophilia, family infighting, medical testing, and the like from police, morticians, undertakers, and even private citizens. I have to admit I was disgusted at first, and then increasingly fascinated."

"How about more detecting, less sharing?" Daniels suggested.

"Of course, of course," Peters agreed. "I'm just nervous, I suppose. Sorry, sorry. My apologies."

There were some moments of blessed silence until Peters came to the charred corpse on the marble slab.

"Now," he softly mused, leaning down to study it closer, "would you look at this?"

Back at the airport and in the Chinese Versailles king's apartment, Gonzales and Lancaster ripped their ear-comms out and threw them down from sheer, agonized instinct, as a screeching ice-pick of pain stabbed their heads. The only one who didn't, from sheer will-power, was Faisal Safar in the jet's rear section, who had been distracted by how the equilibrium earplug control panel had gone crazy.

Key, Daniels, and Nichols would never remember if they heard the screech as their minds were suddenly crushed by confusion, nausea, and pain. Safar wasn't aware that he had already bitten through his lower lip, and how blood was pouring down his chin as he stabbed and wrenched at the control panel's buttons and dials, remembering what he had told Lancaster. "As this machine goes, so goes their brains."

As the machine's readouts settled, the screech in Safar's right ear grew louder and more painful until he, too, had to rip the ear-comm out. By then, however, Key had enough of his senses back to stop staggering. He twisted around to see Daniels hunched almost all the way over, clutching his head, and Nichols in a twitching ball on the squalid ground.

Then he saw Peters. The burned body had rammed its exposed right arm bone deep in the Englishman's left ear. The exposed finger bones of its left hand were hooked in Peter's right ear, eye, and nostril—seemingly almost until the tips were touching inside the Englishman's head. Key saw that the burned body's face was tilted to the right, its lipless teeth wide open. From the way Peter's throat was moving, somehow the burned body had a tongue that was bloating and pumping down the man's gullet.

That, horribly, was not the only thing that was pumping. From Key's angle, he could see a jointed, boney, scimitar-shaped, flesh-covered pipe rammed all the way into Peter's anus from between the burned body's legs.

Key inwardly screamed as pounding waves of disorientation still kept him from completely controlling his spasming limbs. He saw Peter's facial muscles begin to distort and deflate, as the burned body's head began to grow lips.

Key's scream was no longer inward. He didn't dare use his Sig Sauer because both Daniels and Nichols were in the line of fire. The three agents made a triangle around the horrid feeding going on in the center of the abattoir—each one terrified, enraged, and seemingly fighting their own muscles to do something—anything.

Gonzales had all but fallen into the cargo jet's rear section, lurching over to help Safar at the brainwave device. Dr. Helen had done the same for a quaking Lancaster, gripping his arms and whispering. "Too complex— testing too soon..."

"Fuck this," Key snarled, tearing the plugs out of both ears. As soon as he did, a flood of emotions crashed down on him, but he didn't care. His hand was filled, as if by sheer instinct alone, with his own version of the fat black-silver pen. With a shriek he dove forward, ramming the barrel into the body's ear.

He wished the skull had exploded in his face, almost exactly the way his superior officer's head had exploded back in Yemen, because this fucker's head was a lot softer than his commander's was, and had less brains. This time Key wouldn't get knocked out by a piece of skull or have a concussion from it. This time he would make the body dance with the fifty million volts coming from the Lancaster Labs's most recent, most powerful, and most compact stun-stick.

The burned body made another sound as it twitched, its skeletal hand tearing from Peter's yawing face. Everyone soon discovered that the right arm was stuck inside the Englishman's skull because its arm and hand had started growing there. Then the burned body jerked as Nichols's stun-stick stabbed it at the base of its spine and jerked again as Daniel's stun-stick connected with its balls.

It screeched, flailed, and bounced as all three agents stayed with it—seemingly trying to make all three stun-stick tips meet inside the creature's body.

"Dance, you bloodless fucker!" Daniels roared as the thing unavoidably began to dislodge itself from Peters's body. The sounds that accompanied the movements were rancid, drawn-out splats, a waterfall of them, like a pig or steer being gutted, its entrails slopping out.

First came the tongue, and Key saw something that looked like a boney needle sink into the main tongue as it did. Then that ugly, boney male member reluctantly retreated with Peters's life essence dripping off it. Finally, the monstrosity yanked and twisted and shook until its right arm came ripping out the side of Peters's head—with what looked like a fetal arm taking form where its hand should have been.

Still, none of the field team let up on it, keeping the stun-stick tips tight on the creature as they bore it to the ground.

"Who's still got their comm-link?" Key spat.

Everyone was too focused to answer. He repeated the question, but his words were drowned out by the greatest sound they ever thought they'd hear.

It was the distinctive noise of Gonzales's F. B. Law copter right outside. It was the incredibly fast, compact, powerful copter he had created to steal Nichols from her Yemen captors—and the reason he had created the Lawgiver cargo jet to bring it to Varanasi with them.

Its rotors tore the shroud from the abattoir opening and turned the interior into a tornado of filth, but none of them cared. They kept the stun-sticks on the creature until Safar leaped in with a high-powered CO_2 net-gun.

"Clear!" he barked, and all three agents leaped away as he pulled the trigger on the thing that looked like a rifle with a megaphone on the end. Only this megaphone shot a ten-by-ten-foot net consisting of six-inch, reinforced, rubber-coated wire. It emerged with a sound that was a cross between a silenced revolver and a wet kiss.

As soon as it slapped around the creature, Gonzales was there with another one—blasting the creature again as it went down. Then four of them threw themselves on the monster, knotting the corners with the nets before Gonzales returned with Chain-silk duffel bags, as well as industrial straps and chains.

Pure fury fueled them; it was the best accelerant this side of hate. And no one took any chances until the fully wrapped form of the creature writhed at their feet. Only then did a blood-streaked, offal-splattered Nichols look from one to the next with trembling eyes.

"Oh, I am not into toughing this out," she moaned and dropped to the ground, sobbing. No human in the room blamed her. No one moved forward, either; they gave her the moment, and her space. But only a moment.

"Let's get out of here," Key stressed, already tightening his fingers around one end of the creature's packing. "The sooner we get everyone back to Eshe's clinic, the better."

"Everyone?" Daniels echoed, glancing at Peters like a lost cause.

"Everyone," Key stressed.

Daniels did not verbally question the order, only gave his superior an '*are you sure?*' look.

"Come on, *move!*" Key answered verbally...loudly.

Nichols had recovered enough to help Gonzales get what was left of Peters into a body bag before she was inspired to collect all the earplugs the trio had flung. Even so, they were all on the F. B. Law, and speeding back to the airport, within minutes. Only then did Key get on the copter's comm-link to contact Lancaster. He certainly wasn't going to stick the earplugs back in—not after where they had been all over that fire temple.

"Joe," Key heard the retired general say in the radio's headphones.

Just the one name, the one word, communicated dread to Key. "Sir?"

"Assistant Professor Rahal isn't here." He used her actual scientific title, reminding them both that, although she had accomplished some extraordinary things with, and for, Cerberus, she wasn't actually a doctor of anything yet.

Key immediately thought *MIA? On assignment? Injured?* But he wasn't the kind of man who asked "*What do you mean?*" Instead he waited.

"She's AWOL," Lancaster continued gravely, using the military nomenclature for absent without leave. "And so is C1."

Chapter 15

Safar used the eight-hundred-mile trip back to fine-tune the new tech.

Every few minutes the burned body—even from within the layered netting, packaging, straps, and chains—emanated another wave of brain energy—apparently trying to make Gonzales crash the cargo jet with all of them in it. Each passenger dealt with it in their own way.

Key used it to test his ability to withstand it. Daniels used it as an excuse to use his shock stick on the package repeatedly until the emotional wave passed. Nichols cried freely and unashamedly. Gonzales immediately engaged autopilot when it started, then leaned back, closed his eyes, and tried to meditate. And Safar tweaked the new tech's frequency modulator to diminish or eliminate it, occasionally reversing the polarity of the neutron flow.

Daniels didn't need to ask Key whether he thought Peters might come back the way the burned body—who they were now certain was the unclad attacker—and C1 had. As soon as the body bag was aboard Key had, without comment, strapped and chained it tightly around the shins, knees, thighs, waist, elbows, and throat. It lay beside the wrapped, undulating, burned body during the flight.

After this latest mental muddle cleared, Daniels, not surprisingly, spoke first. "Well, I guess there's no doubt now. The burnt bastard with the missing forearm sure didn't have no sleeping sickness."

Key let the comment slide, having much bigger issues to attend to. *Now we really get to see how far and deep Lancaster's influence goes*, he thought. "So, what now?" he asked the retired general via the comm-link.

There was no discernible affront or offence in Lancaster's reply. "In your absence, I contacted the team who rushed out the EQ 'earquilibrium' devices. They offered a lot of gobbledygook about neuronal activity, brain chemistry, molecular pathophysiology, and neurotoxicological research."

Lancaster waited a moment for that to sink in, then continued. "But the bottom line is that they still feel that if anything can prevent this monster from escaping while they continue their research, the containment unit here at Cerberus can."

That satisfied everyone on the jet, except one—the one who was most upset that his brain was being messed with. "All due respect, sir," Daniels replied in a seemingly disinterested way, "but why should we give a fuck what your mystery medics think?"

Again, Lancaster was neither offended nor taken aback. Nor did his reply include any hint of condescension. "A reasonable question, master sergeant. Ever since I decided to create Cerberus, I have been preparing for just such a question by recruiting the greatest suppressed, denied, dismissed, and disbelieved minds in the world."

"A bunch of crackpot loonies?" Daniels blurted, his expression immediately showing regret.

But Lancaster only shook his head. "Now *that* I will chalk up to the brain-scrambling proximity of the naked scavenger, because I'm sure even you know that I'm not a loony hunter. Every person involved has been thoroughly scouted specifically for what I was afraid Cerberus might be needed for."

Key wasn't sure whether Lancaster's very first use of the word "afraid," rather than "concerned," was a good or bad thing.

"Yeah, what about that?" Daniels interjected, needing more time to regain his mental balance. "Maybe now would be a good time to know what the hell I've joined and why."

Nichols, for one, sat up, wiped her eyes, and nodded in agreement.

Key chalked everyone's emotional diarrhea to the unstable mental state caused by dealing with these brain and body pillagers, but it was better to clear the air than further muddy it.

The retired general seemed to agree. "I have seen my share of human evil," Lancaster started.

"More than your share, sir," Safar agreed.

Lancaster paused to acknowledge Safar's comment, then took a breath. "But all too often, especially recently, I've seen evil I couldn't fully explain or understand. And I thought I had seen everything." He paused again, and once he resumed, Key understood why he had paused. "One of the reasons I retired from the military is that my peers, and even my most devoted aides, thought I might be becoming obsessed with the growing shadows just beyond my mental and physical vision."

There was not a raised eyebrow on the aircraft—not even from Daniels, not after what he had gone through.

"But the more successful and wealthy I became, the more apparent this growing darkness was becoming—and all the more threatening to the country and people I had sworn to protect. What was the point of acquiring all that wealth, influence, and knowledge if I didn't use it in a necessary, pressing way no one else was? A way no one else would, because they only believed what was right at the end of their nose? And sometimes not even that. But, if there's one thing I've learned, it's that humankind is more than capable of destroying himself. But I'll be damned if I'll let anything else do it."

That seemed to be the last word, but Key wouldn't leave it at that. As always, he was intent on moving forward, as fast as they could. "Sounds promising, sir, but right now we need something just as important as science." Before anyone could say "what's that," Key continued. "Credulity. I probably don't have to tell you this, but I better. Evil, whether it's a child molester or a vampire, is sick and sad, but also depends on stupid, innocent people to buy their shit because the innocent can't, or won't, believe such evil can exist. Evil feeds on the 'they can't control themselves' and the 'they think what they're doing is right.' What good is all the greatest minds in the world if they allow themselves to be victimized because they believe something, anything, is not possible?"

"Which brings us back to Doctor—I mean, Professor Rahal," Daniels said dourly as he looked at Key. "Someone had to bring it up, Joe."

Key reacted with an understanding shrug.

"She's AWOL?" Nichols piped up, having been informed by Gonzales. "How is that even possible?"

"It's possible," Safar said regretfully. "All the Chinese Versailles security was for keeping people from getting in, not keeping us from getting out."

"But not a single surveillance camera recorded her departure—" Nichols started, then stopped herself. "Oh, yeah, right. C1 was with her, wasn't she?"

"Now we have to find out whether Eshe brought her for camouflage purposes, or C1 was controlling her—" Gonzales mused.

"Or someone or something was controlling C1, Eshe, or both," Key sighed. He nodded at Daniels. "Let's continue our talk with Lailani," he ordered before gingerly standing. "General," he called. "Please have your think tanks collect, study, and analyze everything possible on the myths and stories that inspired vampire legends. Nothing is too obscure or incredible."

"Already in progress," Lancaster assured him. "I am personally editing every word."

Key stood, then nearly lost his balance from his own smell. Daniels put out a hand to steady him. "What do you want to bet Lailani gives us more useful info than all the think tanks?" he whispered.

"I'll bet your ass," Key whispered back. "In fact, I'm betting all our asses." He raised his head. "And general?" he called. "I hope your colleagues have also suggested some cutting-edge sterilization and odor-eating technology, or else we're going to have to walk through a car wash and have a clothes burning as soon as we land."

Lancaster chuckled again. "Understood, Major. Just land safely."

Key glanced at Safar, who looked back hopefully. "Seems to be working," the tech said softly. "Either that or the creature we encountered is *laeib tamarud*." Safar grimaced at his slipping back into Arabic. "Playing possum," he quickly translated.

"Don't give him any ideas," Daniels groaned, gripping his stun-stick tighter.

"I guess we'll find out when the landing gear deploys," Key breathed. "Until then, why don't we all exercise our beat-up brains figuring out what to call this bastard?"

* * * *

There were some new Versailles servants when the Lawgiver landed—safely. They stood around Dr. Helen as she greeted them at the cargo jet door. To the Cerberus agents they looked like a quartet of local farmers, outfitted to battle locusts.

They were completely covered, but in what would seem, to observers, to be standard farm wear: straw hats, clear goggles, colorful scarves from their noses to their necks, billowing shorts, pants, boots, gloves, and aprons. Nichols could even see that their ears were covered by something that, to her enhanced vision, looked like a cross between Cali-brake and Chain-silk. Dr. Helen, who had a large pocketbook on her arm, said something in Chinese to them, and they leaned down to grip four corners of two coffin-sized, insulated, lined boxes that rested on a wheeled platform.

"Bet they're her nephews or grandchildren, or something," Daniels said out of the corner of his mouth.

"At least her relatives," Key commented, thinking of the woman's skills, which he hoped did not fall far from the family tree. "I certainly hope so."

They moved around the agents as Dr. Helen held her nose with one hand and waved the agents toward the Chinese re-creation of the palace's gardens—complete with what was known as the Orangerie Fountain and Swiss Pool. Daniels could take a hint. He was the first to strip down and belly flop in the nearest water, with Nichols, Key, Safar, and Gonzales not far behind. After what they had shared, there was not a shred of shame or embarrassment. And even though the pilot and copilot had only spent seconds in the fire temple abattoir, it was enough to consider their clothes, and especially their footwear, a lost cause.

Dr. Helen reached into her bag and tossed each a plastic bottle of body soap, which they each used quickly but profusely. Then she handed each a remarkably effective towel, then a standard hospital robe. By then, one of the "farmers" had joined her with a plastic hand-shovel and garbage bag. He collected all the soiled clothes and footwear without touching them, threw the now tainted shovel in the bag with them, tied the top, and brought the bag, at arm's length, with him as he left.

They reconvened in Lancaster's office, all wearing new Cali-brake and Chain-silk uniforms, as well as new comm-links and EQs, which they found on the beds of their Versailles *Grands Appartements* quarters.

"Shit," Daniels commented, looking them over. "We look like a German techno band."

Everyone grinned—Key officially acknowledging that occasional humor, and Daniels's humor in particular, was an important weapon in their fight against the seemingly unbelievable. It was either that, or depression, then maybe certifiable insanity.

The second place Key looked was at Lancaster's monitors. They seemed to have sprung an extra image in the team's absence. Each image showed a man watching a monitor. Lancaster noticed Key's gaze.

"For what it's worth," he said. "Double surveillance now. No one watches Z1, or any of our detainees, without someone watching them for safe-keeping." Z1 was the title the team had decided upon—although, for a while during the return trip, they were perilously close to going with Daniels's suggestion: Pee-wee. "And yes," Lancaster continued, "all our new employees are part of Dr. Helen's extended family."

Key was glad to hear it. And heaven knew there were more than enough *grands appartements* to house a lot more. "Good," he said. "Now, first things first, as my dad used to say. Faisal?" He tapped his left ear, "these things working now?"

Safar glanced at Gonzales. "*Hasta ahora, todo va bien.* Speedy taught me that."

Gonzales translated. "'So far everything is going well.' There was no equivalent he could find in Arabic."

Daniels rolled his eyes. "Next time just say 'so far so good.' We'll find out soon enough. If we keep fighting, they work. If we curl up in a ball or our heads explode, they don't."

"Any meaningful updates or upgrades based on continuing research," Lancaster assured them, "will be automatically uploaded."

"Next," Nichols quickly suggested, "we find Eshe, right?"

Key sadly shook his head. "Not blindly," he said before looking at each of the others. "First we have to collect and compare notes. What do we know?"

Key counted on Daniels speaking up first, and the man didn't disappointment.

"They don't die easy," the master sergeant said. "Hell, they may not die at all."

Key nodded—not so much at the comment, but the knowledge that his remark would encourage the others to contribute freely, knowing they couldn't say anything stupider than Daniels.

"Yes, but they are damageable," Gonzales added.

"And they apparently can reconstitute themselves by using the life-force of victims," Nichols observed.

Daniels found himself wondering what they would do if the Z1 did not bleed.

"Not 'they' yet," Lancaster reminded them. "So far it's just 'he.'"

Key made a motion with his head that seemed to combine both a nod and a shake. "But," he said, "'they' can apparently effect human minds. On the basis of personal experience, the closer the proximity, the more powerful the effect." His gaze took in all the others. "And now one has escaped, either by well-meaning accident, or mean-spirited purpose. The question is why."

Daniels threw his hands up. "What else? World domination."

Gonzales snorted. "I've seen a lot more horror movies than you, Morty, and the answer could just as easily be to hide and feed. Vampires"—he started, then knowingly corrected himself—"fictional vampires want to stay in the shadows and control their populations. And if they take over the world, eventually there'll be no one left to feed on."

"So what was this?" Nichols asked in confusion. "A mistake? Did we stumble on Z1 by accident?"

Key nodded, this time without the hint of a shake. "I think so, Terri," he said, unable to erase all worry from his face. "I think Z1 fucked up and has been trying to erase all traces of it ever since."

"So," Nichols responded hopelessly. "What can we do?"

Key breathed deeply. "We can wait for something to happen."

Safar looked stricken. "But what if nothing happens? What if Speedy is right and they all simply blend back into the shadows?"

Key shook his head. "Z1 can't get back to the shadows right now. We already know, pretty much for a fact, that he's fed on at least eight children while we've known him. As he lies in there, strapped and chained, his need to feed will only grow. The same may be true of C1, so the longer Eshe is in the wind, the less chance she'll come back alive. So I believe something will happen, until we stop—"

Key froze. Lancaster recognized his stunned, self-recriminating expression. This time he said the magic word sharply. "Elaborate."

Key returned his gaze briskly. "I think you were right the first time, sir. You suggested that our assignment and Colonel Logan's mission might be on a collision course. So now, I'm suggesting that this would be a good time to prepare for impact."

That left the collected crew speechless for a moment, but just a moment, because Morton Daniels was part of that crew.

"Man, Joe, there would be nothing I'd love more than that to be true," he exclaimed, "but how can you possibly figure that? We got C1, C5, and Z1—!"

"Oh my god, Joe," Lancaster breathed, his face blossoming in remembrance and realization. "Even I forgot. M1 and F1."

Key smiled widely at the retired general's immediate, and accurate, identification.

"Would you stop fucking with us," Daniels exploded. "Just come right out and say it, would you?"

But Key was already almost out the door, on his way to search Rahal's office as it had never been searched before—leaving the rest of the team to stare dumbfounded at their employer, who, for his part, was grinning like a vexed vulture.

"'M' for mother," he told them, "'F' for father. The man and woman who brought the child up to the top of Mount Rushmore faster than it was possible. The man and woman who threw the child off the cliff. The man and woman who eluded the greatest dragnet in South Dakota history after they slaughtered two park rangers in a way a bomb could not. The man and woman who did not appear smudged on surveillance video—they did not appear at all!"

"Vlad the Impaler and Countess Bathory," Gonzales recalled from history. "The king and queen. Overlord and consort. They could be the ones Z1 serves."

Chapter 16

Dr. Val Dearden was everything Eshe Rahal hoped he would be.

He had been from the moment she contacted him on the advice of her students at the Oman Medical School where she had worked prior to joining Cerberus. In fact, within moments of her sending out the text requesting infectious disease experts, she received a simple, unsigned reply via text: Dr. Dearden's name and message number. She reacted to it like a life preserver, only hesitating a moment before using the attached link.

She knew she was risking detection by using the anonymous phone more than once, but she decided it was worth the risk. After all, she had nothing to be ashamed of, or embarrassed about. She was trying to save a tormented young girl the most effective way she could. If she didn't bring some sanity to the proceedings, and hastily, she would not have been at all surprised if Daniels came stomping into the clinic with a cross, garlic, and a sharpened wooden stake.

To her relief, Dr. Dearden himself returned the message—not via text this time but by an actual phone call. Since Rahal had the disposable "burner phone" on vibrate only, she was surprised, but not shocked, when it shook. And his deep, Indian-flavored English voice was remarkably calming. She could practically feel his smile of recognition when she told him who had suggested him, then relaxed for the first time in weeks when he said the six words she had been longing to hear.

"What can I do for you?"

She told him succinctly and clearly of the child who had been abducted, abused, and tormented, and seemed to have awakened from death with enhanced strength, reflexes, and speed—then was as honest as she could be about the girl's subsequent restraint and quarantine. She felt his shock and concern grow with every word. And his reaction was more than she could have hoped for.

"Thank Shiva you called me," he had said. "This sounds precisely like the maladies we are studying. Your case sounds like a possible breakthrough."

"Does it?"

"Yes," he had enthused. "How soon can you bring the child here?"

He offered her transportation, but a plan was already forming in her mind, so she politely declined. Then she pocketed the anonymous phone and immediately set about accomplishing her exit, starting with C1. She fearlessly entered the quarantine, and when she looked at the sleeping, angelic face, she was filled with certainty and conviction. This child was the victim, not the danger.

Wrapping the tiny girl in swaddling clothes, then strapping C1 to her via a baby carrier cocoon, Rahal left the clinic. Even though her certainty that what she was doing was right was growing with every step, she stayed in the unfinished hallways of the palace re-creation, where Cerberus had not bothered to install surveillance cameras yet. Even if they had, Rahal was sure that any sensible person would understand what she was doing and support her goal. But she also remembered what Daniels had said once.

"Better to ask forgiveness than permission."

She was further aided by the grandiosity of the headquarters and the modesty of the staff, who were either on assignment or hard at work. She simply walked to the Chinese Versailles *stables royale*, which now housed dozens of vehicles—both modified by Gonzales and fresh from the factory showrooms. She chose a child-friendly Subaru Outback with the keys in the ignition and drove out the back of the property without delay or opposition.

It had been that simple. She had given Lancaster and the others every opportunity to stop her, short of daring them. But a child's life was at stake, so nothing would stop her, and nothing did. She felt all the more certain when she found that the new Xinjiang Airport, built on the nearby Pamir Plateau, was complete. From there, getting a flight to Indira Gandhi International Airport was not a problem. She didn't even have to use a credit card. Cerberus paid extremely well—so well she hadn't thought twice about securing a first-class ticket. No one even questioned her passport, or requested one of the child. It all went like a dream.

Hours later, with the sleeping child never leaving her chest, she was in Hayana, India, where Dr. Dearden was awaiting her at the arrival lounge. Just seeing him made her feel peaceful. He was a tall, middle-aged, fit man, with a full mustache, graying temples, and a kindly—and relieved—smile.

In his well-fitting gray suit and lab coat, he even reminded her of her late mentor, Professor Davi.

Making sure the airport staff was aware that this was a medical emergency, he easily and confidently guided them through customs and passport control, then led her to a clean, new ambulance with "Frontage Medical Institute" on the side. There, a serene, handsome, loving nurse placed the child in an intensive-care crib—the kind that were used for premature births—as Dr. Dearden led Rahal to a padded seat beside it.

"You've done a wonderful thing," he assured her, his warm hand reassuringly on her shoulder. "An amazing thing. Rest now. It's only fifteen kilometers to the institute—"

"No," she said more urgently than she had intended. She controlled herself, breathed deeply, then tried again. "No, thank you, Doctor," she continued, placing her own hand on his. "I won't rest until I'm sure the child is past any danger. I need to remain aware for any questions you or your staff might have."

He nodded, his face full of respect. "Of course. I'll sit right here by you and answer any questions you might have, all right?" He did as he said, her hand now in both of his.

"You said you have been studying maladies with similar symptoms?" she asked as the ambulance started southwest on Route 48.

"Oh, yes," Dr. Dearden replied in a folksy, assured tone that was both comforting and familiar. "Our newly opened childhood disease facility possesses a complete spectrum of diagnostic and therapeutic expertise, including several state-of-the-art technologies that are first in India, first in Asia, and even first in the world." He paused. "Why are you smiling?" he asked with inquisitive kindness.

"I'm sorry, Doctor," she said, feeling better than she had in months. "But for a moment I thought you sounded like an advertisement."

He laughed sheepishly. "Oh, I'm sorry. It's just that I'm so pleased and even proud to be associated with such a fine institution." He cleared his throat, readjusted his posture next to her, and started again, more seriously. "Yes, I have found an undiagnosed illness with similar symptoms spreading throughout this region, from Vietnam to Kazakhstan. But always the worst sort of superstition gripped the parents, townspeople, or local authorities, so I was unable to properly study the situation."

"Superstition?" Rahal echoed with familiar concern.

Dearden grew grave. "Yes. I loathe sharing with you the details, but yes, there were even dismemberments and immolations, I'm sorry to say."

"That is terrible!"

"Yes, truly terrible." He patted her hand again. "Which is why I am so pleased that you were able to deliver the child from Tashkurgan. I am told that there are villagers there who still might not understand. But here, I can assure you, she will get the utmost care. What is her name, if I may ask?"

Rahal's eyes widened as she remembered the child didn't have one. "We—" she stammered in embarrassment, "we called her C1."

He smiled in rueful understanding. "Well, at least you didn't name her 'patient zero,'" he said sympathetically. He looked over at the child, and his caring smile widened. "Let's call her Angela, shall we? Until she is properly identified, of course."

"Of course," Rahal agreed, her smile also widening. "That is a perfect name."

Dearden looked beyond her, out the ambulance windshield. "Ah," he said, "we have arrived."

Rahal looked in the same direction as he to see what looked like a mall of medicine. It was a widespread glass and metal building, placed just off a busy city street—one that was apparently designed to look like outspread, welcoming arms. As the vehicle drove slowly around it, Rahal caught glimpses of shining marble floors, brightly lit walls, and many beautiful art installations. Finally, the ambulance pulled up to a smaller, starker, separate building in the back, on the other side of a two-story parking lot.

"Our facility," Dearden explained, getting up to prepare the child for delivery to the intensive care unit. "If you want to follow her through the initial diagnostics, I'm afraid you must go through the proper sterilization process yourself, of course."

"Of course, of course," Rahal agreed, just as the stress of the trip finally settled down on her. "But no, that will be all right. I have confidence in your—in your—"

Dearden smiled even more warmly at her. "I understand, Ms. Rahal. The staff will see to it that the child is safe. Let me take you to my office, where you can wait."

The next few minutes were a blur to the Arabic woman, who suddenly seemed to remember how young she actually was—still in her late twenties—and how much she had gone through between Yemen and here. But as soon as her full attention returned, she found herself on a small, well-padded lounge chair in a small, all-too-familiar doctor's office. It was a comfortable recliner, the kind she often saw in old-fashioned psychiatrist offices.

Unlike Professor Davi's office, this one was spotlessly clean, with a high ceiling, wood-paneled walls, an examining table, medicine cabinets, a desk, and several well-appointed chairs. Although there were high-intensity lights designed for diagnostics on the walls, the rest of the room was softly illuminated.

Rahal looked up to see Dr. Dearden smiling down at her, stirring a cup of tea. He sat on the edge of the lounge chair and held the tea out to her. She smelled chai as well as milk, cinnamon, and ginger.

"How—" she started, feeling the dryness of her mouth, started again with greater effort. "How long have I been here?"

"Just a few minutes," Dearden said in a hush, bringing the teacup closer to her nostrils.

"Did I nod off?" she wondered, relishing the sweet and spicy aroma of the creamy liquid.

"You may have," Dearden said. "I would not know, since I was occupied for a time making sure that Angela was safe and secure." He raised his head, his deep, dark, kindly eyes settling on hers. "You will be happy to know that she is."

"I am," she replied, abruptly realizing that she truly was. She also realized how tired she was when her hands started to shake as she attempted to take the teacup.

"There, there," Dearden soothed as he extended his arm to place the cup on the end table beside the lounge chair. The action unavoidably brought his arm and torso across her. "Your *hegira* is catching up with you." He had referenced the Muslim exodus from Mecca to Medina in 622 AD, making her feel even more welcome.

After he had placed the teacup, he curled his palm on the top of the lounge chair directly beside her reclining head. He looked down at her like a devoted father putting his daughter to bed—his solicitously smiling head now just a foot away.

"You no longer should rest," he said compassionately. "You *must* rest. Doctor's orders."

"Yes," she heard herself murmur, feeling her eyes closing. "Yes."

And, as they closed, she swore she saw his head lowering toward her ear. Then she could feel his soft breath on her throat. It was sweet, but also there was something spicy in the aroma. Or was it the tea mixing, and maybe even camouflaging something else? Something stinging. Something.

"Eshe!"

Her eyes snapped open, but for a second she thought she was still dreaming. Josiah Key was standing in the doorway of Dr. Dearden's office, looking down at them.

Chapter 17

If Rahal thought Joe would look reprovingly, or even shocked, at her, she was wrong. Instead he was smiling knowingly, comfortably, even sardonically.

Dr. Dearden had not vaulted to his feet. Why should he? He was doing nothing wrong or compromising. Instead he was just sitting up and twisting around to look over his shoulder at the intruder. "What can I do for you?" he asked with curiosity but no sign of affront.

"Don't mind me," Key said pleasantly, motioning with a rotating movement of his hand. "Carry on with what you were doing."

Dearden looked puzzled. "How did you get in here?"

"I walked," Key replied. "Was something supposed to stop me?"

Before Dearden could answer, Rahal interjected. "Joe, what are you—" She stopped, realizing she knew very well what he was doing here. "How did you—" She stopped again, not sure whether to say "get here" or "find me." Either way, they both knew it was a time-wasting question, designed to help her regain equilibrium.

Key shrugged while coming farther into the room—attempting to look nonchalant, but concerned his cautious care was too obvious.

"Funny," he said. "But there's no such thing as a truly anonymous phone." He looked at Dearden as he pulled up a patient's chair to the other side of the lounge—positioned so the doctor was between him and the young woman, who, to her credit, was blushing. "You know, what with tech today, any device can be identified even from flecks of paint on duct tape. And once i-ID'd, no call or text is actually untraceable."

Dearden looked at Rahal with an expression that asked "should I call security," but the guilt-tinged look of affection that passed her face kept him away from any alarms. Of course, as far as Key was concerned, it could have been more than that. Just like the man's puzzled look could have two meanings as well.

"Are you the father?" was what Dearden finally asked.

"No," Key said resignedly. "I'm another caretaker." He exhaled deeply, leaned back and crossed his ankles. "Very impressive place you got," he commented, seemingly offhandedly. "Practically got the full tour trying to find your office way back here." Key looked directly into Dearden's eyes and all mirth left his face. "Funny how many staff members haven't heard of you."

Dearden didn't bother defending himself. He simply stared back at Key with a face that might have been trying to mirror Key's own but was betrayed by a growing knowing. Rahal seemed about to rally to the doctor's defense but after examining both their faces remained silent.

Finally, Dearden spoke three quiet words. "I'm new here."

Key let the words lie in the air for a second, then seemed to mull them over. "Apparently," he finally said, and let that word lie as well.

Several times in the next few seconds Rahal was tempted to intervene, to break the silence, even to move, but she didn't. Finally she quieted and stilled, letting her insight return to her. This wasn't a macho pissing contest. It might have been if Daniels had accompanied Key, but it certainly wasn't now. Finally, she saw it for what it actually was: a mental chess game. Her eyes widened when she realized that it was Key's king at check. But he wasn't going to concede until he had to.

Key's eyes narrowed and his lips flattened, their ends threatening to droop as Dearden's eyes narrowed and his lips threatened to rise. Rahal saw that both now knew that Key's weakness was through his queen.

"Nevertheless," Dearden finally said a full moment after Key's "apparently" disappeared in the air. "I repeat: what can I do for you?"

Key inhaled deeply, as if saying *"so that's the way we're playing it, huh?"* Then he exhaled again in resignation. "In the spirit of repetition," he said, standing, "we're caretakers, so we need to take care."

Dearden also stood, then moved languidly toward his desk. "If I understand you and the situation correctly," he said with utmost courtesy, "are you requesting to take Angela out of this facility?"

"Angela," Key sniffed. "Nice." He reached into his light jacket and removed his CID badge and identification. "Yes, Doctor, that's exactly what I'm doing."

Dearden looked down at a digital tablet on his desk, taking a moment to tap it twice. "Why on Earth should I allow that?" he asked, not even looking at Key.

"Because you don't know what you're dealing with."

That brought his eyes up to meet those of Key. It did the same for Rahal.

"Don't I?" Dearden inquired.

"I hope not," Key answered bluntly. "This child, if that's what it is anymore, has been infected by something way beyond any known disease. As near as we can tell"—he looked pointedly and a bit reprovingly, at Rahal—"it has little blood and is fueled by the full potential of the body's electrical power, to the point that it can summon enormous strength both physically and mentally."

"Mentally?" Dearden echoed noncommittally.

Key sniffed at what he obviously considered Dearden's disingenuousness. "She can, and has, clouded people's minds. She can even render herself invisible to cameras."

Rahal looked wide-eyed at the man she had chosen months ago to be her lover. Then she looked at the man she hoped would be her new mentor, waiting for his disbelief.

But Dearden only laughed. "Oh," he said. "Children's stories for a sick child? So, like many of the ignorant villagers I have had to contend with, you believe these legends and myths?"

Key was unfazed. "Yes," he answered flatly. "And I think you do too."

That stopped Dearden's laughter—replaced, instead, with incredulousness. "Why?" he exclaimed. "Why, in the name of all that is sane—why?"

"Because you're laughing about it," Key accused him. "That's not a normal reaction. If you thought I was serious or nuts, you would be disbelieving or concerned. I've got a badge. I've got a gun, for what that's worth. But you're behaving in a condescending way, which means you not only believe in them, you *know* they exist."

Rahal's eyes shot back to Dearden, waiting for any reaction Key might find credible. She found a man who was watching the Cerberus agent like a stubborn student.

"Do you know that if you cut down all the nerves going to the human heart from the human brain," Dearden said calmly, "the heart will still beat? Do you know that if you dissect the brain, heart, and lungs, you will find cells that are capable of independent existence?" Key didn't bother answering, knowing Dearden didn't expect him to. "In a world like this, what need do I have of myth and legend?" The doctor shook his head. "Now, especially, I'm afraid you won't be allowed to take Angela from us."

"Afraid?" Key echoed with raised eyebrows.

Dearden smiled sadly again. "Perhaps 'afraid' is indeed ill-chosen," he agreed. "In this case, 'unlikely,' may be more apt."

To any witness other than Rahal, it would appear that the two men were completely within their rights and characters, with no hint of anything more sinister. But to her, the two seemed to be wrestling for her soul: one representing rationality and the other spirituality. Now she was waiting to see which one would overturn the chessboard first.

To her disappointment, it was Dearden. "I am obviously forced to remind you, Agent Key, that to claim custody of a child that has been removed or retained in breach of custody rights, one must first supply the identity of the applicant, of the child, and of the person alleged to have removed or retained the child—in order to prevent further harm to the child, or prejudice interested parties, by taking, or causing to be taken, provisional measures."

"No," Key said diffidently. "You do not."

Dearden raised his hands in the most apologetic way he could. "Now we could call the local authorities and start this long, drawn-out process, but, really, would that be in the best interest of the child—and interested parties?" Dearden seemed as if he was about to continue, but then did not—instead looking at Key as if the doctor was a cat that had just eaten a veritable flock of canaries.

Key grimaced, then looked at a spot on the wall between Dearden and Rahal and muttered, "Chuck?"

"Between Cerberus and the Frontage Medical Institute?" Lancaster said in Key's ear. "No contest."

"Did you say something?" Dearden asked Key. Key held up a cautioning forefinger.

"I'm sure you agree his reference to 'interested parties' could be a veiled, effective, threat," Lancaster continued quickly. "But since you wouldn't want to say this aloud in the present company, I will. If he is something other than a doctor, the clever bastard has not conclusively tipped his hand. But if he is actually who he says he is, it's best C1 stays."

Key lowered his finger. "I'm afraid," he said, using the word knowingly, "we don't have the time to pursue a legal course, do we?" He emphasized the last inclusive word in the statement.

Dearden looked as if Key had just given him a prize. He spread his arms. "I'm always here," he said munificently. "And I can go anywhere."

To Rahal's renewed surprise, Key barked out an amazed laugh at the possible shamelessness of the statement. He lowered his arms and stared at him in something close to admiration.

"I have no doubt, doctor," he said. "I have no doubt."

He stepped over to take Rahal's arm, then stopped and sardonically looked back to Dearden for approval.

"Are you willing to go with him, my dear?" the doctor asked solicitously.

More than anything else, it was his dry, almost patronizing, use of "my dear" that suddenly made Rahal see him in something less than a heavenly light.

"Yes," she said resolutely. She stood unsteadily and allowed Key to help her. "Thank you, doctor. You will keep me apprised of Angela's condition?"

"Oh," Dearden answered, sitting behind his desk as if they were already gone. "Most definitely. You can rest assured of that."

At this point, all Key wanted to do was get out of there. But just as he guided Rahal out the door, Dearden called to him. "Agent Key?"

Key stopped in the doorway and turned.

Since there was just the two of them now, there was no longer any doubt. Key saw, and felt, the human-shaped thing that could have been a doctor ten times over. And the human-shaped thing wanted him to see, and feel, it.

"I rarely get the opportunity to talk to someone like you, Josiah," Dearden said honestly. "I truly enjoyed it." Key waited, robbing Dearden of the opportunity to stop him short again—a fact that elicited an even wider smile from Dearden as he looked pointedly at Key's left ear. "And *you* may rest assured that I will be learning even more in the unlikely event we ever get to do it again."

Chapter 18

A solo Safar was waiting on the roof, the F. B. Law motor running, since Gonzales was busy back at headquarters.

He hardly waited for Key to swing over—after all but throwing Rahal in—when he launched the thing into the sky. As always, Lancaster had already done his magic to clear the multiple countries' airspace for Cerberus's fast, powerful, unusual conveyances—giving the team plenty of planning time.

"Shouldn't we just mount an offensive—go in there and take this smug bastard down?" Daniels immediately suggested in Key's ear.

Key replied as he nimbly cupped Rahal's head in one hand and popped a specially made EQ device into her left ear with the other.

"He's already gone, Morty," he said, managing a smile at Rahal's look of growing, mind-clearing, awareness. "And I bet so is his nurse, the ambulance driver, and Angela. General, if you have any agents nearby, feel free to have them check, but wasting our time on an offensive would be just what they want. The worst thing that could happen is that they'd still be there. Pardon the cliché, but it would be veritable lambs to the slaughter. Comes under the category of standing on a railroad track with your arm out."

"I don't get it, Joe," Nichols chimed in. "Why didn't Dearden just kill you both?"

"Damn good question, Ter," Key replied as he stared off toward the international airport where the Lawgiver waited. "I'm guessing he couldn't take the time, or risk, to hide our bodies. Whatever this guy's end game, it's coming rapidly to a head. He obviously can't afford any distractions or roadblocks."

"What *is* the end game?" Lancaster wondered.

"That's the best question, sir," Key told him. "He gave me a pretty impressive stink-eye at the door that didn't just say 'I know something you don't know,' it said 'I know a *shitload* of somethings you don't know.' He seemed to be looking forward to screwing with us in general, and me in particular."

"Aw, Christ," Daniels groaned. "What is *that* all about?"

Key sniffed, going over the confrontation in his mind for the dozenth time. "He was clearly puzzled when he couldn't get in my head, but then seemed to take it as a welcome challenge. He really came off as a bored brainiac, general. Someone who's seen it all, done it all, and now just gets his jollies tearing the wings off flies."

"I can't believe I'm saying this," Daniels complained, "but couldn't you be mistaken, Joe? Couldn't this guy just be some mad scientist on a power trip? I mean, it's one thing when we're dealing with killer babies and monosyllabic monsters without clothing, but this oily sonuvabitch? Let me add that I really, really want you to be mistaken, Joe."

"Maybe he's the Renfield," Gonzales mused, "and Z1 is actually the Nosferatu."

"What?" Daniels demanded, befuddlement being piled upon confusion and concern. It was a wicked stew for a man easily unfocused.

"The servant," Gonzales clarified in dead-earnest. "The fly-eating domestic serving the vampire lord."

"Stop it," Key snapped. "He wanted to spook us. He succeeded. Let's just stick to what we know without the fiction. The only thing that's obvious is they wanted Angela, and used Eshe to get her."

"But why?" Nichols wondered. "Why Eshe?"

"No," Key informed her. "The proper question here is 'why Angela?' Eshe was just a means to an end."

"To clean up the evidence Z1 left behind," Daniels said as if there weren't any doubt.

But there was. "No," Key disagreed. "Then they'd just destroy her."

"You mean, they *can* destroy her?" Daniels retorted.

"Probably more than we can," Nichols muttered.

"Look," Key interrupted impatiently. "It doesn't matter, okay? What matters is that whatever they are, they still got something bad going down, and now we know that they know that we know, and they are not happy."

That quieted everyone, and in the verbal silence, Key realized how much the race to find Rahal had taken out of him.

"All right," Key sighed. "There's a couple of hours before we can get back. Morty, Terri, use this time to rest. Can't be sure when we'll be able to do that again."

"Gladly," Daniels said.

"Speedy, Faisal, you know what we need and want. General, has Lailani arrived?"

"Here, Joe," he heard her shrill Filipino tone.

"Good," Key said. "Lailani, if you would compile and cross-reference all the information you know or can find on life and blood feeders—concentrating on the powers that most of the myths share—"

"Already started, Major," Lancaster informed him.

"Yes, Joe," Lailani laughed, sounding like she was really enjoying herself. "When you land we'll have everything in one place for you, okay?"

"Okay," he said with relief. "Now, general. Let me talk to Dr. Helen. Private line, please."

He turned to see if Rahal was listening, but she had already curled up on the seat beside him and was fast asleep.

* * * *

Key had wanted to get a head start on his own Vampires' Greatest Hits once they got back on board the Lawgiver but just couldn't muster the concentration. Like almost all the Cerberus air fleet, the Lawgiver had a crew section, with a kitchen, bath, shower, and bunks far beyond the norm. Lancaster took advantage of his myriad industries to stock all his places with advances unavailable to the general public—from bed sheets to toilets.

Key saw to it that Rahal managed to make it to one of those luxurious bunks before he retired to one of his own. Although he was tempted to join Safar in the cockpit, he knew his priorities. But those priorities went out the window as soon as he lay back on the sumptuous sheets and laid his head on the amazing pillow.

He was only wakened by a sensation he recognized—the silken feel of Rahal's naked body sliding next to his. The first time it had happened was when he had found a similar moment of rest in the Hispanic Mechanic's Thumrait Workshop just before he was set to do battle with the Arachnosaurs. Then, like now, it was Rahal who made the decision to share herself with him.

Until then, she had been a young, sheltered medical student more devoted to science than sins of the flesh. But in Key's arms she had learned quickly of its honest pleasures. Using his own strength and experience, combined with her knowledge and love of biology, they reached heights of sensual satisfaction neither had experienced before or even knew were possible.

Rahal had to admit that Key had an optimal body, and Key had done the same in return. Although covered in floor-length *abayasare* sheaths, head scarves, and even masks most of her life, the body beneath, through no plan of her own, had developed its own natural shape without fault— resulting in seemingly perfect breasts, shape, legs, and flanks, all wrapped in soft, buttery flesh the color of café au lait.

Since that first time, they had shared a bed whenever they could, collaborated beautifully in their mutual ecstasy, then slept peacefully and soundly in each other's arms. And because both were dedicated to their important work, it was the most mutually beneficial and appreciated relationship either had ever had, with no emotional fallout, ramifications, or complications. To Key's satisfaction, Rahal didn't even know what those were.

She didn't have to stimulate him now. Her presence alone was enough. All she had to do was slide herself on his firm shank, seemingly fitting as certainly as a Yemini *jambiya* dagger in a specially made, perfectly sized scabbard. The head of his member moved unerringly to her G-spot as his fingers found her clitoris. Her pleasure was his as she undulated, and rode, atop him.

"Thank you," he heard her whisper into his chest when they were done. "For saving me."

He shifted, feeling her firm, teardrop breasts swell against his torso, as her splendid back pressed into his hands.

"Oh, don't think you can bribe me with just your beautiful body," he teased, his hands lowering to her rear. "I'll want a piece of that beautiful mind, too."

He looked down to see she was looking up at him with deep, glowing, haunted eyes. "I hated it," she immediately informed him, surmising what he wanted. It would be what she would want to know if the situation were reversed. "I thought I was thinking clearly. I thought I was myself. But with each illogical moment—when I left without detection, when I went through passport control—I ignored the cries in the back of my mind. Those were the cries I attributed to C1 and even Z1. Those were the cries I thought were trying to hurt me, not help me." Tears began to form at the corners of her eyes. "I was so certain!"

He held her as she quaked against him. As usual, her sobbing was short-lived. The scientist mind took over. "It's an immediate, more effective, more concentrated and focused kind of brainwashing," she decided, wiping her face in his chest hair. "They must have an encyclopedic knowledge of exactly where in the mind to stimulate, and where to dampen."

"Like the Chinese scholars who spent centuries testing every pore with their fingers or needles to find how the nerves all interplayed," he suggested. He felt her stiffen in disagreement and certainty.

"Yet even those scholars were like blind men trying to comprehend an elephant," she said. "They could only feel. Even the ones who could see were outside the mind. These"—she tried to think of what to call them—"these demons are on the inside looking out. We are on the outside looking in. They know things we will never know." She smiled mirthlessly. "The Daoists say that what we do not know can affect us as much as what we do know—and what we *do* know is infinitesimally small about all things."

"I don't like those odds," Key said.

"They are meant to inspire you to engage more with the unknowable."

Key gave her ass one sharp spank, eliciting a look of surprise, then a knowing, accepting, smile.

"These beings—not the Daoists—may know stuff," he said, "but they're turning it into shit."

Her smile widened as her eyes closed, and she laid down on him. "Yes, yes, I know," she breathed. "Villains are stupid, because if they weren't stupid, they wouldn't be villains."

"That's right," he drawled as he held her close. "Anyone who attacks is an idiot, and has already lost. Then it's just a matter of knowing enough to take advantage of it."

Suddenly she pushed up off his chest to stare directly in his eyes. "How do you do it, Joe?" she asked intently. Knowing he rarely responded to rhetorical, baiting, or unfinished questions, she elaborated. "How can you be so warmhearted and loving, but sometimes so cold-blooded and unemotional?"

He smiled as if he had been waiting for that question all their lives. "Seemingly cold-blooded and unemotional," he corrected. "It's just that I know the—"

He was interrupted by the "prepare for landing" alert. The bell was pleasant; less so the sound of the engines decreasing. The respite was ended. They could feel the sensation of the jet losing altitude. Key slapped Rahal's other butt cheek.

"Drop my cock and grab your socks," he crudely advised her, already rolling his legs to the floor. "It's hunting time."

Chapter 19

Key was back in a Cerberus Cali-brake and Chain-silk uniform as he disembarked the jet to find everyone on the core team waiting—except Lancaster, Gonzales, and Dr. Helen, who had more important things to do. The field team's eyebrows rose, and their grins widened, when they saw Rahal coming down behind him, wearing, for the first time, a matching uniform. Before then she had always worn scrubs and a lab coat.

"Welcome!" Daniels boomed, giving her a big hug.

Rahal laughed with unfiltered joy, then went from the big man to embrace Nichols. Key clapped them on the back as he passed, heading for the palace.

"No time to waste," Daniels said, falling in step behind his team leader.

Key didn't need to say anything. Rahal should be in her clinic, Safar in the workshop, and the rest of them in Lancaster's office. By the time they were halfway across the tarmac, everyone but Rahal was at a flat run.

Lailani was already in the "king's quarters" when they arrived. To Daniel's delight, she launched herself across the desk and into his arms.

Nichols looked amazed that they could be this happy given the situation, but Lancaster and Key shared a look of gratification that the team could still be so full of life considering what they were up against. Even though they didn't know exactly what that was yet, they did know it wasn't anything pleasant or optimistic.

Daniels swung the Filipino girl around like she was a Hula-Hoop, then dropped her into one of Lancaster's leather chairs as if they had practiced the smooth move for days.

"*Kamusta ka,* big ape," she said with a big smile. *Hello, you big ape.* She, too, was wearing a Cerberus uniform.

"*Kamusta, ganda*," he replied, calling her beautiful. "What have you got for us?"

"Plenty," Lancaster answered. "She has been remarkably helpful."

"Was there ever any doubt?" Daniels added, plopping his butt on the chair's arm.

"Hey, you can catch up later," Key murmured as he rounded the desk. "Right now I want to know about the vampires."

"Blood demons," Lailani corrected carefully.

"Why?" Daniels asked. "We have to be politically correct?"

"No," she informed him. "The word 'vampire' not exist until eighteenth century."

Lancaster nodded. "Legends go back to ancient times, in virtually every country and culture."

"Where did it start?" Key asked.

"As near as we can tell, Mesopotamia," Lancaster told him. "Predominantly in Persia and Babylonia. Ancient Greece and ancient India also had similar legends of witches and demons that pre-dated vampires, but those creatures all shared some of the attributes."

"We're closest to India," Key observed. "What was their first legend?"

"*Vetela.*" Lailani perked up from the chair. "Demons who inhabit corpses. Hang upside down high in trees. The frightened villagers call them 'elusive ones.'"

When Key grew quiet and still, obviously thinking furiously, Daniels tapped a foot impatiently. "Where you going with this, Joe? How does this help us?"

Rather than be annoyed that the big man's chronic impatience made him interrupt, Key seemed to welcome the question.

"I'm thinking that whatever reality we're dealing with inspired all the myths and legends, Morty. So the more we know about the consistencies throughout those legends, the more we can put them in a realistic context."

"So now we're going to base our strategy on fairy tales," Daniels said. "That's just swell."

"Not fairy tales, legends," Key clarified. "Let me put it in language even you might understand. 'Know fiction, fight fact.' Okay?" Before Daniels could comment further, Key switched his attention to Lailani. "Who was first? And do the stories tell us if there was some kind of Typhoid Mary?"

"There was," Lailani answered. "That was Lilith, queen of the demons. She drink the blood of babies."

"Wait, isn't there a Lilith in the Bible?" Daniels asked.

The others looked at him.

"What? I went to Sunday school," he protested. "That was Adam's first wife."

"The same," Lancaster nodded.

Daniels inflated slightly under a big grin.

"One of the earliest recurring beliefs is of beautiful female demons who subsist on the blood of babies and their mothers," Lancaster said.

"No men?" Daniels wondered.

"No," Lailani told him. "These beings—they sexual predators *of* men."

"Talk about ripe fruit!" Daniels enthused. "Where's the challenge in that?"

"Precisely," Lailani continued. "They went by many names. Lilitu, Lilu, Sumer, Gallu. All beautiful women, drink baby blood, eat mother's flesh, enslave and devour men."

"Then," Lancaster continued, "the legend spread in every direction, through Asia, Europe, and even Africa. There are literally hundreds of iterations."

"Is that another name for them?" Daniels asked seriously.

Key shook his head, not as an answer but with pity.

"Wherever they go, machismo give them what they want...what they need," Lailani said. "Men think they so strong."

Key looked at the woman with interest, because her opinion was probably right. Even though the threat may have been predominantly female demons, over the years, misogynist storytellers turned them into male monsters to protect their own egos. Male enemies made them look brave and angry. Beautiful women made them feel weak and resentful.

"Let's eliminate any myths that dwell on the cause or creation of the creatures," Key instructed. "Concentrate on their powers."

"The ones we macho men *can* defeat," Daniels observed.

Lancaster went right to work, and, while waiting, Daniels grew fidgety.

"Wouldn't the cause help us, too?" he wondered.

Key shook his head curtly, still obviously chewing on the information he had already heard. "Victims trying to comprehend or explain these monsters' behavior and motivations only stir silty waters," he explained without looking at Daniels. "While the monsters' powers might be exaggerated by frightened victims, they're still based on fact, not fears. Beauty, seductiveness, maybe aroma—who knows what's real in the dark, or in the moment?" He looked toward Lancaster. "And let's stick with the core creatures from ancient times," he said. "As the legends spread, they would unavoidably be altered to align with each culture they went through."

"Like martial arts tailored to geography or climate or body types," Lancaster suggested.

"Exactly," Key said. "One nation's karate is another nation's Wing Chun."

"It's all the same beatdown, ultimately," Daniels suggested.

"More or less," Lancaster agreed as he stopped editing.

"Okay," Key said, leaning down and reading from the screen. "This is what they got. Enhanced agility, hearing, smell, speed, and strength." He glanced at Nichols, who looked back with a "oh well" expression. Key returned his attention to the screen. "Night vision, telepathy, flight, hypnosis, regeneration, invisibility, immortality, shape-shifting."

"That's some résumé," Daniels observed. "You know, I'm beginning to miss giant spiders with explosive blood."

Key couldn't disagree. "Okay, then. Now that we got a better idea what we're up against, what's the most mentioned ways to destroy them?"

Lancaster clicked a few keys and stared at the screen, his eyes moving rapidly. "Decapitation," he finally said. "And fire."

There was a moment's pause, then Daniels spoke. "That's it? Sword or flamethrower?"

Lancaster nodded regretfully.

"What about the other legendary stuff, like sunlight? Crosses? A wooden stake to the fucking heart?"

Lancaster and Lailani both shook their heads.

"In ancient tales," the retired general said, "wooden stakes were used primarily to simply nail the creature down so he could be decapitated or immolated. Sunlight only made them comatose. Crosses had virtually no meaning back when the legends began, which was way before Christ. Everything else—silver, garlic, holy water, or any kind of religious relic— only slowed them down."

Daniels looked aghast. "Well, our pal Z1 kind of throws holy water on the fire option, don't he…playing a burned and unburned corpse."

"That appears to be the case," Key agreed.

The others commiserated with Daniels' frustration. But only to a point.

"It *is* true," Lailani sadly added. "I have thought about all the stories I was told. Now I realize all of them ended with the mothers finding ways to avoid or fight off the monster, not kill them. Families put glass in dead bodies' mouths, or eggs under each armpit, or needles in their palms to prevent them from becoming monsters. They would hang thistles around doors and windows, hoping maybe monsters not enter."

"Superstition," Nichols murmured sadly. "All superstition."

"They were just throwing shit at the wall to see what sticks," Daniels complained, standing up to start pacing around the office.

"So, Joe," Nichols asked, "what are we going to do?"

Key gave the question some serious thought before shrugging. "I guess we better start throwing some better tactics at this problem," he decided. "Speedy," he called to the air. "Ready?"

They all heard the reply in their ear canal comm-links. "As ready as we'll ever be."

Key headed for the door, motioning for them all to follow. "Bring your A-game," he advised.

Key led them to the quarantine section of the clinic. It had been enhanced since their last visit. Now it looked even more pristine and stark—a single square room made up of seemingly glass walls, a metal floor and ceiling, with a single metal chair in the center of it, surrounded by eight huge, seemingly glass, rooms of the same size.

Seated in the chair was Z1.

Perhaps "seated" was not the most apt description. He was strapped there, by seemingly elastic metal bands around his neck, chest, waist, thighs, knees, shins, feet, shoulders, arms, wrists, and even fingers. He also had on a skullcap, made of the same seemingly elastic steel.

"Fuck a duck," Daniels breathed before looking at Lancaster. "Is that what I think it is?"

Lancaster nodded. "An electric chair, but not like you've ever heard of." He, in turn, looked at Key. "Not just bolted down. Anchored into the bedrock below us as far as it would go. Then ten feet more." He motioned, seemingly passively, at the panes of what seemed to be glass. "Electrically conductive polymethylmethacrylate," he explained musingly. "Reportedly stronger than tungsten, harder than chromium." He shrugged philosophically. "We'll see."

Daniels was distracted when Gonzales appeared, slapping what looked like a cross between a KRISS Vector submachine gun and the flamethrower from the movie *Aliens*into his hands.

"Congratulations, Morty," he said. "You can now shoot lightning. And not just out your ass."

Daniels took a moment to be surprised, then beamed like a kid on Christmas—as Gonzales turned his attention to Key. No one had to ask whether the big ape needed some practice shots, an instruction book, or a refresher course.

"If you think whistling that up was fun," Gonzales said, "you should have been here for Z1's coming-out party." The engineering wiz looked at where the monster was strapped down. "We did it one limb at a time, with electrified animal control poles that had nooses of both wire and iron rings. Put the netted bag on the chair, started with the left ankle, then the right, then up the body." He looked back at Key. "His limbs have regenerated even more, by the way, but he acted like he was suffering one big cramp."

That would have been as a result of the starvation diet Cerberus had unavoidably put him on. Key didn't have to ask Gonzales if the EQ devices held up. The team wouldn't be there if they hadn't.

"Sorry I wasn't there to help," Key apologized.

Gonzales shrugged. "Right back at you, Joe. But Dr. Helen's family is pretty amazing. If I asked them to get me proof of alien life I'm pretty sure they'd hand me an 'I Visited Area 51 and All I Got Was This Lousy T-shirt' shirt the next day."

Once more Key was pleased that the team handled enormous pressure with humor. He got quieter, they cracked more jokes. He took one last look around the room, noting that Safar was across the way, ready with a line of net-shooting guns that looked even more powerful than the ones they had used in Varanasi.

Key was about to turn back when he did a double take. At the end of the line of net guns was, apparently on the express orders of General Lancaster, a decapitation-worthy-sized machete. He was about to go check it out, but stilled when Dr. Helen and Eshe Rahal entered the room.

The old Chinese woman, still in a lab coat, stopped and looked meaningfully at Key. Key looked meaningfully back at Dr. Helen, who noticed, and then at Rahal, who didn't. The Arab scientist only had wide, concerned eyes on Z1. Key then looked back to Dr. Helen, who shook her head and pouted so minutely and quickly it almost read like a tremor. That meant the old woman had done as Key had asked.

"Test her," he had instructed on the private line back in the F. B. Law. "Test her like crazy."

Apparently Rahal had passed the tests. Key found himself exhaling with relief he didn't even know he had, as Dr. Helen started preparing her acupuncture kit and Rahal started preparing her autopsy tools.

Key looked away, to the thing in the electric chair. "Okay Z1, whatever the hell you are," he said. "We have no more time to spare and nothing left to lose." He turned back to the others, who stood at the ready. "Open him up."

Chapter 20

Stuart Gullan inwardly laughed at himself.

He used to shake his head sadly at all those New Yorkers who lived their whole lives in the Big Apple but never visited the Statue of Liberty, the Empire State Building, or any of the other justly famous tourist attractions. But here he was, born, raised, and a lifelong citizen of Philadelphia, the City of Brotherly Love, and he had never visited the Liberty Bell.

Until today. Gullan had woken up that morning, almost the same way he had for thirty years—on the comfortable bed in the master bedroom at the crown of the little suburban house—only with two big differences. First, his wife and two daughters were already up and out—the former taking her first physical therapy client of the morning, and the latter duo to their jobs at the local florist and pet store.

And second, this was the first day of Stuart Gullan's retirement. The hospital where he had served as night manager for decades was trimming staff, and, although he would have been fine remaining, when they offered him early retirement, complete with a not-too-subtle hint that the decent retirement package might not be so decent if they offered it again a year down the road, he gratefully took it.

But now what was he going to do? He had enjoyed tennis and golf in his college days, but a night manager position didn't exactly lend itself to making, and keeping, day friends. Besides, with his kids eyeing college, he didn't have the kind of money needed to maintain a club membership, or even to get decent equipment.

Gullan got up, fully intending to make a nice breakfast, read the paper—some old habits die hard—and relax. But, by the time he got downstairs, the sheer quiet and emptiness of the house was getting to him. So much so that, by the time he showered, shaved, dressed, and retrieved the paper from the front stoop, he took the small article on an anniversary of the Liberty Bell as a sign.

Why not? he thought. There was nothing keeping him there. The Phillies's season was over and the Eagles didn't play until the weekend. What was he going to do? Twiddle his thumbs until someone came home? Do yard work?! That last thought really motivated him. Within minutes, he found himself on the Southeastern Pennsylvania Transportation Authority's rapid transit train heading for Fifth Street.

It was a fine, crisp autumn day, and, for a while, Gullan enjoyed the sense of freedom he got watching and pitying all the others on the SEPTA train, who he imagined were burdened with responsibilities and the worries that came with them. Not him, he could do what he wanted now—at least until his family got home. He got off at the Fifth Street station and took his first look at Independence National Historical Park.

Even for a jaded, somewhat introverted, gentleman such as himself, Gullan was impressed. Independence Mall and Independence Square stretched as far as he could see—the National Constitution Center directly in front of him, the Visitor Center to its south, the Liberty Bell Center beyond that, Independence Hall next, and finally, the Tomb of the Unknown Revolutionary War Soldier—who Gullan strangely identified with. At least that poor fellow's early retirement was a lot worse than his.

He got an immediate pang that his family wasn't with him. He imagined that the girls might have gone as part of a school outing when they were tweens, but he didn't know for sure. That gave him another, long ruminated-upon, pang. He had many a late-night talk with the wife about his parental philosophy. Like his father before him, he believed in teaching what he knew, then leaving them alone. His wife had no problem with the first part but thought he was a little too good at the second.

"Hey," he said, "if they have problems, they'll come to you." Which they did. Reportedly, often to complain about him—how he acted, how he looked, how he drove, how he dressed—all, according to his wife, code complaints to cover their feelings that their father wasn't "there for them."

Gullan nodded. He would have to do something about that—starting that very evening, he decided. But first, he had come to see the Liberty Bell, and that was just what he was going to do. He took a quick look around. He had all day, and while the park was nicely populated with tourists and visitors, there was no mob or crush. It didn't look like he'd have to wait in line, even at the main attraction.

Gullan passed by the Christ Church Burial Ground, across from the Visitor Center. He wasn't even tempted to go in. He figured any brochures or souvenirs there he could get later. Instead, he surveyed the expanded Liberty Bell Center, which looked like a steel and glass exclamation point lying on well-groomed, manicured, and tended gardens.

He remembered his older brother talking about the times he and his hippie friends would protest nearby when the bell was on display in the 1960s, then reading about how it was moved from Independence Hall to a glass pavilion on Independence Mall in 1976, and finally the minor funding controversies when the Liberty Bell Center was being constructed at the turn of the latest century.

Lot of fuss for a darn bell, he thought, *and a cracked one at that.*

That attitude got an immediate adjustment when he stepped inside the building itself. But first, of course, he had to stop at a desk for a quick security screening. Gullan quickly identified with the guard, who reminded him of the hospital's security guard, whom he had spent many a break meal with. Like the hospital guard, this one took his job seriously, but not too seriously, and he had an extra layer of pride. In the hospital guard's case, it was from helping make sure sick people were safe. Gullan imagined that, in this guard's case, it was working at a place that had so much history and unpretentious patriotism.

"Another day, another bag search, huh?" Gullan said with an empathetic smile.

The guard swung his squeaking "magic wand" up and down Gullan's form and returned a pleasant grin. "One guy shows up with a hammer in 2001, and here I am," he said, referring to the lone incident that changed the layout of the center. "I wish I could thank him for giving me a second career."

Gullan snorted. "Say, good idea. Today's my first day of retirement!"

The guard beamed. "Great. Enjoy. Just don't go fishing for my job, y'hear?"

"Deal," Gullan said, feeling better already. "Guess you've seen it all, huh?"

The man shrugged. "It's not too bad. As long as you don't show up with a pocketknife or pepper spray we're okay."

Gullan chuckled and resisted making a joke about shoe bombs or containers with more than three ounces of liquid. "Deal," he repeated.

The guard nodded, seemingly appreciative that no wisecrack was forthcoming. "Have a great day and a great visit," the guard said.

"Thanks," Gullan replied, and stepped into the center.

It was nicely laid out, with inlaid bricks in a herringbone pattern as the floor, a wood panel ceiling of the same color, a white granite wall on one side, brick columns framing tall windows on the other, and handsomely designed displays in between. Gullan was planning to just saunter past them to get to the main attraction, but they were cleverly created to catch the eye.

"...like our democracy, it is fragile and imperfect," he saw emblazoned on a larger placard placed above some documents and pictures, *But it has weathered threats, and it has endured....*

That hooked him, and he found himself almost a half hour later filled with respect and admiration for what had happened here, and around here. Now he knew that the two-thousand-pound bell was ordered for the Pennsylvania State House in 1751 and cracked on its very first toll. A repaired version was made in Philadelphia and served well for nearly a century when the crack reappeared. Gullan was most surprised that the now-famous crack was actually the repair job—a widening to prevent further cracking and return its tone.

So, by the time Gullan reached the big, rectangular display "point" of the building's exclamation-point design, he was completely in the spirit of the thing. So much so, that he realized he had hardly noticed anyone around him. Now, however, entering the viewing room, he surveyed the nineteen other visitors—all in their hoodies, jeans, T-shirts, running shoes, and jackets.

As he looked, he felt that now growingly familiar pang. In addition to the teens, young adults, and middle-aged tourists, there was one small child. Like him, she was in the minority—Caucasian. He looked quickly away when she reminded him of his youngest daughter, Emily, when she had been this little girl's age. This little girl couldn't have been more than four years old.

Gullan purposely looked away, concentrating on the bell. It wouldn't do for a single, older man to be caught staring at a young blond girl. So, instead, he admired the elegant silver, thigh-high fence encircling the bell, which was elevated off the floor to about eye level by two silver posts. It was also framed by a large picture window looking out over Independence Hall, where the United States Declaration of Independence and Constitution were debated and adopted.

He watched and listened, because, instead of music, there was an informative lecture playing. "The Liberty Bell consists of seventy percent copper and twenty-five percent tin, with residue of lead, gold, silver, zinc, and even arsenic...."

Try as he might, Gullan couldn't get the little girl out of his mind. She was so different from everyone else in the room, including him.

"It hangs from its original yoke, which is made from American elm...."

She had been standing there, in a little raincoat and rain boots, holding what looked like a little orange juice container in front of her—as if it were an offering. Bet the security guard certainly checked that before he let her in.

"It remains a shining beacon for lovers of freedom everywhere."

Gullan's face clouded. The little girl couldn't have come in alone. She was too young. He quickly glanced on either side of him, expecting to pick out her parents, but, for the life of him, he couldn't.

"And it will remain forever steadfast in the inscription from Leviticus 25:10 that it bears upon it—"

Could she be here with a nanny or maid? He saw only three women of the correct age, and what was he going to do, walk up to each and ask, "Is that your charge?"

"To 'Proclaim liberty throughout all the land—'"

Gullan was trying to decide whether to go ask the security guard when he noticed movement in his peripheral vision. The little girl was walking toward the elegant, open fence that encircled the bell.

"'Unto all the inhabitants thereof—'"

"Hey," said Stuart Gullan, taking a step toward her, his hand out. He wasn't even totally aware that he had decided to take care of her in a way he hadn't for his own daughters.

The little girl kept walking—slowly, calmly—holding the orange juice container in both her hands. As she reached the thigh-high silver partition, Gullan was being jostled by others who had started noticing her.

"Hey," he repeated insistently, taking another step toward her so the others wouldn't crowd him. "Don't do that."

The growing concern dissipated when the girl, seemingly from his exhortation, stopped. Suddenly the room was quiet—the recording had finished, and was, apparently, rewinding. Gullan found himself holding his breath as the girl started turning around, as if she were on roller-skate shoes.

When she did, her clear, almost crystalline, blue eyes focused on Gullan's brown ones. He thought she might raise the juice carton, but she didn't, so he could only concentrate on her face. He wanted to look away, but found he couldn't. He wanted to involve the others around him, but couldn't. He even wanted to look beyond her, to the bell or the picture window, but found he couldn't.

All he could do was stare at her beautiful, tranquil, ethereal face. He could think of only one word for it. *Angelic.*

Then she spoke in a tiny, sweet, innocent voice.

"Zaman will keep going until you stop him."

Stuart Gullan did not have time to comprehend what she had said. It wasn't because it was so unusual or unexpected. It was because as soon as she pronounced the "m" at the end of "him"—as soon as her little lips touched—she exploded in his face.

Chapter 21

The Cerberus team thought they were ready for anything. They were wrong.

They had been fully expecting Z1 to try escaping. They expected him to try attacking mentally, and even physically, even though he now looked like a baked potato whose skin had erupted all along his body. Even his new fingers looked like mashed potatoes that had puffed up out of their skin. They were expecting pretty much everything except what they got.

Laughter.

But it wasn't just Z1's laughter that unnerved them. Had the creature laughed in a way that was understandable—hateful, mocking, evil—that would have been easily comprehended. But this laughter seemed honestly happy, delighted, even gleeful.

Key got over his surprise about as fast as it arrived. He looked with great interest at the thing in the chair—practically feeling the powerful energy of their bodies, as well as the nearly staggering technology involved.

Electricity surged through Z1, ebbing and increasing as he reacted. The same was true of the team's brainwave-modulating earplugs. They altered their frequencies depending on the surges and dips of the energy brought to bear on different sections of the team's brains, either by themselves or outside forces.

Then there were Dr. Helen's needles. She apologized for the "crudity" of her approach since the chair didn't allow access to most of Z1's underside. So she tried to compensate by actuating rarely used nerve clusters. At first, it looked as if she were dancing not just around him, but for him. Every place her hand waved, needles were left behind. They made his skull look like a pinhead and his body look like a pincushion.

"His *linghun* tormented," she gasped. "His soul—"

"He still has a soul?" Lancaster asked incredulously.

The old woman nodded. "Some is left. Some. But his *wugu*—innocence—is destroyed. So he seeks to torture and destroy others."

"The more innocent, the better," Gonzales guessed with disgust.

"Pure," the old woman said, defending the choice as if she were talking about water or milk.

Rahal stood stiffly off to the side, holding a scalpel as if it were a wriggling worm. She stared in shock at the doctor's dance, seemingly feeling every needle the old woman placed. Finally Dr. Helen stepped back, her fingers waggling in the air like she was getting set to play an invisible piano.

It looked like Lancaster was going to ask something, but he held his tongue since all Dr. Helen's considerable energy was concentrated on the thing in the chair.

Z1 started to laugh. He laughed and laughed and laughed until his head began to nod and hisgaze started to dart from one team member to the other. Only then did Key step forward. He moved between Z1 and the rest, all but demanding the creature's full attention.

"I know what it is," Key said directly into Z1's face. "Something was bothering me, but I know what it is now." He glanced over at Daniels. "No blood. There's no blood in his veins, so there's no red in his skin or in his eyes." Key turned his head to look into the creature's mirth-twisted face.

"What are you laughing about, you disease?" Key asked as he motioned at Safar to engage the translating machine.

The laughter was interspersed with robotic sounds that filled the room. Key glanced at Safar with a quizzical expression.

"A mix of likely Indian languages," the Arab-American quietly informed them. "Hindi, Tamil, Sanskrit, Vedic Sanskrit, Prakrits, Middle Indic, Kannada, Telegu, Malayalam…"

But then the laughter changed. It was a second before even Key realized that the laughing had become a song—a song like the one they had heard from the Indian movie musical that led them to Varanasi. A song that Z1 was cackling in English.

"You," Z1 said with a whisper. It sounded more like an exhalation than a word.

"What?" Key demanded.

"I am laughing about you, my friend," the creature said as clearly as he could from his warped mouth and ruptured throat. "For you, with you, to you." He looked at each of the others from around Key's head. "Yes, I know English. Of course I know English. English is the language of the oppressors."

"No," Key countered, shaking his head and attempting to hold the creature's attention. "You are only laughing for you. You, like your master, know something I do not. So even here, seemingly trapped, you are free."

Key succeeded in getting, and holding, the creature's attention. The creature studied Key the way Key was studying him—almost as if they were doing a mirror exercise. Then Z1's head dropped back, his jaw fell open, and his laughter returned.

"Yes, free!" he cried. His head dropped to lock eyes with Key again. "Now, after all this time, I am free. Because, finally, I know the truth."

Key leaned closer. "You need me to ask you?" he inquired. "All right—if you require me to ask you, I'll ask."

Z1 moved his head closer in return, the needles rippling. "Yes, *hadda*," he said. "Ask."

The translation machine quietly said "wasp."

"Then *hadda* asks," Key said.

Z1's head cocked to the left. "Yes," he said. "First you were *mait*." The translator quietly said gnat. "Then you were *machchhar*." Mosquito. "Now you are *hadda*."

Daniels was sorely tempted to comment "*Moving up the food chain*," but, with great effort, resisted. The thought was nauseating and he was afraid to open his mouth for fear of vomiting. Instead, he took the moment to grip the lightning rifle tighter.

"So they know me, then," Key responded.

Craven nodded with pity. "They know you. But they do not fear you. They merely admit your sting."

Key moved a hair even closer, his head on the same level as Z1's. "And you?"

The creature's face calmed. "I thank you," he said with sadness. "For showing me freedom."

Key straightened, nodding, and playing his advantage. "Then I will not sting you," he said, "if you tell me your name."

Z1's barking laugh was bitter this time. "I have no name."

"Then what do I call you?"

The laugh was even more bitter. "You can call me what they call me. *Krevan*." He said it in Hindi, but they all heard it as Craven. Daniels's expression clearly communicated the moniker's suitability.

The "they" clued Key that his supposition about Craven's master was correct. "So, Craven, tell me," he said. "What is the truth?"

"Pilate."

"What?" Key asked.

Craven grinned. "You are so...provincial. The same question is always asked, never answered. Consult your holy book."

Key understood, then: Pontius Pilate...Jesus. The question, *"What is truth?"* It was tough enough to stay focused with this impossible being. He didn't have time or frankly the knowledge to match wits, traipsing through theology and history...though he did wonder, briefly, what Biblical figures might have been vampires. Was that how Lazarus came back from the dead?

Key repeated the question, and the creature almost winked at him. His laughter turned hollow and accusatory. "They would never turn me. A little, yes. Each time, a little. But they would never make me one of them. Not completely. Not ever."

Key glanced at Dr. Helen, acknowledging that she was right about Craven's remaining soul. He was a monster, but not yet a complete Blood Demon. That almost made what he did to those children even worse. "You know that now, Craven."

"I know that now. They had used me before. But then they needed me. And, when the day, the hour, the moment they no longer need me—"

"Needed you—?" Lancaster blurted, stopped by Key's hand snapping back to shut him up. This was not the time to divide the creature's attention.

"Needed you how?" the team leader pressed. "What did they need you for?"

Craven's head started rocking, his laughter becoming more strident. "You *maanav,*" he finally gurgled.

"Humans," the translating machine said.

"So *moorkh.*" Stupid. "So *goonga.*" Silly.

"Why?" Key asked without shame. In fact, he couldn't help but agree. It was this honesty that recaptured the creature's attention and made his disfigured look show interest as well as derision.

Craven started nodding, a look of realization and recognition in his bloodless eyes. "You are like I was," he said. "So impressed, so envious, so afraid, so excited by their power. How could you know? How could you guess?"

"Know what?" Key answered with consummate patience. "Guess what?"

But Craven started trembling. Key snapped his head toward Gonzales as the mechanic's hands flew across the chair's controls while Safar raced over to help.

"Careful, careful," Lancaster quietly warned them. "It could be a feint, a trap."

But when Key turned back, he could see little flashes of lightning going from pinhead to pinhead, all across Craven's body, until it looked like he was being woven into a net of fire.

"Shut it down!" Key ordered.

"No!" Lancaster countermanded. "We don't know if we can—"

"*Doesn't matter!*" Key said, stabbing his hands at Daniels holding the lightning gun, and Nichols holding an electrified animal-control noose. "Shut it *down!*"

Lancaster took a split second to decide, then slammed his own hand down on the abort button. He turned immediately back to Key, but Key had already turned back to Craven, who was drooping in the chair, his skin smoking. Key put his hands on a needle-free part of the creature's right shoulder and left forearm.

"Tell me, Craven," he said softly. "Tell me what you need to tell me."

Through trembling flecks of flesh that used to be lips, two breaths emerged. Key heard something that sounded like "haaaa—naaaa." He didn't understand it, and neither did the translating machine.

"What?" Key pressed, letting his grip tighten, feeling the noxiousness of the creature's flesh. "Tell me again." He lowered his ear to Craven's mouth.

Later, Lancaster would examine what happened next the same way he studied how Craven had dodged Nichols's bullet in the school cellar. The Cerberus alarm went off a microsecond before Craven's tongue almost knifed into Key's ear. But Key was already straightening from the surprise of the claxon. Then the stabbing tongue was gone, no one having seen it.

"What the hell?" Key exclaimed.

"Emergency," Lancaster grunted. "Set my news feed on alert." He slapped on the electric chair's controls again; at the same time he dialed the potency down. "Everybody out," he ordered.

"But—" Daniels started, indicating the creature.

"Craven'll keep," Lancaster assured them, his tone broaching no contradiction. "Rahal, Dr. Helen, keep watch. Let us know of any change immediately."

The two acknowledged. Then he was out the quarantine door.

Key shared a look with the others, then he rapidly followed, already accepting that the retired general was not one to cry wolf, and that the interrogation was all but over in any case. Now all they had to do was figure out what "ha-na" meant. But, as his dad said, "first things first."

As Lancaster ran toward his office, he was already realizing that he needed to have extensive stations so he could access the alerts from anywhere in the palace. And virtually everyone who was following him was planning to suggest the same thing.

Safar, however, was way ahead of them in terms of the simplest, and most obvious, tech—he had pulled out his phone and was staring at it as he ran.

"*Waa faqri!*" he swore.

Gonzales knew it was serious, because he had heard Safar use the Arabic term that translated as "damn" before.

Then they all knew, since all of Lancaster's monitor screens were on in his office as they entered. Everyone approached with trepidation, as if they wanted to draw out these last moments of relative ignorance and innocence, of not-knowing. And then they saw. The monitors were all showing the same thing from different sources: the Liberty Bell attack. A third of the screens showed witness interviews, a third showed tourist videos, and a third showed the museum's security footage. All agreed that an angelic blond girl holding an orange juice container had set off a bomb—killing her, killing the man closest to her, and tearing the bell in two. The obscene image was replayed over and over, in fuzzy slow motion, the colors blanched by the explosion. It played in a nauseating loop: the iconic landmark, big and heavy, lifted upward by the blast, parting along the crack that raced to the top in a mighty leap, just ahead of the rising smoke of the explosion. Then they saw the two halves of iron falling to the sides, into the ugly white cloud and out of frame like a shelled peanut, the ancient wood from which it was suspended sighing upward as it was relieved of its great, historic weight. Then it, too, was lost in the obscene cloud. There did not seem to be any shrapnel, at least nothing jetting through the cloud or toward the security camera. The old bell had taken the hit like a titan, the solid metal from which it was made refusing to splinter. The edges of the crack had peeled back and up and it just—broke.

"Fuck them," Daniels finally seethed with uncommon, heartfelt anger. He stood stiffly still in the middle of the room as the callous carnival played around him.

Lancaster got behind his desk like a commander about to launch his ship. He engaged contact with his network of associates and informants around the world. Nichols tightened her fists repeatedly while Daniels pounded his on the top of the nearest easy chair.

"Was the bomb in the carton?" the redhead asked, unafraid to admit that she couldn't tell.

"No," said Safar, still checking his phone screen. "It was full of tissue paper. That was why the security guard didn't confiscate it. It was full of a harmless roll of paper that he could only see the top of." Safar looked up from his screen. "Paper that floated everywhere after the explosion. Paper that had written on it, over and over again, 'I will keep going until you stop me.'"

Key's head snapped up. "*Moorkh!*" he exclaimed. "*Goonga!*" he cried as he raced back out the door.

Although Daniels and even Nichols quickly followed, Key slid, standing up, back into the quarantine area seconds before them. So he was first to see Craven in a crumpled heap on the floor.

As the others were seeing that, Key's eyes snapped over to where Dr. Helen lay at the knees of Eshe Rahal—the young lady's fist in the old woman's hair as her opening mouth lowered toward the old woman's neck.

Just as the others assumed the scientist was helping the old woman after an attack by Craven, Key snapped up the lightning rifle and shot his lover in the face.

Chapter 22

"Come in, General."

Lancaster didn't know if Pat Logan's earnest rather than ironic use of his rank was a good or bad sign. He hadn't even used the usually sarcastic "retired" as a kicker. He supposed he was about to find out. He stepped into Logan's command post, which took up an entire long, half-circle bivouac tent that was just one of four erected side by side between the Bagram Airbase runway and its control tower.

The retired general was flanked by Master Sergeant Morton Daniels and Corporal Teresa Nichols—both in full assault gear uniform. Lancaster wore his dress blues—the only U.S. military uniform that used all three colors of the American flag.

"You dressed for the occasion," Logan said drily, glancing at him as he leaned over the desk of his personal aide, First Lieutenant Rita Jayson.

Lancaster caught her eye as it went from the files to her commanding officer. It glinted as it passed. He was glad to see she was still working for Logan after having revealed to Lancaster the mission wavelength of the last attack on Zaman.

Each one of the Cerberus people would have sworn that Logan could not have caught the look that passed between aide and general. Nonetheless, the savvy ladder climber looked from her to Lancaster anyway.

"You two have met?" he asked as he took the file and headed to his own, much larger, desk in the center of the tent.

"I saw her on the runway the last time I was here," Lancaster said truthfully as he and the two agents shouldered their way through the hive of activity. This time the area was predominantly filled with intel officers rather than soldiers—obviously assigned to triple- and quadruple-check their latest findings. Lancaster nimbly changed the subject back to his uniform. "I thought it was only fair, considering your latest promotion."

Nichols took a second to check if Daniels could control himself. To his credit, he didn't roll his eyes, but he couldn't contain a flattening of his lips and eyebrows. When the team first heard of Logan's seemingly inexplicable ascension to brigadier general following the Paktika Urgon fiasco, Daniels had grunted, "I never met a man who could fall *up* stairs before." To Daniels's debit, however, the reason his eyes weren't rolling was that they were locked on the handsome flank of Rita Jayson.

Logan sat and meaningfully picked up an expensive cigar from a box on his desk. It was obviously a gift from friends in celebration of that promotion. He took his sweet time lighting it, clamped it in his teeth, and leaned back.

"You know as well as I do that it was a face-saving upgrade, Chuck," he said with a wide, shrewd smile.

"Do I know that?" Lancaster asked insincerely.

Logan continued as if the other man hadn't spoken. "And you also know that it comes with its very own razor-lined trapdoor. I said I would fall on my sword if I fucked up again, and I will. But until then—" He let the unfinished phrase hang as he took a long pull on the cigar and sent up three perfect, ever-widening smoke rings. "Until then, I'm going to enjoy it." He leaned back even more, wove his fingers together behind his head, and crossed his ankles on top of his desk.

Lancaster was sympathetic, but largely unmoved. "I gather you knew I was coming."

Logan dropped his feet back to the floor and jerked forward to grab a file. "Oh, yes, First Lieutenant Jayson's line rang with each link in the chain of command you reached." His eyes ticked down six lines of notes on the paper. "By the time you buzzed in the C.O.S.'s ear, we started cleaning off the red carpet."

Lancaster frowned, remembering the chief of staff's words of support for their new Johnny-on-the-spot, who was, of course, the old Johnny-on-the-spot who had most recently screwed the pooch, then ran away.

"I'm here for the same reason I'm always here," Lancaster said evenly.

"Say it—just so we're clear," Logan replied.

"I want what you want."

Logan looked down, smiled, and shook his head. They *could* play this game for an hour; the man wasn't going to commit to anything, not really. But Logan wasn't going to let him get away with it. When his head raised again it had less of his usual suspicious cunning and more charge-of-the-light-brigade acquiescence.

"Okay, we can do it this way," Logan said quietly. "What do *I* want? Glory? Fame? Respect? A cushy job with a great pension?"

"You tell me," Lancaster said, continuing to pass the buck to Logan.

Logan took the cigar between his right fore and middle finger, then waved both the tobacco smoke and the words away. "Let me make this easier," he said. "The only reason I let you in is that I realize all of the above has always been true." He looked the retired general dead in the eye. "So where does that leave me? Us? What can I do for you? Or, more importantly, what can you do for me?"

Lancaster took a few steps to the side of the desk and plunked one ass cheek on the corner. "This setup is the same as before," he said, taking a brisk, professional tone. "Too easy."

Logan raised his arms in surrender. "I know," he said, taking a less-formal tone. "Another impossible terrorist attack seemingly designed to elicit just the right, contained, reaction. Instead of a big body count, we get a kick in our pride. If one witness hadn't gotten so close, probably only the suicide bomber would've died." Logan shook his head heavily. "A four-year-old suicide bomber."

"And another dare to catch him if we can."

"Not catch," Logan interceded. "Stop. He doesn't want a carpet bombing. He wants it personal. Eye to eye."

"Only this time," Lancaster mused. "No big neon scar across the mountain range saying 'secret base here.'"

"No," Logan grunted, looking at the busy intel guys. "This time the anonymous tips were as frequent and continual as the messages that you were on your way up the chain of command." He shrugged. "But what was I going to do? Say 'I think this is a setup'? Not with that same chain of command nipping at my ass." He motioned at the activity. "They spent all their time collecting data. I spent all my time seeing if I could debunk it."

"And smoking fat stogies," Lancaster reminded him.

"And smoking fat stogies," Logan admitted without rancor. "You get the little pleasures where you can, in our business. 'For tomorrow we die,'" he went on, quoting 1 Corinthians. "But even if I smoked the whole box, it wouldn't change the intel. Even without the anonymous tips, satellite and ground surveillance is unimpeachable. Aarif Zaman is pinpointed in the Hindu Kush Mountains of Badakhshan Province." He caught Lancaster's eye. "That's practically in your backyard, isn't it?"

Lancaster nodded. The mountain range—a militarized combat zone created after 9-11, as well as the ongoing al Qaeda and Taliban fight—was practically sandwiched between Bagram and Tashkurgan over a distance of four hundred miles. Cerberus couldn't help wondering whether Zaman's new "hideout" was positioned knowingly to eventually prep a kick in its pride as well.

"Yes," Lancaster said slowly. "He couldn't have done much better at getting our attention even if he had mooned the spy satellites."

"And what are we going to do?" Logan said hopelessly. "We're a hammer, remember? And right now, Zaman is the biggest, baddest, sweetest nail there is."

"He's also the one that's sticking up the most," Lancaster reminded him. "Like he's begging for it."

"Ah, martyrdom."

"Maybe," Lancaster agreed. "Let us track him for you."

Logan sniffed. "No more time. You may be in a position to say 'thanks, but no thanks,' but I'm not."

"You don't want to throw good soldiers after good soldiers."

"Don't you think I know that?" Logan almost exploded. Instead, he stood straight. "At oh five hundred hours tomorrow morning, we're going in. And this time, no matter what happens, I'm not leaving without him."

Lancaster stood up as well, then, all too knowingly, and saluted the newly minted brigadier general. Despite himself, Logan's face was washed with gratitude. But then the crafty suspicion made an unwelcome, but understandable, return.

"Okay, Chuck," he said. "What do you want?"

Lancaster was the picture of knowing innocence. "Me, Pat? Why nothing, absolutely nothing."

Logan waited for the 'but,' and soon he got it.

"But, if you're in the mood not to leave without something, I've got two good Marines you would be wise to find a place for."

* * * *

The new, seemingly improved brigadier general knew what he was being loaned here.

At least part of the deriding sniggers about Cerberus in the halls of power came from envy over their seemingly bottomless budget and the exceptional equipment that bought. Besides, both Daniels's and Nichols's reputations were reaching legendary status amongst the enlisted men—the former even before the Arachnosaur incident.

So, just to make sure there were no distractions, each got their own bunks—which were essentially simple master sergeant rooms off the main sleeping quarters. Neither minded. Although basic and utilitarian, they each got their own, lone, cot, sink, shower, and privy. Daniels was grateful for the privacy. Neither he nor Nichols held any illusions about their roles in this possible snafu—situation normal all fucked up—so a good sleep might be their only actual reward. A reward that had been in short supply since the start of this bloodless corpse investigation.

At least that might be the case for the redhead. As Daniels stepped from the privy, wiping his freshly shaved face, his nostrils flared. There was a scent that hadn't been in the quarters prior to his toiletries. It was of jasmine, lilac, mint, cinnamon, rose petals, musk, and one aroma he couldn't quite put his finger on. He lowered the towel and looked toward the door.

First Lieutenant Rita Jayson stood there, in her form-fitting skirt uniform, one hand on the upper frame and the other on the doorknob lock. As he watched, she twisted the bolt to the right. They both heard the clack.

"Sir?" he said, lowering the towel and facing her, wearing only his Cerberus underwear.

"It's ma'am," she answered, either correcting him or taunting him, it was not at all clear which.

He decided to pursue the former opinion. "Ma'am," he said. "To what do I owe this welcome visit? Good fortune? Karma?"

She looked him up and down, her lips in a cross between a pout and a purse. "My predecessor in this assignment, Lieutenant Strenkofskl, said if I ever met you I should pass on a message from her."

"Oh?"

The woman frowned. "Innocence doesn't seem to become you," she observed, taking one step into the small room. It was not as small as the student rest closet of the Oman Medical College where he had drugged and abandoned Strenkofski, but still.

"Is that what I'm being?" Daniels asked innocently.

"Trying to be," she affirmed.

There was nothing uncertain about this officer. He looked from her mane of luxuriant mahogany hair to the swell of the shirt intersecting with the strain of the jacket lapels trying to contain her mighty chest, before sweeping down to the impressive curves of her trim waist, hips and shapely legs.

"You have something for me, ma'am?" he asked, managing to retain formal military protocol and demeanor both.

"I do," she replied, and then the world shifted. She reached for the top button of her shirt with one hand while pulling up her skirt hem with the other.

Daniels tossed the towel he knew not where and closed the distance between them just as her white lace demi-cup bra and stockinged garter belt appeared.

"This is a very interesting message," he whispered huskily in her ear as he unsnapped the bra—through both the jacket and the shirt—while unzipping the skirt.

"That's only the subject heading," she whispered back, her warm hands curling behind his neck and down his shorts.

If there was ever a clear distinction between natural blondes and soulful brunettes, Strenkofski and Jayson set the standard and the rules. Both had been willing to lay beneath only after they got to ride on top. While the blonde's skin was flawless cool cream, the brunette's was smooth warm tea.

Barbara's breasts were pendulous teardrops always about to cry, while Rita's chest was ever-cresting ocean waves. The second lieutenant's body was a sleek rocket ship, while the first lieutenant's was a well-oiled sports car. One was sky, one was earth, and both were hungry.

Even so, Jayson had it way over Strenkofski. Because, with the brunette, Daniels got to finish. Twice.

By then she had jammed the towel deep into her mouth so the Marines sleeping outside would not be disturbed by her moans and gasps. She had taken all of him, and her inner walls seemed to consist of twenty of Lailani's expert fingers. Daniels had been hard-pressed to time their release right, but somehow he managed.

But finally she undulated, contorted, and stretched beneath him, clamping him to her—the cry coming from beneath the towel like a kitten on its ninth life. Only then did she collapse, coo, and cuddle, all seemingly at the same time.

As she buried her face in the crook of his arm and chest, he caught the scent of her again. And there was that last aroma, even sharper this time. But he still couldn't place it.

"Rita," he said, for the want of anything better to say. "What sort of name is that?"

"Sanskrit," she immediately, absently, replied, her legs, feet, arms, and hands almost everywhere across and around him. "I guess I was created to return to this area of the world. It means 'brave.'"

Her lips started suckling on him—on his wrist, forearm, shoulder. "And Jayson," he wondered. "Sanskrit as well?"

"Sinhalese," he heard her murmur as she kissed his right clavicle.

"Sin," he breathed, not recognizing the region. "Well named."

Her giggle was both charming and ravening. "I was named for Ritigala Jayasena," she said softly, raising the hairs on his back. "A fierce warrior."

"I'll buy that," he acknowledged as her fingers started to curl around his chin and neck. Her nails began to both tickle and scratch. "Hey," he said as her lips adhered to his Chain-silk undershirt.

He felt something thin, sharp, and strong stab at the top of his spine. Then he heard a sound that seemed to combine a drowning bat's shriek with a frightened wolf. The cot bounced, even with him on it, and the next second he was alone in the room.

Daniels looked everywhere, but the door was still closed. It was even still locked. Her clothes were gone. It was as if she had never been there at all.

Normally he might have gone after her, but this was far from normal. Especially since he finally recognized the final aroma of her scent. He had smelled it often enough on all the battlefields he had walked away from, but it had taken him too long to separate it from the stench of piss and shit that always overwhelmed it.

It was the scent of freshly dead flesh.

Chapter 23

"I'm already dead, aren't I?"

Eshe Rahal stared at Josiah Key through the clear, electrically conductive polymethylmethacrylate wall of the cube that had recently housed Craven. The electric chair he had been strapped into was still there, but Craven was not. He was back in the padded box they had transported him in from Varanasi. Or at least the husk that was left of him. Rahal was now strapped in the chair.

After having shot her in the face with the lightning gun, Key had dragged her there himself and started strapping even as the others had run around babbling questions and expressing confusion. But the security footage soon bore out Key's fears. On it they could see a "smudged" Rahal do something to the top of Craven's spine, then send Dr. Helen to the floor when the old woman tried to intervene.

Key looked at the doctor now. Her face still bore the bruise of Rahal's slap, but her expression obviously bore something worse for her—the shame of not having known Rahal's condition even after all her tests. As much as the others had assured her that she had not lost face—an important aspect of respect in her culture—she was the final arbiter, and, apparently, had found herself guilty.

She had tried to make up for it by immediately performing a more thorough, front and back, acupuncture examination on the creature known as Craven, which eventually became a complete autopsy as well. The findings of both had done little to make her feel that she had regained any face.

"*Mei yinying*," she had said unhappily.

"*Chhaaya nahin*," the translating machine's voice had said.

Key had shown consternation for the first time in a very long time when he remembered that Safar was not there, then went to the machine's controls to find that it was still set to Hindi dialects. He yanked the controls over to English, then made a "repeat" motion at the old woman.

"*Mei yinying*," Dr. Helen had said again.

This time the voice in the air said "no shadow." When Key had looked perplexed, Dr. Helen had gone to the control's keyboard and started typing. The machine's voice had done its best to translate as she went.

"No blood. No electrical activity. Empty."

Everyone remaining in Cerberus headquarters had seen their share of corpses. And when the bodies were undamaged, they all looked like humanoid-shaped flesh and bone vehicles devoid of any drivers or crews. But Eshe Rahal looked nothing like that. Even strapped in the electric chair, she looked as alive and thoughtful as she had on the first day Key had seen her.

Key sniffed, cleared his throat, and answered her question. "Seems that way," he told her. As always, he saw no reason to lie. "What did Dearden do to you, and when?"

"I don't know," she said. "I must have dozed off in the ambulance or his office. It could have happened then, but I don't know. I felt no different either before or after."

"What did you do to Craven?"

"I don't know."

"What were you about to do to Dr. Helen?"

"I don't know!" she cried. "I wish I did. I've been wracking my brain ever since I woke up, but I can't remember. I really want to, but I really can't." Her beseeching eyes ratcheted around the room, then returned to Key. "It's like—it's like I've become a visitor here. I'm sitting in the waiting room of my mind and the rest of my brain is controlling my body."

Key inhaled and exhaled deeply again. There were really only a few options. She was lying or she wasn't. Dearden was controlling her or he wasn't. Key decided, at least for now, she and Dearden weren't.

"How are you feeling?" he asked.

She looked honestly puzzled. "What do you mean?"

"Well, let's start with your immediate comfort. The electrical current running through you is elevated for a normal person."

She snorted with mild derision. "I don't feel it. I don't feel anything but hunger. Like I haven't eaten all day."

Key shook his head sadly. "You must have fed on Craven," he surmised. "Drained his life force. That would explain both your conditions."

Her head dropped, her face etched with misery. "I thought they'd target Morty. All he has is weaknesses."

"No," Key corrected her. "All he has is vices. They only become weaknesses if he starts being ashamed of them."

"*Allaanah*," she cursed. Tears began to form in her deep brown eyes. "I should have listened to you. You were right. It's because I wouldn't believe in them that I was vulnerable to them. *Allaanah*!"

Key could tell she wasn't trying for pity. She was just trying to come to terms with her predicament. What made it all the more tragic and effecting was that he couldn't disagree.

"All right, all right," she gasped through her tears. "Talk to me, Joe. Keep me sane. You said 'let's start' with my immediate comfort. What else?"

"How do you feel?" he repeated. "Try to get beyond the hunger and your mind's waiting room. What does it feel like to become—" He had to stop there, unable to find the right term—or deal with the thickening in his throat.

"*Shaytan alddam*," she said for him. "Blood demon. The hunger grows each time I think about it. It's a want—not yet a need. But I feel the need coming. I still can't decide whether the need will be a physical necessity, like air, or a loud, insistent, mental demand." Her eyebrows raised. "It's like desire."

"How?" Key managed to choke out.

"Well, like, we don't need sex, but we want it. Sometimes really bad. And the more we have, the more we want, to recapture the first rush or see if there's even more."

"How does this kind of desire feel?" Key asked, studying her all the closer.

Her tears cleared again and she stared at him wide-eyed. "That's it. That's it. The hunger is physical and mental, not physical or mental. It's a mix of sustenance and sensuality. Hunger and desire as one, building, threatening, overwhelming thing. Want-based need. Oh, shit, oh shit—"

"What?"

She started to cry again, beginning to writhe in the chair. "I lied to you, Joe. Back near the very beginning of all this." Her sobs became worse and worse, the wracking overtaking her words.

"How, Eshe?" he interjected. "Tell me how."

"I—I—saw Angela's true face," she gasped. "From the very start." She stared at him, her fingers clawing the air. "It was worse than just seeing it. It was a frightening sensation, a dreadful feeling, an unformed, desperate emotion." Her head dropped, her chest heaving. "But—but I kept it to myself. I wanted so badly to prove you wrong. I just *had* to show you she wasn't a monster, she was just sick—"

Rahal suddenly spasmed, her body exploding off the chair, the straps barely holding her. "Like me!' she screeched. "Now, like me!"

Key stepped back despite himself. He heard Dr. Helen typing furiously behind him, then heard the calm voice of the translation machine struggling to interpret.

"Her responses surpassing human thresholds—"

"Eshe!" Key yelled at her as, one by one, the straps holding her to the chair snapped. She somehow managed to stand, legs wide and arms outstretched, across, over, and in front of the electric chair—pure energy radiating all around her.

He was about to shout her name again, but then, before Dr. Helen could stop him, he wrenched open the dividing door, stepped into the room, then locked the door behind him.

"Eshe," he repeated, standing directly in front of her.

And suddenly she was herself again, her face showing confusion. But only for a split second. Then she became something far better, and far worse. He felt caressing fingers in his brain, softening his thoughts of her. She seemed to change inside his eyes, becoming sweeter, more attractive, and more needing of care.

"Yes, Joe?" she asked in a voice that combined everything she ever was, or ever could be, to him.

"Just wanted you to know," he said flatly as he pulled his Sig Sauer 9mm automatic from under his jacket. "I love you." Then, with an enormous feeling of déjà vu, he shot her directly between the eyes.

* * * *

It took what had been Rahal's brain forty-five minutes to reconstitute after they had moved her body to the intensive care unit, then removed her short-lived Cerberus uniform.

While it had reformed, Dr. Helen, through her tears, used both Western and Eastern medicine to check what the old Chinese woman called her newly formed *gyonshiology*—*gyonshi* being the Chinese term for vampire. Once again, she came up empty.

Key had helped the Eshe thing along with a steady dose of electricity. He had conferred with Lancaster via comm-link about injecting some blood into her, but they decided against it.

"Don't wait for me," Lancaster said from his jet en route from Bagram.

"I won't," Key assured him, then had gone to prepare a wooden stake from the leg of a chair in the Hall of Mirrors. He placed the sharpened tip between Rahal's beautiful breasts, and waited.

He wouldn't have cared if it had been hours, but, in the meantime, he watched the hole in her skull scab over, close, and develop skin as if his eyes were time-lapse cameras. He imagined the crater in the back of her skull was an even more impressive repair job. By the expression on Dr. Helen's face, she had found out what future generations of her family would be studying for the foreseeable future.

When Key returned his attention to the naked body on the examining table, Rahal's eyes opened. She looked calmly at Key, then at the stake tip just under her sternum, then back at Key with growing hunger and despair, but also certainty.

"Do it," was all she said.

Key did as she instructed.

It didn't take her heart as much time as her brain. In fact, it didn't take her heart at all. After the sharpened tip of the wooden stake plunged through her body, she closed her eyes, obviously hoping it would work, but within minutes opened them again, reached up, gripped the stake's shaft, and pulled it from her chest.

"Well," Key said sourly. "Worth a try."

"With no blood," Rahal sighed. "No need for the heart."

"Yeah," Key murmured. "Figured that when you didn't bleed."

"Interesting sensations though," Rahal told him from the table. "Both during the destruction and reconstruction. Too bad I didn't have these heightened feelings when I was—human."

"How's the hunger building?" he asked her quickly.

She seemed to consider the question for a moment. "It's there," she admitted. "It seems to grow as fast as the flesh reconstitutes." She frowned, gritting her teeth. "This is awful. It's like my body is laughing at me. Like I have dual personalities—one me, one a monster who wants to be me. I feel it waiting, knowing it will win."

"If there was blood," they heard the translator's voice say, "we could test it, maybe find an antidote or cure, but—"

Key glanced over to where Dr. Helen was typing furiously.

"No blood," Rahal finished for her, then looked directly at Key. "You have to kill me before the hunger overwhelms my reason."

"I'm trying," he managed to grunt.

"No, you're not," she told him as he looked away. "Not really. I understand the gun, and even the wooden stake, but we already know electricity and fire won't work. There's only one thing left. You know you should have already done it, but I know why you didn't."

He felt her hand on his cheek. Finally he looked back at her, but still he couldn't speak. So she did.

"Every time I come back, there's less of me. I don't want to exist if it's only for the hunger. I can already feel what it's like. Aching, agonizing, all the time. Endless agony, endless urges. Only slaked when fed, and less and less every time."

Key nearly jumped back when her fingers clawed at his neck. When he looked down it was into the face of a drowning woman desperately trying to break the water's surface, but not being able to. It was the worst helplessness he had ever felt.

"They—" she gasped. "*We*—don't steal the soul. We feed on it! *Ealaa qayd alhaya walakun bila ruh!*"

He saw her go under, her last dying gasps only able to emerge in her native tongue. As the calm machine voice translated, Dr. Helen appeared beside him. With a simple, seemingly effortless touch she sent him flying ten feet across the room.

So he watched from the floor between two chairs as the old woman raised the machete. At the same moment, he comprehended what the machine voice had translated.

"Alive but soulless."

Dr. Helen brought the machete down on Eshe Rahal's neck, separating her head from her body as easily as if she were preparing Peking duck.

Chapter 24

It was a completely different Patrick Logan who rode the command MV-22B Osprey tiltrotor copter over the peaks and valleys of the Hindu Kush Himalayan range—a difference both Morton Daniels and Terri Nichols studied carefully from their flanking positions just behind him.

The redheaded corporal thought it was a difference that came from more than just being bumped up to brigadier general. The master sergeant thought it was a difference that came from more than just being within frequent proximity to Rita Jayson—who had been MIA since her exit from Daniels's room. Both Cerberus agents had already communicated their concerns to retired general Lancaster, who remained in constant communication through their ear-comms.

Now, however, they all agreed the difference was in Logan's conviction. His eyes were steady on the horizon, and his jaw was both jutted and set. As he had promised Lancaster, he had no intention of leaving these mountains without his quarry, and he wasn't going to let anything or anyone distract him from his mission—least of all the Cerberus agents who shadowed him.

All the troops behind them could clearly distinguish the difference between their commander and his reluctantly accepted "advisers." Logan looked like John Wayne, ready to take on all enemy armies in full camo uniform, while the Cerberus duo looked like refugees from the latest sci-fi superhero flick in slightly glowing, sleekly armored Cali-brake. Logan had his Marine sidearm. The agents flanking him held weirder, less familiar weapons that seemed like mutated Tasers, or even videogame guns.

As the copter started losing altitude, Daniels looked over to the Super Stallions beside and behind the command chopper—the bellies of which were each filled with fifty fully equipped troops. Including the twenty-five soldiers behind them, that seemed to be more than enough person-power to mop up the mountain folk who awaited them.

"Prepping to land now," Daniels muttered. He didn't even hear the words over the Bell and Boeing engines, but Lancaster did, loud and clear.

"A humbled Logan is a cautious one," the retired general told his agents from nearby, in his own command post inside a Discrotor Jetcopter—an aircraft so advanced the military didn't even know it existed yet. So much so, in fact, that Logan wouldn't see it even if he was staring straight at it. The small, versatile, fast, Gonzales-perfected little beast had a first-generation cloaking device and anti-heat-seeking tech. "He's trying to take no chances—at least from his limited imagination."

Daniels sniffed. "Very inspiring, sir. Thanks for the confidence." The master sergeant had been testy since recognizing Jayson's scent, a fact that had sent Cerberus into overdrive, but given everything that was happening with increasing speed, intensity, and need, that only resulted, as far as Daniels was concerned, in wheel-spinning.

Lancaster's lips tightened, biting back any trite, essentially useless, hollow advice like "be careful" or "keep your eyes peeled." The Cerberus standard equipment all over their uniforms was already taking care of that. Instead, he fed them information Logan might not share.

"The area is under constant infra-radiation radiological tech," he reported. "It reveals a network of caves and tunnels that are filled with successive groups of attackers waiting to ambush anyone entering."

Daniels's eyes narrowed as the copters floated down some fifty feet away from a cave entrance. He looked from it to the armament hanging on either side of the Osprey doors. In addition to the craft's standard Gatling guns, Hellfire missiles, and Hydra rockets, he recognized new, laser-sighted, computer-controlled, "leapfrog" landmine cannons. "Well, that explains that," he murmured, looking forward to seeing the cannons in action.

He didn't have long to wait. As soon as the Osprey settled, Logan signaled the leapfrog tech. The brigadier general and the Cerberus agents watched the techie's screen, which looked like an animation that foretold the future. A line went from the cannon to inside the cave, then skipped, like a flat rock on the surface of a pond, through the tunnels, even around corners, leaving small discs in its wake.

The animation had hardly stopped when the techie's thumb twitched, and the cannon blasted out with all the energy and power of an electromagnetic thrill-ride launch ramp. Logan, Daniels, Nichols, and all the troops watched as what looked like a hat box disappeared into the cave. Then only the latter trio, plus the techie, watched the screen as the hat box seemed to divide into slim, discus-shaped sections that sped deeper into the caverns—leapfrogging each other to get there. Then they all heard the *whomps* of the detonations from inside the caves, saw the cave walls crackle, and felt the ground shake.

"These mines combine the most effective attributes of explosive, napalm, shrapnel, sound, and sight assaults," Lancaster's voice said into his agents' ears. "Designed to kill, incapacitate, blind, and/or deafen."

Logan wasn't done, however. As that was happening, the hundred troops had emerged from the Super Stallions. As soon as they were out, crouching, their copters relaunched, floating above the cave systems. As the troops watched, the undercarriage armaments launched what Daniels recognized as new injector lance missiles, designed to burrow into landscapes before detonating. More *whomps* followed until the entire area seemed to wobble.

Logan turned expectantly to his techie, who studied his screen carefully before giving his commanding officer a thumbs-up. The screen was clear of infrared shapes that could be identified as living humans. Daniels and Nichols shared a look. Both knew that the screen didn't, and couldn't, show living dead humans. Thankfully, even Logan wasn't dropping his guard, but probably not for the same reason.

He hauled himself up and scuttled toward the copter door. Although both Daniels and Nichols had started after him, their boots hit the ground before his, their bodies between his and the smoking cavern entrance. As Logan watched the Osprey troops deploy, the Cerberus agents only had eyes for the cave entry.

"There's nothing for it," Daniels heard Logan say tightly. "We'll have to go in."

Everyone had hoped they could have made this a small-unit, nighttime assault, like the team that took out bin Laden, but, as with everything else so far, the Marines had to dance to Zaman's tune. This wasn't so much a surprise attack, but an early morning RSVP to an obvious invitation. They could only hope that the terrorist had underestimated the speed with which they had managed to mount the assault. But everyone in Cerberus doubted that.

Daniels and Nichols carefully placed themselves around Logan so the brigadier general didn't get the impression that they were restraining him as he, like a baseball coach, gave silent commands with his arms and hands. The troops responded expertly, approaching the cave from two sides, weapons at the ready. As two backed up one, the lead man went in, made sure the area was clear, and signaled the others to follow.

Logan heard their reports on his own earphones and grinned rapaciously as one team after another announced "all clear." He nodded, then gave an order that was music to Daniels's ears. "Strafe the walls, floors, and ceilings."

Lancaster grunted in response himself. "Ah," he said in his agents' ears, "seems he can learn from experience."

They all heard a renewed chorus of "all clear," but that didn't seem to cheer Logan at all. His face remained grave until he heard a quiet comment from the team leader up front.

"Got something."

Logan stepped toward the cave, Daniels and Nichols moving with him as if they were his moonshadows. "What?" he asked.

"Can't be sure," came the team leader's report. "Body too disfigured by damage, but it might be Zaman."

At the mention of the name, Logan started striding toward the cave. It took all of Daniels's not-considerable willpower to keep from wrenching the brigadier general back. Instead, he and Nichols quickly followed, subtly sandwiching the man from possible harm. They both wanted to offer warnings, but remembered their place—as well as the likely effectiveness of that.

Whatever their concerns, they found themselves in eerie green night vision light, standing amid the leading squad, looking down at a disfigured, crumbled, shattered corpse. The Cerberus agents' night-vision glasses were superior to the military issue, so they could see the man's face, body, and clothing better than the others.

"Yeah," Daniels muttered, "Looks like Zaman all right."

"It's not outside the realm of possibility," Lancaster told them doubtfully. "The bombing was intense."

"Only one problem," the normally quiet Nichols said, surprising both her boss and partner. "It's only his corpse. Where's the others? Where's anybody else?"

"Shit," Daniels snapped. "She's right."

"Wait, wait!" Lancaster warned. "It's entirely possible that—"

The phrase was as far as he got before several things happened at once. Logan was leaning down to check the body when the team leader spun around at the sound of a rifle. The soldier next to the team leader grunted and staggered as the rest of the soldiers' helmet lights converged on a turbaned, burnoosed man holding an AK-47 at an outcropping at the far wall of the cavern.

The other soldiers opened fire as Logan fell atop what appeared to be Zaman's corpse. Daniels placed himself between the brigadier general and the other men as Nichols grabbed a fistful of the corpse's remaining clothes and threw him in the opposite direction. Daniels was again impressed by her strength as the body that might be Zaman smacked into the wall by the cave opening they had entered.

Daniels tried to look everywhere at once as the sounds of the soldiers' shouts filled his ears. "Shit," he repeated. "Don't chase him!" But it was too late. Like starving cats spotting a mouse, they raced after the man who had shot at them. "What do you see?" the master sergeant asked his boss.

"They can't get a bead on him," Lancaster replied, expertly deciphering the jumbled images Safar had hacked from the soldiers' camera feeds. "The tunnels are getting smaller and twistier the deeper you get into the caverns."

"Of course they are," they all heard Key say from their Chinese Versailles headquarters. His clear, strong, voice was welcome, but not so much after what he said next. "Trap, trap, trap. Get out of there. Get Logan out of there."

"How is it a—?" Daniels started, but his body was already responding to Key's orders as his brain tried to catch up to the fact that no good ever came of questioning Key's deductions. He took one step back toward the copters just as Logan ran by him in the opposite direction. "Shit," he said a third time as he tried to grab the man, but Logan was too fast.

The brigadier general got to the outcropping just as Nichols sidled in front of him like an electric eel. But despite her enhanced speed and reflexes, Logan's intensity and bulk slid her back. By then Daniels had caught up, and the two Cerberus agents crammed the commander between them.

"Get out of the way," Logan barked. "My men—I have to reach my men!"

Both Cerberus agents saw the truth of Key's guess. The outcropping was more than that. It disguised an opening into a deep, multi-tiered cavern—a cavern that was even now being cut off by a sliding slab of rock.

"Fuckaduck!" Daniels seethed, unable to figure how the slab of rock was being moved, or from where. All he knew was that if he stayed where he was, he would be crushed in seconds.

Logan was blocking Nichols's exit. She'd never get out in time. Daniels could simply step back and escape, but he had his orders. He grabbed Logan by the arm and head, then practically threw him over his shoulders like a rag doll. He could have used a German suplex to hurl them both to safety, but there was no way he was going to save himself at the cost of Nichols.

Instead, he tossed Logan the way Nichols had tossed the corpse, then purposely stepped to the redhead's side as the slab of stone slammed across the opening, sealing them in the darkness with the other soldiers. Even her enhanced reflexes couldn't help her dive out now.

"Trap sprung," Daniels announced to whoever was listening. There was no answer. "Logan out, us in." No answer. "Stay tuned." No answer.

The master sergeant grimaced as the truth sank in. Not only were they trapped, but they were trapped in a space that somehow cut off all communication. Daniels lowered his head until he could see Nichols only by the glimmer of her green eyes.

"We're screwed," he whispered to her.

No answer.

Chapter 25

Josiah Key couldn't think of anything that could stop him from joining Lancaster to find out what had happened to Daniels and Nichols. Within seconds of their ear-comms going silent, he was already collecting the tools he'd need for an extended field assignment.

In fact, he was on his way to Gonzales's hangar to see which aircraft he could pilot when both Dr. Helen and Lailani blocked his way. The Chinese woman had no translation device nearby, so the Filipino was the one to tell him.

"The naked malfeasant," she said. "Not dead."

Lancaster may not have heard Daniels and Nichols any longer, but he heard the woman's words as clear as day.

"Go," he told Key from hundreds of miles away in his command post aboard the Discrotor Jetcopter high above the clouds of the Hindu Kush battlefield. "Or, more accurately, stay. See what this is all about, and what you can find out. One thing we don't need right now is another helpless agent wringing his hands and walking in circles."

"That an accurate description?" Key wondered, marching down the Hall of Mirrors toward the clinic's morgue, flanked by the two Asian women.

Lancaster looked toward Safar in his corner of the craft's cabin, all but banging his fist on the ear-comm's control board. "It'll do," he told Key before checking his own readouts and screens. "Logan's on the ground with the surviving copter crews, raising holy hell for additional forces to drill through the rock wall. He doesn't want to use a missile in case it kills the trapped troops."

Key nodded as he entered the cold, sterile medical examination room. "Logan's a shitload of things, but he's not dumb," the team leader said tightly. "He knows that operational HQ will want a positive ID on the corpse he's got ASAP."

"Or negative," Lancaster agreed. "Although he's had a crisis of conscience, if I know Pat, he'll get over it soon enough. Better a live possible hero back at base than an impotent commander in the field. If that body is Zaman's, the powers-that-be will be satisfied, no matter how many troops were lost." Lancaster paused, taking just enough time for a nod. "Yup. The Osprey is taking off now. Faisal, stop trying to get through to Daniels and Nichols. It's a waste of time and effort at this point. Keep apprised of the military chatter." The retired general returned his attention to Key. "What do you think?"

Key stopped in his tracks, looking at the withered, wizened corpse of the monstrous old man that had haunted them from India and back. He lay, naked, looking like a ruptured human-shaped balloon—but one that now had grown ragged fleshy patches on lumpy outer extremities. Key looked at Lailani, who nodded.

"Once creator is gone," she said, "many legends state that victim's curse fades."

It tragically fit. Now that the one who fed on the creature's feeble life force was beheaded, her victim was returning to his previous state.

"Doesn't matter what I think," he told Lancaster. "Now it matters what Craven knows." Key motioned at Dr. Helen, who started unwrapping her largest acupuncture kit with one hand while motioning at the body on the metal table with another.

"She says," Lailani interpreted, "she needs his whole body."

Key quickly studied the room, seeing metal tracks in the ceiling from which thin chains hung. "Do you need his thumbs?" Key asked her, then, when she looked confused, pointed at his own thumbs. Dr. Helen took a second to tap the tip of Key's thumbnail. He responded by pointing to the base of his thumbs. The old woman curtly shook her head "no," then went back to her preparations. "Okay then," Key said dourly.

When she was ready, so were Key and Craven. The former had strung up the latter with bands tight around the base of the knobby, nude, corpse's thumbs. Craven hung from the ceiling with his toenails just scraping the metal floor—allowing Dr. Helen access to every centimeter of his body except for a half-inch band where his thumbs met his hands.

Key hefted the lightning gun, parked one buttock on the edge of the examining table, and watched with Lailani as the Chinese doctor did her needle dance. It took almost a half hour, but finally Dr. Helen stepped back, revealing the pincushion that was now the child murderer. There had to be hundreds of needles in the thing's form, with the most being in his arms, legs, feet, and ears. In fact, the latter two places could hardly be seen through the steel pin forest.

She nodded at her work, then at Key, then stepped over to the medical console. She sat on a wheeled chair there, and switched on the electricity. Both Lailani and Key saw the monitors light up—their graphs veering wildly. Craven seemed to tremble in the air, but otherwise Key waited for no approvals.

"Friend," he said to the seemingly passive thing that passed for a face. "*Chhaaya nahin.*" Craven's eyes opened. They were dry and still bloodless, but clear. "You think I'd forget so soon?" Key told him. "No, friend. Now you may answer. *Chhaaya nahin.*"

It looked as if Craven was trying to smile. At least the corners of his ruined mouth were twitching. "No shadow," the creature breathed, the words carried to Key's ears as if by dust and wind. "They had no shadow, so I became their shadow."

"And the children became yours?"

This time Craven managed to turn his head, and the mouth corners twitched again. "*Goonga,*" it breathed.

Key nodded, finally understanding why this monster would think him silly. "Not your shadow," he realized. "Your reward."

If Craven could beam, he would have. "Yes," he said. "Finally, yes."

"For being their shadow," Key urged.

"Yes," Craven said, then became silent as, with every word, it seemed as if extra vitality was pumping into his body from an invisible tank. As they watched, his nose, lips, fingers, and toes began to take on a more familiar form.

Key looked back at Lailani, who was staring at the thing like a bug. "Legend says vampire have no shadows," the young woman whispered, as if Craven would react badly if she was heard.

Key looked from her back to Craven, his mind chopping at the puzzle, trying to figure out where that legend came from. "Vampires avoid light," he muttered. "Light casts shadows."

"If they in light," Lailani said, "people see no shadows."

"They see nothing behind them." Key sat up. "People would see no one behind vampires." He turned from Lailani's confusion back to Craven. "They let you have children as reward," he said. "For being behind them, for backing them up. For—"

Suddenly the puzzle pieces started clicking into place. Key wasn't sure whether to nod, shake his head, or both. Instead of either, he raised his hands, bringing the lightning gun with them. "Oh, God," he chastised himself. "So *moorkh*. I am so *moorkh*."

A noise emerged from Craven's mouth that combined wheezing and choking. He was laughing at Key. "Yes, *hadda*. You stupid before. Not so much now, henh?"

Key opened his mouth to continue, but before he could, Lancaster came back on his ear-comm line. "Major," he interrupted, "the corpse has been positively identified. It is Aarif Zaman."

"Of course it is," Key replied.

"What?" Lancaster responded. "Never mind, that's not important. What is important is that, as far as command is concerned, the mission is complete. But at a terrible cost. They've done an even more intensive infra-radiation radiological search, and there's not a sign of life in the entire cavern any longer. I am truly sorry, Joe."

"Don't be," Key snapped.

"What?"

Key ignored his boss, keeping his attention on Craven, while answering them both. "You brought them Zaman, didn't you? Zaman and his men, who would then bring them more men, better men."

Craven's exultant, bitter laughter filled the room. "Yes, *hadda*. They did not want me. They wanted you, and the others."

"What?" Lancaster exclaimed again in Key's ear. "Why?"

"Because they had no shadows anymore," Key said to whoever was listening. "What happened, Craven?"

This time the creature did not pause or gloat. "You happened, *hadda*. You, and all the other gnats and mosquitoes became so rich, so fat, so poisoned, so polluted—"

"Oh Christ," Lancaster nearly gasped. Key smiled grimly as he realized that Lancaster was figuring it all out just a few minutes behind him. "We were—we *are*—their food chain!"

"Yeah," Key seethed. "Faisal could tell you. Any computer wiz could tell you. GIGO. Garbage in, garbage out."

"HIV, AIDS, SARS, Ebola," they heard Gonzales say. "All the modern plagues."

After everything he had been through—after everything he was going through—Key had to throw back his head and laugh along with the monster. "What, did we think that vampires would be immune?" he spat at the ceiling. "These are blood demons. And as our blood got tainted, so did theirs!"

"So," Lancaster struggled to get his head around this. "All the surviving blood demons teamed with Zaman. But why?"

"Not all the survivors," Key shot back. "Two survivors. They're shape-shifters, remember? The Mount Rushmore 'parents.' Dr. Dearden and his nurse. Rita Jayson and—Aarif Zaman."

Lancaster managed not to exclaim "what" again. He was simply thunderstruck into silence.

"He must have been killed in the first explosion," Key pressed on, interrupted not by Lancaster, but by Craven this time, whose laughter became even more strident and triumphant.

"That was me!" it cried. "That was me!"

"Good for you, you bastard," Key snarled. "But you wanted more men, didn't you? You had to lure more men, so your master became the new, resurrected, unkillable leader of the terrorists, didn't he?"

"Did he?" Craven mused, shaking in his chains.

As the truth began to sink in, Key and the others were distracted enough to ignore Craven's words, attributing them to the creature's growing strength and substance.

"But to what purpose?" Lancaster wondered. "Just to kill soldiers rather than civilians?"

"No!" Lailani suddenly cried. "Not to kill! To turn!"

Key smiled with grateful appreciation at their blood demon expert. "Exactly. They had no more shadows, General, so they have to create them. And to make more certain they wouldn't be nearly wiped out again, they wanted the best of the best. They wanted more than a few good men. The terrorists were used to entrap their quarry, and I bet they will wind up as lifeless food eventually. But the Marines who attacked Paktika, and the ones in Hindu Kush? They may be lifeless, but I'm betting you anything they're definitely not dead—"

Lancaster heard a horrible screech as Craven tore out of his chains, his thumbs spinning in opposite directions like rubber bullets, and clamped his needle-encrusted form onto Key's body.

Chapter 26

The last thing Morty Daniels remembered seeing was the glint of Terri Nichols's green eyes and saying "we're screwed." But he couldn't be sure of even that now.

The blackness that surrounded, and eventually consumed, the jade glint also enveloped him as well. Not just his eyesight, but his entire mind. When his consciousness slowly rose to the surface of his awareness, the first thing he felt was the ache of his shoulders, then pressure on his jaw, and finally pain at his scalp.

His eyes snapped open to see only rock and dirt. When he tried to change his point of view, the ache, pressure, and pain only intensified.

"Fuck. A. Duck," he grunted, hearing a clacking from his wrists and a squeaking from his chin.

He couldn't shift his position enough to see what was clamping onto his head and arms, but he could sense them well enough. He was in a small stone grotto, his arms wrenched behind him, shackled together, and somehow shackled again to the cave's ceiling. The position, called a strappado by ancient torturers, insured that he was bent double at the waist and would remain that way.

But at least in a basic strappado, the victim could move his neck a little bit. Something else had been added to prevent him from making anything but the most minute of chin-wagging. From what he could feel, it was some sort of head halter that cupped his chin and stretched his spine to its optimum length. From the restriction of his skull shackles, it seemed to be somehow attached to the cave wall, or ceiling, as well.

Otherwise, he seemed unfettered. In fact, most of his uniform was missing save for the undershirt and shorts. Before he could completely process that, he heard two words.

"Ah. Awake."

He couldn't be sure whether he heard it in his ears or his mind. Ultimately it made no difference, because they seemed to relax him. He was about to test the strength of the restraints, but once the words reached him, he felt calm, even soothed. He even recognized that they seemed to communicate relief and appreciation. His eyes strained in their sockets until he saw the one who pronounced them.

Rita Jayson stood before him, but it was not the same Rita Jayson who had been in his room the night before the ill-fated assault. This woman was even more sensuous, with an expression of sexual hunger, and a uniform that was even more extreme than before. Her starched, tight dress shirt was open, revealing the frilliest, skimpiest, and laciest of push-up bras. Her skirt was slit, revealing lace-top, thigh-high stockings. And the tan heels were impossibly high. The fact that they were all an almost mocking satire of military protocol made them even more potent.

She was rubbing his EQ between her elegant thumb and forefinger.

The body inside the mock uniform was even more perfect than he remembered. Breasts impossibly strong and full. Waist impossibly small, legs impossibly long. Even her ears and feet—which were, to his experience, what ladies seemed to like least about themselves—were perfectly shaped and sized.

"Accent on 'impossible,'" he murmured, trying, but failing, to look away.

"Ah," he heard again. "Sergeant." He felt her impossibly cool, and impossibly warm, hand caress his face right after she crushed his EQ like it was a popcorn kernel.

"Ma'am." He almost chuckled. "You got me at an obvious, purposeful disadvantage, don't you?"

"Please," she said softly, the sound settling his mind more than her fingers did. "Feel free to call me by my name."

Both her hands settled on his jaw, bringing his head up as far as it could go, so her bulging chest practically kissed his eyes.

"Rita?" he choked.

"Ritigala," she corrected, letting one hand course through his hair, deftly avoiding the clamp that attached the follicles to another hook in the cave ceiling. "Ritigala Jayasena."

Daniels cleared his throat, unable to think of anything else to do. "Nice name," he grunted. "Not exactly 'Bond, James Bond,' but it kind of rolls off the tongue, don't it?"

He felt, as much as saw, her appreciative smile. Her hands kept caressing his face and hair as she looked approvingly down at him.

"Ah, Mort," she replied, clearly referencing the French word more than his name—the French word meaning death. "Always making jokes, even in the worst of circumstances." She crouched in front of him, giving him a glimpse of her thighs. "It is yet another admirable thing about you. Just another thing that so attracted me to you—that made me want to help you join us."

Daniels grimaced as the dead flesh aftertaste of her otherwise sweet and spicy breath reached his nostrils. "Aw, what's the magic word, sweetie?" he growled. "Never heard of 'pretty please?'"

She grabbed his hair in a fist and shook his head dismissively before standing and taking a step away. "I underestimated you," she said firmly. "I always underestimate you."

He remembered the sound she had made when her mouth had touched his Chain-silk dickie. "Well, you certainly underestimated my tailor," he reminded her. "But before we go any further, might I suggest a breath mint?"

She turned back toward him, her crossed arms creating a balcony for her buoyant breasts. She made a sound between a giggle and a sniff.

"Tried everything," she admitted. "But when you've eaten as much shit as I have?" She walked beside him, idly rubbing his back as she went toward his flanks. "I was only lying a little when I said I was descended from a great warrior. I was actually created from one after I was decapitated in battle."

Daniels raised his eyebrows. Her words were so soothing, and she was speaking so matter-of-factly, that he was unsure how to respond, or even joke. It got worse, or better, when she coolly crouched by his thighs and reached into his bike shorts.

"My first regeneration wasn't pretty," she serenely mused, tenderly fondling Daniels's penis. "'Great demon of the graveyard,' they called me. So what was a poor girl to do—but go on a thousand-year feast of flesh and blood?" She paused in her speech, but not in her gesticulations. "Odd," she pouted disingenuously. "My subjects are usually erect by now."

"You tell them the same story?" Daniels asked incredulously, the head harness creaking angrily as he tried to look back at her.

"Oh, no," she laughed prettily. "I reserve that for only the most special of recruits, sergeant. The ones I know can take it. Like you, dear Mort."

She seemed honestly happy as she continued her consummate hand job. "Oh, I've heard them all. How I was torn from my mother's breast as a demon. How my skin was blue or green or purple or yellow. But always blotched with blood. How red rays erupt from my eyes and smoke pumps from my ears. How I wear a necklace of skulls or intestines, and a skirt of bloody arm or leg stumps." She paused, pouting. "Funny. The only thing they ever got right was my tongue and my breath."

"Do me a favor, would you?" he groaned as her expert, even somewhat supernatural, ministrations completely hardened him, despite the situation. "Treat me like a regular Joe, would you?"

Her giggle was annoyingly delightful. "Oh, very well," she sighed. "If you insist."

He felt her mouth envelope his manhood in a way no woman ever had, could, or would. Her oral cavity was like a warm, wet tunnel of flesh that could contain his erection without pause or problem. Then her beyond-perfect fingers were back at his scrotum and even anus.

"Oh, God," Daniels moaned, knowing he shouldn't ejaculate, but also knowing he had no choice, even with his vaunted willpower. "New world's record," he grunted as more semen he ever expected he had all but exploded out of him in a torrent unlike any other he had ever cannoned.

Then he felt something else. As the semen left, he felt a thin, sharpened, bony needle enter his penile canal. Whether it spit something itself he couldn't be sure, but as he shuddered, he felt another sort of warmth wash over him—a warmth that sedated him more effectively than any man-made drug.

She sucked down everything he shot like an open dam accepting gallons of delicious milkshakes. She patted his ass as she rose.

"Now, that's more like it, soldier," she said.

Daniels was completely prepared to glare proudly and defiantly at her when she came back into view, but the woman who appeared to him was not Rita Jayson or even Ritigala Jayasena. It was a perfected vision of a nineteen-year-old Cathy Kelly, complete with summer dress, freckles, strawberry blond hair, and light blue eyes. She was Morton Daniels's mother.

"Hey!" he moaned. "No! No fair!"

But his young mother—the one before she married his father—the one who was impossibly pretty and effortlessly sexy—only laughed at him.

"Can't help it!" she said in Jayson's voice. "This is from your own mind. I asked it who you loved the most, and—" She moved her arms up and down her own form. "Ta-da."

"You fucking bitch," he hissed.

"Ah, sergeant," his perfected teenaged pre-mother sighed as she placed her hands on his skull and back. "You don't know how right you are."

Then her mouth sank onto the top of his spine, and the needle-like tongue inside her liver-like tongue, unimpeded by any Chain-silk, stabbed into his first vertebra.

Chapter 27

"Ah. Awake."

Terri Nichols opened her eyes to see Aarif Zaman standing before her, holding her EQ in one hand and her ear-comm in the other.

Before she even checked her own position she saw the yawning cavern behind him. Her enhanced vision allowed her to see what Daniels would not have seen: piles of bodies, but bodies unlike any she had seen before.

Even at her relatively young age, she had seen her share of corpses—both in person and on film. At first glance, these reminded her of the piles of emaciated cadavers that had been bulldozed into mass graves throughout history and the world. But then she saw they had more of an order than that. These bodies were, for the want of a better word, filed. They looked like gigantic jigsaw puzzles made of human forms, laid side by side and one on top of the other.

And, while she couldn't make out any specific breathing, they seemed to pulse. Shining, pulsating, nerve wires seemed to stretch over and between them—either feeding, or being fed, for the want of a better term, life force. These bodies weren't so much resting as they were, somehow, gestating.

Only then did she take stock of her own situation. She was chained to the wall of a small grotto off the cavern, naked. She was instantly reminded of her captivity by Usa Awar as he tried to make her the first human Arachnosaur weapon back in Yemen. But because she had experienced, and survived, that horrid internment, it freed her brain to think clearly. So clearly, in fact, that she felt no need to respond to Zaman's comment. She looked at his smug face evenly, even calmly.

He seemed to take that as an annoying challenge. He held her earpieces closer to her face to make sure she could see them. "Do you know where you are?"

Again, she didn't answer, but took the opportunity to closer study her surroundings. The medium-sized chains held her wrists above, and on either side, of her head—as well as holding her ankles wide, a foot or so above the ground. As such, they allowed her to look directly into the tall terrorist's eyes. Considering what she had seen the blood demons do before, this was not a promising position.

Unlike her Cerberus comrades, Nichols hardly spoke at all. But like at least her team leader, she watched, listened, and studied intently. Nothing got past her, which was probably the reason she had lived so long, even against what many might consider impossible odds. Her nudity didn't shame her, and her predicament only inspired her to consider all the more options.

Again, Zaman took her silence as a chance to gloat. "Wherever you think you are, you're wrong," he said. He glanced back at the cavern full of stacked bodies. "Wherever your people think you, and they, are, is also wrong." He looked back at her with what she supposed was a superior smile. "Oh, they may drill through the rock blocking them from where you were last seen, but even if they do, they will discover you are nowhere to be found. In fact, you are miles away from where you landed, with no connecting caves or tunnels to lead them."

Nichols stared at Zaman, her eyes narrowing. The longer he spoke, the more unnatural he sounded. Try as she might, she could discern no Afghan accent of any kind. In fact, no Middle Eastern accent at all. If anything, she recognized tones of South Asia.

And "miles"? If he were truly Afghan or even Asian, he'd use "kilometers" or even "*li.*" She tested the chains' strength, making them rattle, but still said nothing.

"Oh, you wish to escape?" Zaman said, his smile widening. "Please, feel free to try. I can assure you that, even if you somehow manage to, you will be in for a great surprise." She looked at him incredulously, considering the circumstances, which seemed to inspire him to step closer. "Do you know who I am?" he asked, just inches from her face. "Do you think I am your hated enemy, Aarif Zaman?"

He held up her ear-comms in front of her eyes and popped them as easily as Jayson had. "Could your hated enemy Aarif Zaman do that?" the man in Zaman's skin and clothes bragged. "I think not. Because, no matter what you think, I am not him. I am your true enemy."

To Nichols it looked like God's thumb smudged the man's face, and, when He was finished, a new face had replaced it—a dark, swarthy, handsome, commanding face, with a strong brow, straight short black hair, crimson eyes, high cheekbones, and a strong chin.

"I am Mahasona," he said, slowly and purposefully, putting his left hand flat on the stone to the right of her face. "Do you know of me?"

Nichols exhaled. "The greatest demon," she said, remembering what Lailani had told them and the research Key had shared. "Shape-shifter. Mind and body thief. Chief to thirty thousand demons."

It was Mahasona's turn to snort. He straightened, then started slowly, purposefully, unbuttoning Zaman's shirt. "No longer," he said, jerking his head toward the bodies behind him. "These will be my new army. The rest? All gone."

The truth settled into Nichols's brain as it had for Key and Lancaster. It was the only thing that made sense in an experience that stretched the very definition of "sense." But by the time she realized what had gone, and was going, on, Mahasona had finished removing his shirt and started unbuttoning Zaman's pants.

"What was it?" Nichols asked quickly, bunching the muscles at her wrists and ankles. "A slaughter?"

"A plague," Mahasona said sadly. "A plague of bad blood, bad energy. It made us sick. It made us die." He glanced accusingly at her as he pushed the pants off his legs one by one. "And with no souls we were dwindling in these flesh shells as they withered and became part of the ground." He stepped out from the clothing, naked as she. "But not me. Never me. Never again."

"But what of your soldiers?" Nichols asked hastily, stretching in the chains. "I see what you're doing to my soldiers, but what of yours—I mean, Zaman's—the ones who helped you arrange all this?"

Mahasona huffed as he stepped back toward her. "Of no consequence. Wretched refuse. They served their purpose. Now all who are not integral will join my kind in the dirt!"

Even before he finished speaking he was on her. His hands had turned to claws that clamped both sides of her head. His bulbous, inflating tongue plunged into her mouth, coiling into both her cheeks. And his penis had become a scimitar-shaped hook of boney flesh that stabbed up into her.

What saved her was that she didn't go into shock. She was preparing herself with every second he took and every word they spoke. She was not surprised or frightened, so when he came at her, her mind slowed him down. He was obviously expecting a normal human female, not one whose reflexes had been enhanced by her previous ordeals.

Even so, she knew she only had a second before his infection delivery assault would lock in. Then it wouldn't matter how enhanced her strength was. She had already seen that the chains on her wrists and ankles were merely looped, and affixed in place by small padlocks. The "wretched refuse" who had chained her up obviously had no idea of her reflexes either.

With a constriction of her hand muscles and a twist of her wrist, her hands slid free. The same was true of one foot. But not the other. To her sudden fury, one link dug into her left heel, trapping her left leg in place. Mahasona didn't seem to notice. His claws kept clamping, his tongue kept surging, and his member kept shoving as his eyes seemed to exult in the grotto ceiling.

"God. Damn. It!" Nichols hissed through gritted teeth, using her free hands to return the monster's favor. She grabbed his head in both her hands and took a good hard look at him.

Okay, you bastard, she thought. *Maybe you can't be killed, but let's see how good you are flying blind.*

Sinking her fingers as tightly as she could in what passed for his face flesh, she plunged her thumbs as deep into the center of his eyeballs as they would go—fixating on the mental image of crushing grapes.

The howl that came from him echoed through the caverns but only served to deafen her. He did not relax his grip on her, but he did start staggering around the grotto. But with her thumbs deep into his eye sockets like they were a bowling ball, he could only go so far since her left ankle was still chained to the wall.

She felt his impaler go as limp as it could, while his tongue flopped disgustingly around her mouth like a virgin on prom night. His claws, however, remained clamped to her head as tightly as her fingers were clamped on his.

"Come on, come on, come on!" she seethed at her left ankle as she tried to twist it loose while still dealing with the way he was wrenching her back and forth. But it just wouldn't pop free.

He had started babbling in the Sinhala language until he suddenly stiffened and shouted something incomprehensible in anger. Then still holding her up, he slammed her back against the cave wall, nailing her there with his shaft.

"*Modaya!*" he screeched—*fool* in Sinhala. "You want it this way? Then this way you shall have it!"

For the first time since the Cerberus team had rescued her from the Yemen weapons auction, Terri Nichols felt fear. She had done everything she could, but, because of bad luck and a far superior adversary, her mind cried that he'd have her. She could feel the contagion building in his tongue and penis, ready to infect her. She no longer had even a second.

Terri Nichols screamed in agony and frustration as Mahasona screeched in triumph.

Then, only one of their shrieks changed. And it wasn't hers.

Suddenly he froze, and just as suddenly recoiled with sickening convulsions. His claws snapped away from her head, his tongue snapped back into his own mouth, and the scimitar-shaped thing rammed back into his own body as he lurched.

"*Monavada*," he gasped, hunched over as if suffering cramps. "*Monavada oba kaja?*" *What have you done?*

Nichols didn't know what he was saying and didn't care. The second he released her, she snapped off the left ankle chain with a combination of reward and rebuke, then went speeding out the grotto opening without shame or pause.

If there's a way in, there's a way out, she thought, already letting her unpopped eyeballs scour every centimeter of the cavern for it. *And I don't care if it's only big enough for a squirrel. If it can get out, I can.*

In the darkness, she saw a glimmer of light. In the stagnant atmosphere, she felt a whisper of moving air. In the enveloping cave of rock, she smelled the sun-baked aroma of grass. Hardly even controlling it, she let her body take her toward it, only allowing a single instance of checking where her blind rapist was. She saw him stumbling out of the grotto, but the scent of the other hundreds of bodies was already masking her own.

As she gained speed toward the as-yet unseen exit, she didn't know whether she said it or thought it, but she didn't care because it was true.

"I've been held captive by better assholes than you."

She said it, and Mahasona heard it. He managed to take one step toward her when he felt a restraining hand on his arm. He didn't need his eyes to know it was Tajabana. The smell of honeysuckle, rose, and dead flesh was pungent in his nostrils.

"No, my great master," she said. "Do not sully your magnificent hands with this *wen rui*." Gnat in Sinhala. She saw that his ruined eyes were already beginning to reconstitute, then turned her head to watch the naked little redhead disappearing into the twisting cavern tunnels. "I have a much better idea."

Then, with a small smile, she called forth the remainder of the armed, angry, integral Zaman followers.

Chapter 28

It was a macabre sight, made all the more macabre by taking place in bright sunshine.

The Hindu Kush spooned the Pamir Mountains where the borders of Afghanistan, China, and Pakistan met, and, while the area once had been a significant center of Buddhism, it was now littered with the remnants of statues and temples destroyed by Taliban Islamists.

Nichols emerged from a hole in a sandstone mountain wall. As soon as she dove out, she fell twenty feet but rolled in the air like an Olympic diver and somersaulted across a sand and gravel beach. Coming up in a crouch, she spun her head in every direction to get her bearings.

She stood between what looked like a massive sand castle that bordered a swath of deep flat grassland, leading to trees that looked like frozen explosions of branches and leaves. It was a remarkable wilderness— obviously once a holy land that had been demolished by extremists, and then grown over. As she stepped back, the visual effect was of a gigantic death's head that had been savaged by both a psychotic dermatologist and dentist.

Nichols was about to sprint toward the copse with the thickest mass of trees, but she heard something ominous behind her. She spun just in time to see robed, burnoosed, turbaned Zaman followers emerging from many other holes in the cliff wall—looking like a desiccated face that was ejecting its own blackheads. They were popping out from cavities all over the cliff face, making her consider trying one of the most extreme life-or-death games of Whac-A-Mole ever.

Thankfully, the holes seemed too small for them to bring their assault rifles with them, but every one, to a man, was gripping at least one Gurkha,

Khyber, or Peshkabz knife, which, in close combat, were even more deadly than any gun. Nichols clearly remembered what Daniels had told her.

"Rule one, don't get in a knife fight. Rule two, what, didn't you hear rule one? Rule three, if you ignore rule one and two, remember: you're going to get cut. The trick now is to minimize the damage."

After recalling that, Nichols played out a literal example of "fight or flight." One foot slid toward the grass and trees, but the other flexed, sending her up toward the nearest emerging man. He was taken totally by surprise, obviously thinking he was too far up to be reached, but he hadn't counted on the naked woman's enhanced abilities. Nichols yanked the man out of the cliff face like a veteran fishmonger yanking out a squid's guts.

The man's frightened screech was music to her ears as she let her altitude and attitude bring him down to the ground like she was John Henry nailing a railroad spike. The man's screech was cut off with a sickening thud as Nichols popped the Peshkabz knife out of his grip with one hand while tearing his robe off with the other.

As the man slid to a stop, leaving a bloody streak where his face had smashed the rocks, Nichols was already spinning away. When she stopped, she had already wrapped herself in his short robe, using his turban as a belt, and brought the Peshkabz up for a closer examination.

Hollow-ground, tempered steel, single-edged, full tang blade—broad at the hilt, then beautifully tapered to a needle-edge, triangular tip. She wrapped her fingers over its pair of handle scales, which were fixed to a full-tang grip that had a nicely hooked butt. The seventeen-inch-long weapon snuggled into her hand like a newly born kitten. *Nice.*

She seemed oblivious to the men who dropped behind her back, to her left, and to her right. They just saw a slim, almost feral, redheaded woman in a robe-dress, hunched before them, her back to them, seemingly paralyzed with indecision or fear. They had the more standard machete-like Gurkha knife or the sword-like Khyber, and raised them like they were going to easily carve her for a cannibalistic pita. They were even smiling in anticipation. They weren't smiling for long. Just as their arms got to their highest positions, the young, little, redheaded woman moved.

At first she looked like she was trying to dodge or avoid them, but her arms and legs were moving too purposefully for that. The impoverished, desperate, poorly educated men immediately thought of the dancing girls they had been promised in the afterlife as this nymph-like creature quickly weaved among them. Even so, they swung their blades wildly, trying to slice, cut, or chop her as she seemed to get near. But then she was several steps away, her pace quickening.

They stepped after her, not wanting her to escape, only to find that their hands were now empty. They looked around them to find that their knives were on the ground several feet away in three different directions. For a moment they felt elation because they saw that each weapon was bloodied, but then they realized that the blood was not on any of the blades.

The man to the left looked to see his right hand was missing. The man next to him saw that his burnoose was sliced open from hip to hip. On closer inspection, he saw his intestines beginning to throb out over his lap. The third man's head began to fall back, his eyes filled with sky. It just kept going, the cut from ear to ear giving it no anchor.

Nichols danced back, making a quick count of the others emerging from the cliff wall. There were a dozen, appearing from holes that stretched for fifty yards. No way she'd be able to outrun them forever. And run where? The Cerberus ear-comms were crushed. According to Mahasona they were miles away from where they were last seen, and the Hindu Kush was five hundred miles long and a hundred and fifty miles wide. There was no way anyone on her side would find her in the foreseeable future.

Fuck it, she thought. *As Key always said his dad said, "first things first."* Nichols gripped the Peshkabz tighter and raced toward the trees.

Sure enough, the burnoosed men came from every direction behind her, like heat-seeking missiles after a jet. She could outrun them, but they would be relentless and knew the area much better than her. Besides, they had comrades all over the place. The Hindu Kush had almost always been a battlefield, dating from Alexander the Great to al Qaeda. But it was also always a hideout, with venal backstabbers tucked into every imaginable refuge.

She found that out when she reached the trees. Thinking they would give her cover, she was saved from certain death by her enhanced hearing. No matter how quietly the ambushers tried to drop from branches on top of her, she heard them with seconds to spare—just enough time to switch position to avoid their knives, then use their dying bodies as cover when snipers tried to back the knifers up. She heard them too—especially the *clack-clack* of their bolt-action rifles.

Thankfully, these were mountain villagers, so they were using old Lee-Enfield or Mosin-Nagant rifles that might have had better range and accuracy than AK-47s but only allowed one shot at a time. That was all Nichols would allow them.

Only three tried to ambush her. Each tried to jump on her from above as she passed. She would avoid their knives, hands, and feet, but wouldn't let them hit the ground. Instead, she plunged her knife up into their chins, chests, or backs, held them up by their heads, sternums, or spines, then let the sniper's high-caliber bolt-rifle bullet thud into their bodies. No matter how small they were, she was smaller and slimmer, and no bullet could reach her.

By then, some of the knife-wielding terrorists had caught up with her. Not surprisingly, they had learned nothing from what she had already done. Maybe they were too busy scrambling, climbing, and running to have witnessed it, so they simply charged at her, screaming and brandishing their blades—perhaps hoping she'd react like the innocent women, children, and animals they usually used that tactic on. She didn't react that way. Daniels and Key had taught her. Fighting was as easy as A, B, C.

A, avoid. Don't be where the knife is aiming. B, balance. If she avoided well, the attacker would automatically be off-balance, so if she was balanced, then it just became a matter of "so many ways to kill you, so little time." C, closure. A fight wasn't over until the attacker was incapable of attacking anymore. So Daniels and Key had taught her an encyclopedia of ways to devastatingly end it, the fewer moves the better.

She shifted as the screaming man brought the knife down. At the same time she plunged her knife into his hurtling-past eye with one hand, she dug the thumb and forefinger of her other hand into the nerves of his attacking hand, so his Khyber knife popped free. As the man fell heavily to the ground, already in the process of dying, she plucked his knife out of the air and threw it into the throat of the man just behind him.

As that man stumbled, not quite cognizant of his mortal wound, Nichols grabbed the arm that held his Ghurka knife and used an aikido technique to use the man's own aggressive energy to spin him in midair so, like a bowling ball, he took out the two men nearest him. Seeing how they fell, Nichols kicked the nearest man's forearm, so his knife was plunged into his own throat, and tossed the first man's Ghurka knife into the head of the other.

Then, moving in a quick circle that seemed to be the natural extension of her defensive actions, she located the remaining half-dozen. As she turned toward them in the forest's clearing, her Peshkabz at the ready, they stopped dead—their eyes wide as they realized that the sheep they thought they were attacking was actually a lioness. A really pissed lioness.

"Enough!"

Nichols let her head cock to one side and her right knee bend as she exhaled, because she recognized the voice. Mahasona appeared from behind a tree some ten yards away, his arms out, his hands open in the universal sign for "stop."

"That disappearing and reappearing trick is great," Nichols sighed. "But please don't give me the 'slow clap' thing."

To her surprise, the man laughed. "Actually I was going to," he admitted with a wryness that shouldn't have chilled her, but did. "But since you beat me to the punch—" He motioned his hand back to the tree he had emerged from, and bowed.

"Oh shit," Nichols groaned when she saw who was with him. "Oh fuck."

Tajabana smiled at her. There was no mistaking the woman. She stood in a simple robe that was open down to her navel and up to her thigh. Her body and face was Nichols's idea of perfection. Since Nichols was a green-eyed redhead, she was envious, for some reason, of soulful, statuesque, serene, brunette Earth-mothers, complete with a light dusting of freckles and deep blue eyes. Tajabana was the most beautiful one she had ever seen.

But that was not why Nichols had cursed. She had cursed because Tajabana's elegant, tanned hand was resting on the elbow of Morton Daniels. One look and Nichols knew that the difference between Daniels before and Daniels now probably existed inside the smiling mouth of the brunette.

"I believe you two know each other," the extraordinarily beautiful woman said in the most soothingly disingenuous tones imaginable.

"We did," Nichols breathed, trying to get ready to face her teacher, friend, superior, and what she was now certain was a just-infected blood demon thrall. "Once."

Their eyes locked, and Nichols saw something beyond cold emptiness. She saw Daniels behind his own eyes, locked inside his own brain, feverishly fighting against the darkness that threatened to engulf him at every second. She saw his lips move. She could have sworn she saw him mouth, "I'm sorry."

Then he attacked.

Chapter 29

"Anyone who attacks is stupid," Key had said. "How do you know they're stupid? Because they're attacking."

Daniels and Nichols knew that. Mahasona and Tajabana didn't.

Nichols had seen Daniels's inner struggle just before he charged her. Trusting the man's great strength, Nichols used her superior reflexes to A, avoid. He had come at her like Frankenstein's monster, lurching and grabbing—something he would have never done on the battlefield, and something he had only done once in the gym.

It had been a joke. He was laughing with her about all the bad fight scenes they had seen in movies and on television.

"Yeah," he had said. "You ever see how the bad guys either lurch around like Frankenstein or, better yet, do that Incredible Hulk thing of just grabbing someone and throwing them? Hell, the Hulk could tear their heads off like taffy, and all he does is toss the guy? Come on!"

She could take a hint, and did—ducking low, spinning, and skittering away. During her retreat she scoured the area for the new landscape. Mahasona and Tajabana were still by a far tree, but now a bunch of terrorists and villagers had made a large, wide, circle around the two Americans—all brandishing or holding their knives or rifles at the ready.

The blood demons were clearly struggling to control the big man, but, even without her EQ, they seemed to be having no effect on her beyond a small mind massage—the massage that perfected their beauty in her eyes. As Nichols kept her distance between the circle and a growling Daniels, she finally had a split second to remember Mahasona's reaction to his sexual assault on her. He had recoiled with seeming revulsion.

She knew that was important. Now all she had to do was somehow escape Daniels, the blood demons, and every terrorist in the surrounding two hundred miles, and she might be able to do something about it.

She returned her full attention to Daniels, who seemed to be struggling more with himself than with her. He had first attacked like Frankenstein's monster, giving her time to get her bearings. She trusted him enough to know what should be coming next—that is, if he still was managing to hold off the infection from taking complete hold. It was worth a chance.

He came at her again, arms outstretched, and she seemed to dodge, but let one arm swing back just a little too much. Daniels grabbed it, and, sure enough, used it to throw her through the air like a rag doll—right over the nearest terrorists.

She landed on her feet and ran directly at the blood demons. The circle of terrorists broke and came after her just as Mahasona stepped back. But Tajabana smiled. At that moment it felt as if they had reached into Nichols's head and clamped their fingers deep into her brain as if it were pizza dough.

Nichols dropped to the ground on all fours, panting, just as the nearest terrorist was about to plunge his knife deep into her back. But then meaty hands grabbed him and threw him into the tree. He smashed into the tree trunk with a wet thud, making Mahasona take another short step away—lest he be splashed with the man's sweat.

But Tajabana remained, head lowered, lips frozen in her knowing smile, as Daniels grabbed Nichols by the hair and neck. He then threw her back to where they had started as the terrorists stumbled and began to scatter. The brunette looked sharply at her master, who snapped at the terrorists.

"Back! Back to your places, dogs!"

The men began to do as ordered while Daniels stomped toward a rolling Nichols, who came up lightly on her feet, peering at her adversary. The Daniels she knew was all but gone. She could just make out a silver sliver deep in the back of one eye before he grabbed at her.

"No muscle," she remembered Key telling her. "If you use female muscle against male muscle, you'll lose. Use their muscles against them. Use their aggression against them. You just help them defeat themselves by redirecting their energy back to them." Then he had showed her how to do that.

Daniels grabbed at her. Nichols curved herself under his attack and placed her arm under his, her palm under his bicep. Having avoided the strike, she let his momentum carry him forward. Then all she had to do was cross his off-balanced ankle with her balanced one, and he somersaulted forward, smashing down, back first, with a ground-shaking boom.

Daniels's back was to her. Without hesitation, she dove forward, all her strength and energy lancing from her toes through her body, then into her right forefinger's second knuckle—which she had curved into an arrowhead. She landed perfectly, in the tender spot behind his earlobe, to cut the blood from his brain just long enough to render him unconscious.

She had done it better than she ever had before. It was as close to a perfect "phoenix eye" attack as she could imagine, so she was already moving forward to take on every terrorist from the circle who got near her.

Then she stopped from no fault of her own. Stunned, she looked back to see Daniels, sitting up, barely conscious, gripping her left ankle in both his meaty paws.

The phoenix eye hadn't worked. The contagion had become more powerful. His blood flow was clearly compromised.

Nichols felt her heart breaking because she knew what she had to do. She couldn't let Daniels become their slave. Nor could she let herself be killed by him. Rather than struggle to free her ankle, she stepped back with her free foot and swung the pinky-side of her right hand like a scythe—directly into the side of Daniels's head just above where his jawbone met his skull.

Even if she had used half her power, the tiny, vulnerable connecting bone there would break, even shatter—flooding the rest of his skull with blood, drowning his brain. She heard this was what had killed Bruce Lee as well. But she didn't use half her power. She used everything she had left.

Daniels's fingers snapped open. Nichols jumped back, ready to spin and fight. But, while still turning in the air, she fought the lump in her throat and the tears coating her eyes. She never thought it would end this way. Just the opposite, in fact. She always thought it would be Daniels who wound wind up crying over her mortally wounded body.

No time now, she yelled at herself. *First things first!* She had to get away from the blood demons.

This time she ran in the opposite direction, ready to eviscerate any terrorists in her way. She was only feet from them, but even then she saw they were smiling, not preparing for battle. A moment later she found out why.

She felt Daniels's meaty paw clamp around her neck from behind. There was no mistaking it. A moment after that, she felt herself being launched high off the forest floor, the grip not weakening. He used her head like a sledgehammer, throwing her down as if trying to bury a stake in the ground. If she hadn't been enhanced and gone totally limp, her skull would have cracked like an egg and her neck would have snapped like a twig.

Even as it was, Corporal Terri Nichols crumpled onto the ground like a marionette whose strings had been cut. She moaned, twitching, astonishingly grateful she could do either. But then Daniels's knee plunged into her stomach and his left claw clamped to her throat. When she looked into his eyes this time, there was no Daniels there.

Then he looked up, away from her. Her eyes rolled to see him staring at Tajabana like an obedient pet. Mahasona smiled with consummate pleasure, then started toward her while reaching for his pants.

"No," said the brunette, her hand lightly on her master's arm. "Let him kill her." She turned her overwhelmingly soulful eyes to his. "For me."

Nichols could not recognize the emotions that were crashing over the blood demon's handsome face. They went too quickly and were too confusingly contradictory. But she recognized all too well the last emotion that settled on his countenance. It was the look of any emperor about to give the thumb down.

"Very well," he said with a hungry, anticipatory, smile. "For you."

The blood demons turned back to their unwilling gladiators and waited with satisfaction. Daniels looked back at Nichols like she was a pinned specimen. His fist rose, ready to plunge into her face until there was nothing between it and the ground.

In that split second, Nichols used her arms, legs, feet, hands, knees and elbows to rain a flurry of blows all over Daniels's body. But not one seemed to have any effect on him. And, by the way he was straight-arming her throat, she just couldn't reach his eyes.

He wouldn't talk, and she couldn't talk because of the way he was strangling her, so she mentally said what she figured were her last words.

Maybe I'll suffocate before he smashes my bones and brains.

She closed her eyes, and didn't die.

What's with the high-pitched, barely audible whine? Did imminent death give me dog's hearing?

Terri Daniels opened her eyes and saw the terrorists scattering. She looked up to see a frozen Daniels staring blankly off toward the tree where Mahasona and Tajabana had been standing. The blood demons were no longer there. Instead, there was an astonishing aircraft hovering two feet above the forest clearing.

It was a small, camouflage-colored plane with advanced helicopter rotors attached to its fuselage just above its dual cutting-edge jet engines. It looked like a metal hummingbird had mated with a spaceship and given birth to a chopper-jet. It all but screamed "Gonzales," and, as Nichols watched, the side door flew open.

She saw the lightning gun first, and then that it was being held by Faisal Safar, who pulled the trigger to give the full blast directly into Daniels's face and chest. The sergeant twitched, jerked, shuddered, and shook at the same moment another figure came leaping out, carrying a net gun in each hand.

Nichols saw Josiah Key, with what looked like a serious case of acne afflicting his face, pump one net over a recoiling Daniels, then, before the big man had even stopped rolling, hit him with another. By then retired General Charles Lancaster was already gathering Nichols up and hustling her back to the aircraft.

"What?" Nichols managed to choke out as Lancaster launched them inside while Safar ran to help Key collect Daniels. "How?"

"Later," Lancaster grunted, jumping into one of the cabin's six seats.

"Strap in!" Gonzales yelled from the cockpit. "We got to be gone as fast as we came."

Nichols managed to find a seat and click the restraints in place just in time to hear the cabin door slam. She looked to see, incredibly, that everyone, including a heavily netted Daniels, was back on board. It had been a hit-and-run surgical strike deep within enemy territory. Even so, she couldn't even begin counting the international laws they had somehow circumvented or rocketed under.

Then she felt something she hadn't experienced since her first takeoff from an aircraft carrier. She imagined it was something similar to what astronauts felt when leaving the launch-pad. She couldn't breathe for a minute, but it was better than being dead.

When the pressure on her chest, and the ripples stretching her facial skin, finally subsided, she took her first full breath since leaving the blood demons' cavern. She opened her mouth to ask every question that was demolition-derbying inside her mind, but then saw gray creeping into the corners of her eyes.

Oh, no, she thought. *You have got to be kidding.*

But then she remembered everything she had just been through, cut herself some slack, and let her body and brain collapse.

Chapter 30

Nichols couldn't decide whether she was having a nightmare, dream, or something in between. But by the time she saw Cerberus Chinese Versailles Headquarters out the aircraft's window, she knew things she hadn't known before Daniels had hurled her headfirst into the Hindu-Kush ground.

"Welcome to my latest, greatest baby," she could've sworn Gonzales had told her. "S.H.E. Silent Helejet Extreme. What the U.S. Defense Advanced Research Projects Agency couldn't perfect, Cerberus did. Part spaceship, part chopper, really fast, and all but silent." He shook his head, sheepishly realizing he was talking like a fanboy geek. "High speed vertical takeoff and landing, rotors retractable into an aerodynamic spoiler, and an airspeed of more than—oops, got to go. Autopilot disengaging. Sleep tight, we'll be back in no time."

She lost him after that, and the next thing she remembered in her dream-state was Key's pock-marked face. Her own hand came into her vision, seemingly attempting to touch the man's visage, which looked dotted with freckles made of popped, scabbed-over, pimples. He gently caught her hand in mid-reach and sympathetically put it down by her side.

"Not what it looks like," she remembered him grimacing quietly. "Got head-butted and body bumped by a pincushion." He grinned grimly. "You should see the other guy, though. Which you will, in time. But for now, rest, recover."

Finally, when she rose momentarily from her stupor, she saw Lancaster sitting by her, looking on with paternal concern. When he saw her eyes were open, his expression changed to understanding. "You asked me 'how,' remember?" he told her quietly. "Well, I take 'no one left behind' very seriously, so you don't think I'd send you into the field with only traceable earpieces, do you? No, Corporal. You'll get full details when we've time, but for now, rest assured that if you're findable, Cerberus will find you."

Despite its remarkable hovering abilities, Nichols's enhanced senses felt SHE touching down near their Chinese Versailles and, rather than make sure her dream-like visits were true, she got up from the reclining seat ready to help Key and Safar move the netted and wrapped Daniels into the isolation unit. The work they still had to do was far more important than any confusion she might still have.

As soon as they entered the warren of electrically conductive polymethylmethacrylate cubes, Key motioned Nichols toward Dr. Helen as he and Safar started securing Daniels in the electric chair even more stringently and strongly than they had for Craven. When Nichols hesitated, Key insisted.

"Got to make sure you're a hundred percent," he reminded her. "Or, at least fifty. We're not anywhere close to out of the woods yet. None of us."

Nichols nodded, quickly telling them all how Mahasona had recoiled during his assault on her. "And, even without my EQ, they didn't seem to have much power over my brain."

Key looked pointedly at Dr. Helen, who started typing, until Safar stopped her, motioning around the room to let them all know the automatic translator was on.

"It is possible," the calm, disembodied voice said in English as Dr. Helen spoke Mandarin, "that your brains have already, and automatically, adjusted to protecting your mind's wavelengths that the blood demons have attacked."

"Or, they are getting weaker as we continue to frustrate their plans," Lancaster suggested.

"I wouldn't count on that," Key grumbled as he strapped in Daniels's legs with all his strength. "Nor start from that assumption."

"Of course not," Lancaster agreed, taking up his place in front of a wall of monitors. Ever since they had been distracted by the Liberty Bell alert, he saw to it that there were command centers in virtually every major room in the HQ. "Not when they still have hundreds of our soldiers being turned into God-knows-what."

"Your God has nothing to do with it," said a voice that was obviously Mahasona.

Every member of the team froze where they were, then started looking for where the voice could be coming from. Key placed his left ear near Daniels's still covered head and mouth. Safar started reprogramming the translator furiously. But Lancaster pressed his forefinger into his own ear, then waved at the others before pointing to his auditory canal.

"Yes, yes, naturally," Mahasona told them all through their ear-comms. "While I crushed the devices that blocked your minds, I saved one communication device for just such an occasion as this."

Everyone looked to Key, who looked only at Daniels. "White flag, Dr. Dearden?" he asked simply. He and Lancaster were certain the blood demon would know the meaning. The tradition had started as far back as the Han Dynasty and Roman Empire just a hundred years after Christ's crucifixion.

They all heard the blood demon smile patiently. "White flag, Major Key. And please, don't call me by my assumed name. I don't suppose you'd consider calling me 'Master.'"

"Not yet," Key immediately replied.

Everyone, maybe even Daniels as well, was amazed and riveted by the civilized conversation, as well as what seemed to be the blood demon's subsequent chuckle. "Oh, save me from the man with a sense of perspective and humor," the creature said. "That's been the problem all along, you see. I've spent too much time dealing with the likes of Craven, Logan, and—well, we'll just leave it at that."

"Good idea," Key replied drily, knowing that the creature was about to include Rahal in his list. "What can I do for you, Dearden?" He stressed the name, putting an end to the question of monikers. He would not call him "master" in any form.

They all heard the creature sigh. "I was thinking of asking you the same thing, Major. It seems we're at something of a—what do you racist Americans call it? A Mexican standoff."

Key was unfazed by the baiting comment. "How do you figure that?" he immediately retorted.

"Oh, come now."

"No, I have ideas," Key interrupted. "I just wanted to hear your take."

The creature sighed again. "Oh, very well. I suppose that's the cost of establishing communication between our races. I believe the term 'Mexican standoff' started in the seventeenth century when a bandit told a tourist that he would take his money but spare his life. Over the eons it has come to be thought of as a situation in which no one in a confrontation can safely advance or withdraw. I believe that is what our little conflict has become."

Key and the others played out all the variations in their minds. Cerberus's position was severely hampered by the hostages the blood demons had, as well as their shape-shifting and infection abilities, no matter how weakened.

However, the blood demons had suffered setbacks, no matter how minor, with every direct contact with the Cerberus team.

"Well," Key shrugged. "As contactor, you have the right of first offer. What do you propose?"

"Can't you guess?"

"Rather not."

They all heard another big sigh. Lancaster looked to Key, but he was still staring at Daniels's covered head. Realizing that the team leader needed his full concentration, Lancaster looked to Nichols instead, but she only stared at Key.

"You cannot destroy us," Mahasona told them. "We have existed for millennia. It is too late. There are too many of us."

"Not what I heard," Key retorted flatly.

"Consider your sources," the creature suggested smoothly. "This—skirmish—is only our latest rise and fall and rise again. Through the centuries, our kind has fed on your kind. And there were many years when they—we—stole essences—leaving your kind alive, but soulless."

"Well, that explains a lot," Key muttered, thinking about the people who made, and ruined, history.

"Yes," Mahasona promised. "You will never be rid of us, because you'll never know for sure who is us and who isn't."

Key snorted impatiently. "You call that a proposal?"

"No," the creature said flatly. "That was the preamble. This is the proposal. Surrender to us, Major. We will leave your kind alone and return to the shadows if you and Corporal Nichols—the only two who can truly threaten us—give yourselves to us."

Key's eyebrows rose. He knew better, but responded anyway. "What sort of deal is that?" he complained. "What's in it for Nichols and me?"

This time the creature laughed. "Eternal life."

"Eternal hunger, you mean," Key corrected.

"Safety for your species," Mahasona countered.

"When you, your consorts, Nichols, and I aren't feeding on them?"

The creature took a moment to consider that. "Relative safety for your species, then," he amended. "After all, we've always fed on humanity, and you didn't really even know it until recently. Besides, you know as well as I do that we cannot be killed, and have always been, and always will be, with you."

"Again," Key snapped, "not what I've heard."

"Again," Mahasona replied in tones that held complete assurance. "I strongly advise you double-check your sources."

Finally, Key lost his temper—already feeling like a failure because he had let the creature hit his soft spot. "Sources?" he barked. "My source can't say a fucking thing for the very reason I know you're lying. She can't talk because she's—"

Dr. Helen interrupted him with a noise. It was a cross between a hiss and a click made by snapping her tongue on her teeth. Finally, Key looked away from Daniels's covered head. He looked over to where Dr. Helen stood in the entrance to the quarantine unit, holding onto a rolling examining table. An examining table on which Eshe Rahal was propped up on her bent elbows.

Key didn't appear to move, but in everyone's mind they saw his jaw drop, his heart sink, and his stomach turn over.

Her neck had grafted back onto her body with what seemed like hundreds of flesh hooks that appeared to be melting into each other. Her facial muscles were twisted and her skin discolored as her infected system seemed to be struggling for some kind of control she couldn't understand. Her limbs and fingers twitched as they sought some sort of system with which to exist.

Safar couldn't help but think of a smartphone searching for a service signal or Wi-Fi, only this was from a reactivated brain searching for lifeblood or life force. No one said anything. The only one who would have been so crass as to speak at that moment was Daniels, but he was electrocuted and netted. Gonzales thought *fuckaduck* for him, but said nothing.

No one said anything until Rahal did. "I couldn't help it," she choked through a twisted mouth. "It's in the blood."

Chapter 31

Mahasona greeted them personally.

When the major and corporal landed in the F. B. Law—the heli-thing Gonzales had created to help rescue Nichols from her captors when she was being experimented upon to create the first weaponized Arachnosaur-human hybrid—the blood demon was standing between the cliff opening the redhead had originally dove out of and a tall, statue-shaped cavern that used to showcase a Buddha statue. That was, before the Taliban had destroyed it.

Key took one look at what the creature was wearing, thought about shaking his head, but then decided to simply be honest. So he laughed. Mahasona, back in his Zaman face, was knowingly dressed in a three-piece tuxedo and red-lined cape.

"Save me from a monster with a sense of humor," Key shouted at him over the whine of the slowing rotors.

"Thought you might appreciate the irony," the false Zaman yelled back as the Cerberus soldiers emerged from the small, nimble aircraft. "You should have seen the faces of my followers when I demanded they find me this." The Maha-Zaman thought back on that moment. "It was in a Gaz Khun costume shop. They were as surprised as I was. Just shows you how pervasive our legend has become." He motioned for them to follow, then turned.

Key followed without hesitation. "Wonder if he has plastic fangs? Or, given the situation, real ones?"

Nichols grimaced. "The attacks, the assaults?" she whispered to Key as they followed. "That I could take. This chummy hypocrisy?" She motioned at the flowing cape and made an incredulous face. "Not so sure."

"We'll make the best of it, Terri," Key murmured. "Until we don't."

The Maha-Zaman stopped at a crevasse in the cliff wall. "Look familiar, Corporal?" he asked Nichols. "Not by location, but by design? We've become quite adept at creating entries that look like solid rock, even if you stare directly at them."

To prove his point, he slipped into the seemingly impassable crevasse and disappeared. Key looked knowingly at Nichols and followed suit, seemingly without fear.

Despite the further negotiations that had occurred over the comm-link after the surprise reappearance of Eshe Rahal—whose death turned out to be slightly exaggerated—the time between Cerberus's agreement to the blood demon's terms and the two agents' arrival at the Hindu Kush crypt was relatively short. The realization that the opposition couldn't be killed had a way of short-cutting any pesky details. The only real delay was the travel time needed for the heli-thing to get from Tashkurgan, and that seemed to take all day.

The Maha-Zaman led them through tunnels Nichols recognized. She had a nearly overwhelming fantasy of unleashing a flame-throwing scythe on everything in sight, but, knew, even without Key's input, that it would ultimately only slaughter her own comrades while simply delaying their captors. The result would simply be that she would be infected by a burned body rather than a mind-massaging beauty.

Key, however, had other things on his mind. "So," he started. "You're the original, huh? The thing that started all the vampire legends?"

The Maha-Zaman shrugged. "Who can say? Certainly not I. All I know is that I have been feeding on humans for as long as I can remember, but it all changed when my companions started collapsing and withering away."

"Dying?" Key asked, perhaps too quickly.

The creature shrugged once more. "Again, who can say? What is death, Major? In my many millennia of observation, human death simply looks to me like a captain abandoning his desiccating ship." He glanced back at the humans. "As someone who feeds on life force and lifeblood, I can assure you I have never been tempted to take a bite out of your flesh, organs, or bones—contrary to some of your more elaborate legends that attempt to communicate our power." He turned back to pay closer attention to the cave networks. "No, our soulless simply were trapped in themselves as they disintegrated."

"Why didn't that happen to you?" Key asked pointedly.

Maha-Zaman looked back with a small, knowing, smile. "For the third time, who knows? I suppose that, perhaps, I was more careful and considerate with my diet." He turned away. "Not for me the 'McHuman.' No, for me, only the best would do."

"Like us?" Key mused.

"Don't flatter yourselves," Maha-Zaman tsked. "As you know by now, your little friend there nearly made me sick. What are you feeding her back at your fake palace? Chips and dip?"

They walked silently for a few steps before Key replied. "Maybe it was what you fed her that made you sick. Nothing like a little tongue and rocky mountain oysters to turn the stomach, huh?"

Maha-Zaman paused, turning back toward the soldiers. "No need to be crude, Major. Don't make me regret my peace offering."

"You call this peace?" Key immediately retorted. "This is a lesser of two evils if there ever was one. And all the civility in the universe can't disguise what you did to her."

Maha-Zaman surveyed the major coolly. "I suppose you feel you have nothing to lose by being blunt." His expression soured. "Don't be too sure."

"I'm never too sure, Dearden," Key said pointedly. "But I'm here, aren't I? So let's get on with it."

There was a moment when the two stood their ground, but then, as if becoming aware that he was the host, Maha-Zaman bowed slightly and returned to the path. Finally, their calm, almost unctuous, host turned the corner of another camouflaged crevasse.

"I will admit," he said, "that I was relieved that you so readily saw the futility of continuing to fight."

Key followed the creature into the second crevasse, and shrugged. "Don't believe in beating a dead horse," he sighed.

"Ah, yes," said the Maha-Zaman. "Politician John Bright, yes? 1860s England, I believe."

"I'll take your word for it," Key replied.

The creature mirrored Key's shrug. "Just trying to make your transition as pleasant as possible," he assured them. "'If you can't beat them, join them,' yes? Senator James E. Watson, 1932."

Key shook his head. "Now you're just showing off," he complained.

"Actually, trying to prepare you for the sight that originally sent Corporal Nichols running," the creature explained. "If anything will make you back out at this late date, it will be that."

"She already gave me a full debriefing," Key said, somewhat petulantly. "And I'm already convinced of the cost if I back out now."

"Yes. A full-scale battle against an enemy that cannot be killed—one that you could not win no matter how hard you tried—would be ugly indeed. Still…" the Maha-Zaman said cautiously, then stepped out into the main cavern, turned, and spread his arms.

Nichols's words had not communicated the full, gut-punching effect of the blood demon incubation chamber. The literally inhuman sight of the perfectly stacked and layered bodies interwoven with glowing webbing that both fed, and fed on, them was bad enough, but added to that the smell of both preserved and rotting flesh was enough to make Key dizzy.

He took a step back, but felt Nichols's hand on his arm. When his vision cleared and his equilibrium returned, he saw that they had been joined by Rita Jayson in her open-shirt, slit-skirt uniform, as well as the men who had surrounded Nichols during her fight with Daniels.

Behind them were many more villagers, all carrying their rifles and knives. Key counted at least thirty, who lived up to their reputation by surrounding the Americans again—only this time with the master and his consort within the circle as well.

"Welcoming committee?" Key guessed.

"You could say that," Maha-Zaman said

"Do they know your secret identity?" Key wondered aloud, certain that the witnesses didn't understand English.

"Would it matter?" the creature mused. "These people are willing to blow up themselves and babies. All you need to do is give them a reason they can die with."

"How is Morty doing?" Jayson interrupted with sardonic self-assurance.

Key was unimpressed. "Speaking with forked tongue," he replied. "As if you didn't know."

"I look forward to seeing him again," she quickly added, while placing her hand on Maha-Zaman's shoulder and her thigh over her master's leg.

Key raised one eyebrow. "Speaking of showing off," he muttered. "Into threesomes, are we?"

Maha-Zaman smiled with no offense. "The more, the merrier," he replied, motioning at the gestating bodies of the captured Marines.

"Then I look forward to our first night," Key said.

Maha-Zaman reacted as if he had just remembered a trifling point. "Oh, yes," he breathed. "About that—"

Key stilled at that comment. He reached over and carefully placed Nichols behind him. "About what?" he asked slowly.

"Well, my dear Major, my dear Corporal," the Maha-Zaman said with pseudo-sadness. "I already articulated that our only true threat is you two. So, could you imagine what mischief you might get up to if we made you one of us?"

"You lying bastards," Key started, backing up only as far as the circle of terrorists would allow.

The false Zaman reacted as if complimented. "Well, after all, I am Mahasona, the great demon. You were expecting truth?"

Key felt Nichols shaking against him, her face buried in his shoulder, until three of the terrorists surged forward and grabbed her by the arms, dragging her away from her team leader.

"No!" she cried, writhing in their grip. "No!"

"Yes!" Jayson shrieked as the Maha-Zaman let his cape drop to the cavern floor. The powerfully sensual consort walked indolently over to the corporal and gripped her chin in one claw. "But don't worry, my dear. The master will not sully himself with your tainted blood. Not again."

She spun on Key, whose face had set in shock. "But you. You will get the rare pleasure, the supreme honor, to experience what only your most sordid ancestors experienced. You will get to find out where the true legend of the vampire originated!"

She hadn't even finished the word "originated" before the creature in the three-piece suit was on him impossibly fast, and with incredible strength. Key was slammed to the ground, the creature's hands a blur as they knit firmly into his hair, pulling one way, and clasped tightly around his chin, as if it were a doorknob, pushing another.

Before Key could even react to the initial onslaught, he felt teeth plunging into his dorsal scapular artery, and saw blood—his blood—spurting into the creature's mouth.

Nichols howled in fear and rage, but that only returned Jayson's attention to her. "Shut up, you bitch!" she snarled. "You should be so lucky! By the time these men get done with you, you'll beg for Mahasona to drink your blood. But even then, no! I will dance on your bullet-ridden flesh!"

"Enough!" they all heard Charles Leonidas Lancaster boom. "Now!"

Chapter 32

Everyone except Mahasona, Key, and Nichols looked around the cavern for the source of the voice. But when Jayson returned her attention to the redhead, Nichols was not where she had been—and the men holding her were already trying to staunch the blood erupting from their faces and throats.

Jayson turned to see where the girl had gone, only to wind up staring into the widening neck of one of the terrorists—who Nichols was holding by his hair and chin, aiming his sliced-open throat. A moment later, his jugular vein gushed a torrent of blood directly into the brunette's stunned face.

At the same moment, Key's left hand came hurtling across his shoulders to slam into the Maha-Zaman's upper face, his thumb going into the creature's left nostril and his first two fingers going deep into the Mahasona's only recently healed eyes.

Once blinded, twice shy, so the Maha-Zaman recoiled away as if being yanked by a cable. Key was up almost as impossibly fast as the creature, already pressing his bunched Cali-brake jacket against his throat punctures.

"Good performance, huh?" he croaked, hunched down and gasping. "You assholes have gotten jaded, arrogant. You think any human is stupider than you, huh? Think again." He turned to see Jayson running from the chamber into the curve of the camouflaged crevasse. He dismissed the Maha-Zaman with a wave of his hand. "Let him have it."

Key then hustled after the woman, frustrated that he had to miss the execution of his plan, but Nichols had been too busy killing the rest of the terrorists with her razor-sharpened fingernails to prevent the brunette's exit.

As Key slipped through the camouflaged corner he caught a glimpse of a dark figure rising from the stacked and layered bodies, holding a handgun with a goblet-like muzzle and multi-banded barrel. Desperate to stay to see if it worked, but equally desperate to leave no loose ends, he squeezed through the opening as something began to course out of the goblet and curve through the air toward Maha-Zaman—something interwoven and filmy, like Silly String mixed with cotton candy.

But then Key was in the tunnel, staunching the flow of blood from his neck as he chased the woman, whose slit pencil skirt and high heels slowed her down just enough for him to start catching up. As muddled as his thinking was after the attack, he knew she could have thrown off the shoes and torn the skirt into a more sprint-friendly loincloth, but she hadn't.

Maybe it was because the horrible screams and whomping detonation that came from back in the cavern had unnerved her. Maybe it wasn't. But, for whatever reason, he eventually slid to a halt in what was obviously her chamber. It was filled with jewels and treasures from many famed eras of history. It actually looked like any Middle Eastern potentate's parlor, only every single item, from rug to bed to pitcher, was a glorious, plundered work of art.

She stood before him in her standard low cut, high slit outfit—the one both Craven and Daniels knew so well—but with a face that combined the soulful eyes of Rahal, the flaming hair of Nichols, and the lips of Kay Arnold, Key's high school prom date.

Key nearly doubled over, trying not to laugh. "Tajabana," he said. "You look terrible."

Her face registered surprise, dismay, and insult. "It is only a reflection of your own mind!" she accused angrily. "I am beautiful. It is your thoughts that are not."

"Naw," Key countered, keeping his distance as her face wavered in his eyes. "Just an echo of my chaotic condition." He placed one hand flat on the rock wall and leaned on it while keeping the pressure on his still bleeding puncture wounds. "You're trying so hard to massage my mind that it's coming out muddled." He looked up, directly at her eyes, whose colors were swirling from brown to blue to green to red. "You know it's over, right? It's been over for a while, hasn't it?"

She looked shocked, then grew wide-eyed and strident. "It is not over," she declared fearfully. "Not while Mahasona lives! We are all merely his victims. Go! Go stop him, by any means necessary!"

Key shook his head, trying to clear his thoughts and keep up his strength. "That's what I'm trying to do," he sadly assured her. "Stop Mahasona."

"What do you mean?" she asked in a tiny, trapped, voice.

"You are Mahasona," Key told her flatly. "Like Aarif Zaman's face on your poor dupe out there, Rita Jayson and even Tajabana were the faces you wore to protect your true identity. Isn't that true, Mahasona?"

When she just stared, seemingly motionless, Key breathed deeply. "I agreed with our Filipino vampire expert, you see. Male egotist storytellers changed the sex of the greatest blood demons over the years, but even then, the huge majority of the most powerful legends were female."

Key looked back up at her, noticing she was one step closer to him. He compensated by leaning his entire back against the wall. "Besides, your dupe wasn't very good at maintaining his disguise, was he?" he mused. "Constantly making mistakes, blustering rather than dominating. Where'd you get him anyway? Bargain basement sale at the Roman Colosseum? Last vampire standing?"

There was a significant pause. Key just waited, and sure enough, it was the woman who broke the silence. And when she did, it changed the timbre of the room entirely.

"Just a terrorist I turned," she sniffed, all pretense in her voice gone. "The tallest, strongest one of Zaman's followers I could find. Just one in a long line of fronts, I'm afraid." She looked knowingly, as well as apologetically, at Key as she took another step. "A girl's got to eat, and 'beggars can't be choosers,' John Heywood, 1562."

"Showoff," Key automatically said as he leaned back even more. "Is Morty Daniels scheduled to be your next present consort and future meal?"

The brunette seemed to be considering it, but not for the first time. "Who knows?" she said idly. Then she raised her head and locked eyes with him. He noted that her visage and form had taken solid shape as a feminine ideal—seemingly a combination of every optimal female trait she had experienced over her millennia.

Her hair was lustrous and thick. Her eyes were a combination of hazel and violet her nose straight and dusted with light freckles, and her mouth rich and rose-colored. The body had settled into a smooth, supple, strong, crowd-pleasing thirty-six, twenty-four, thirty-six. The ears and feet were perfectly shaped.

"Why not you?" she suggested gently.

Key only grinned weakly and listlessly waved her away. "I'd only be a disappointment," he promised her.

"Not at all," she countered, taking another step toward him. "I can honestly say you are the most remarkable man I have ever met."

"Human man, you mean."

She made a dismissive face with a slight wave of her hand. "Human, *vaempayar*," she sniffed, using her original Sinhalese language. "What's the difference now? You know as well as I do that as long as I live, this will never end. And I will always live, so why not let the deal stand?"

"What deal?" he asked softly.

"Let me walk away," she immediately replied, leaning toward him, starting to reach for him. "Come with me, or not, but let me walk away and I promise I'll return to the shadows. I promise not to try re-raising my army. No one will know I am there. Like before. As it ever was."

Key breathed deeply, and started to shake his head.

"No, no," she pleaded, actually taking his face in her cool and warm hands. "Don't say that, don't decide. Not yet." Her own head moved in rhythm with his, trying to find his eyes again. "Because you know, don't you? You know the alternative. I will walk away, no matter what you do."

That did it. Their eyes locked, and this time neither looked away.

"What did you do to my front out there?" she asked him imperatively. "Electrify him? Net him, like you did the others? Do you think I can be electrified, netted, strapped down? Many have tried, all have failed. You will fail. You have only three choices. Either watch me go, go with me, or be one of the dead behind me."

Her head was lowered to his shoulder. He felt her cool hands on his hair and on the fingers holding the jacket. Her hands felt good, even healing. He did nothing when she moved the Cali-brake away and tenderly fastened her succulent mouth on his seeping puncture wounds.

He gasped, then sighed, closing his eyes and murmuring. "You certainly set the bar high for us," he whispered. "We had to create an EQ so effective we were essentially invisible to you. But not to your followers. So we decided only one or two should risk infiltration while you gloated."

He waited until he felt her tongue lick the wounds, then suction onto them, the tip of her tongue pressing against the larger of the two punctures.

"Nichols was already here. You know about her, right? Tainted blood. Living proof that your food chain is already irrevocably compromised. So that gave us a fourth choice." Key looked sympathetically at the woman who was undulating against him, suckling his life liquid, pressing him to the cave wall. "Kill you."

The bone-needle inside her tongue plunged into his wound. He felt the infection starting to pump in, but rather than recoil, he grabbed her hair and held on for dear life.

"You know why her blood is tainted?" he asked while his other, now gloved, hand rose above her face. "Because someone tried to make her a weapon. This weapon!"

He smacked his Arachnosaur-web-covered glove onto her flesh as his blood streamed into her.

Mahasona shrieked and tried to get away, but Key would not let go.

"'It's in the blood,' Eshe told me," he choked. "That gave me the idea."

Mahasona started to spasm in his grip, her skin reddening and her entire body getting increasingly heated.

"My blood is tainted, too," he hissed. "I gave Nichols a blood transfusion. So guess what Arachnosaur webbing does to human blood? Go ahead, guess!"

Key wrenched her head away from his throat, splattering the cave wall with his plasma, then kicked her full in the chest, between her breasts, with the flat of his boot.

Mahasona slid back, still juddering, her mouth and eyes wide with pain and confusion.

"It makes it incendiary," Key spat at her. "Enjoy your very own personal big bang, baby."

With one hand Corporal Terri Nichols grabbed Key by the arm and threw him out of the way, bringing up an M32 Multiple Grenade launcher modified with an extended spray muzzle and two side-by-side tanks on its barrel. They ducked behind a solid-gold, sitting Buddha statue as Rita-Tajabana-Mahasona detonated.

Since Key's blood had not quite completely circulated throughout her body, the ignition was very messy. Her tongue ripped open, cleaving her mouth's upper palate, then her esophagus erupted, just before her sternum split open, tearing her chest from her clavicles to her gullet. Her stomach didn't so much explode as perforate and shred at the same time, splashing hydrochloric acid into her pancreas and gallbladder—both of which began to burn.

By then his blood had seeped into her liver, which popped like a crushed balloon, smearing bile across her intestines, which burst in a chain reaction until all her inner waste exploded out her rectum and sphincter, peeling her legs from thighs to shins.

The Mahasona went down like a slaughtered pig in a flesh sack, her robe awash in almost every liquid except blood—little explosions dotting every part of her body like her pores were erupting, self-immolating volcanoes.

Key staggered to his knees just in time to lock eyes with her a final time—immediately before his volatile blood seeped into her optic veins, tearing open her eyes like a half-dozen swiping razors. He both saw and felt Nichols surge to her feet beside him.

"Come back from this, bitch!" she snarled as she unleashed the fury of Gonzales's Fluoroantimonic Flamethrower on her.

Her impossible scream might have only been in their minds, but it was still a sound they could never forget. But it quickly died, because what the fire didn't incinerate, the acid dissolved, until her corpuscles couldn't be distinguished from the scorched stone.

"That Zaman-faced guy must've had more of your blood," she grunted to Key as she lifted him up. "He blew up and burned much better. Need help walking?"

But by then Lancaster, Gonzales, and Safar had encircled him, applying germ-killers, medications, and bandages, which Key gratefully accepted.

"Mop up in here," Lancaster instructed the others, while taking Key's arm. "Meanwhile, you come with me."

Since the major was certain the retired general wouldn't take "no" for an answer, he didn't give him one. Instead, he thankfully appreciated the assistance and walked out with him to see Brigadier General Logan in the Hindu Kush clearing, leading a brigade of new Marines and helicopters to rescue the incubating hostages.

As soon as he saw Key and Lancaster, he broke out in a huge, beaming smile—without even a hint of shit-eating—and gave them an unironic, even delighted, double thumbs-up.

"I *told* you we were smart to keep that spider shit!" he shouted at them.

Lancaster shook his head and continued leading Key toward Gonzales's S.H.E., which was parked in the forest clearing where Nichols had first taken on Daniels.

"Know what tonight is?" the retired general asked as he helped Key aboard.

"I ought to," Key sighed, enjoying the sensation of finally lying down on the bedding Gonzales had specially prepared for him. "The irony and coincidence of it was too great to ignore."

Key just managed to say it before his eyes closed and his brain happily accepted its well-deserved rest.

"It's the Night of the Demon."

Epilogue

"How do you know Mahasona won't come back?" Eshe Rahal asked in a thick voice. "After all, I did."

Josiah Key sat next to Rahal's bed in the intensive care unit of Cerberus's "mockatectured" Chinese Versailles headquarters. A phalanx of Chinese and Indian doctors both tended and studied her, not with disinterest.

Although she had reconstituted enough while the rest of them were battling in Hindu Kush, she still had months, if not years, of mental and physical recovery to deal with. At first glance she looked whole, but, on closer inspection, the seams showed.

As Gonzales told Key when he was awake enough to visit her: "It's like she had a stroke and polio at the same time." Speedy wasn't exaggerating.

"We don't really," Key answered her honestly. "Because, as far as we can tell, she was the last, and maybe first, of her kind, so we only have what we experienced and best guesses to go on. Because, Lord knows, we can't believe anything she told us."

"Why not?" Rahal managed to mouth, unable to keep hope out of her slurred voice.

Key sniffed, shrugging philosophically. "Near as I can tell, these *'vaempayar'* are like ninja. They need your fear to fool you into thinking they're unstoppable." He looked at her with a kind smile. "How did I know she was lying? Her mouth was moving. She had no reason to tell the truth."

Rahal looked concerned. "So she may come back."

Key frowned diffidently. "She may. Never say never. But it would be quite a trick." Key looked over toward an observation window, where yet another Lancaster command center had been constructed. "Chuck brought an electron microscope into the cave to see if anything of whatever served as blood demon DNA was identifiable. No luck. Besides, Terri kept burning and dissolving the area until the fire and acid fumes threatened to melt her skull."

He leaned back and took Rahal's nearest hand. "Besides, you're different. You were a victim, not the victimizer. As best as we can tell, there's definitely something to the legend that once the victimizer is destroyed, or, at least their human-shaped container is destroyed, the soul energy they've stolen returns to the victims. You, the hostage soldiers, and even the captive children seem to be bearing that out. That's how we can judge Mahasona is truly gone. I guess, just like everything else, there are checks and balances in the afterwards."

Key looked over when he felt her hand sidle out from his. He saw a face that was still afflicted, as well as haunted. She looked off to where Dr. Helen and her family were busy compiling everything they could about what had happened.

"I've still got a lot to learn," Rahal admitted before twitching in what could have been an attempt at a laugh. "Now that's a huge understatement. So, I think you should know that I won't return to Cerberus until I think I'm ready to truly help you. Or, at least do the opposite of what I did during this assignment."

If she was expecting Key to try dissuading her, she didn't know him very well. Thankfully she knew him all too well, so she wasn't disappointed.

"Yeah," he agreed, "but once Cerberus, always Cerberus. Lancaster got you covered." He patted her hand. "That's why I stay with this freak show. Best health care coverage in the business." He could tell she was embarrassed and uncomfortable, so he stood. "I'll let you get back to it."

He was on his way out when her labored voice stopped him. "What do you say at times like this? *Au revoir? Ciao?* Farewell?"

He smiled back at her. "You know me. I always like the truth plain and simple." He gave her a little salute. "Be seeing you." He left her wondering whether it would be in reality, dreams, or the afterwards.

Key enjoyed the exit from the sedate clinic and entrance into the Hall of Mirrors, where the sky always streamed in through the many tall windows. All roads led to that central hall, so he was not surprised to see Nichols, in Cali-brake T-shirt and bike shorts, coming out of the gym, patting her sweat with a fluffy, folded towel.

"Joe," she called, and he detoured to face her. "See Eshe?" He nodded. "So she told you, huh?"

"She told you first?" he wondered.

"Girl talk," said the redhead sheepishly. "Commiserating."

"Commiserating?" Key echoed. "Commiserating about what?" he asked, although he already thought he knew.

"She needed a break," Nichols admitted. "And I think I do, too."

He put a reassuring hand on her shoulder. "Can't say I'm surprised," he told her empathetically. "You didn't get to waltz through this one, did you? But you know as well as I do, we couldn't have done it without you."

That snapped her out of her regretful funk. "Oh, yeah, I know, Joe. And believe me, if you need me again, I'll be there." She paused and glanced away through the nearest window. "But if you don't—"

He clapped her on the other shoulder. "I know, I know, *'Ter, no wux,'* as some Aussies say. Cerberus got Eshe, Cerberus got you too. Whatever you want, need, or think best."

Suddenly she was embracing him with all her strength, which knocked the wind out of him. But he tried not to let her know that. So she got in a big, long hug before he started laughing and patting her on the back.

"You take care of yourself, Corporal," he suggested, "because I happen to know very well, you can."

"Yes, sir," she said brightly, her green eyes a little wet. "Be seeing *you*."

Then, thanks to her enhanced reflexes, she was gone, back into the gym.

"Took the words right out of my mouth," he murmured, and, now that he mentioned his mouth, headed for the cafeteria, which was still being run by one of Dr. Helen's relatives—who, apparently, had been a three-star chef back in Beijing. It had been so long since Key had a good, full meal, he realized he could probably eat an entire buffet.

As he was going in, he nearly ran into a laughing Daniels and Lailani, who were coming out, his arm around her shoulders.

"Bad timing," said the master sergeant with a big grin. "I just ate them out of cow, chicken, pig, cat, dog, and whatever else they put in that stuff." He hugged the Filipino to him and gave her an admiring smile. "Hungry enough to eat a horse, wasn't I?"

"And back to nearly normal I gather, huh, Morty?" Key asked.

"Nearly?" he retorted with mock chagrin. "Back and better than ever!" He looked to the ex-escort for corroboration.

She made a *"comme ci, comme ca"* motion with her right hand. "Almost," she said with a sarcastic smirk. "Just a little more practice."

Daniels, being Daniels, was undaunted. "Then what are we waiting for?" he exclaimed, slapping her on the rear. He winked at Key before following her to his quarters. "Back to the coal mines, Joe. Be seeing you."

And then, they too, were gone.

Thankfully, Key had just enough time for a bowl of ma po tofu and eggplant as well as pork, shrimp, and pineapple fried rice before Lancaster found him. The retired general leaned over the table and said only five words.

"Craven wants to say goodbye."

Without a word in reply, Key rose to follow his boss. They walked side by side through the gallery and garden before they reached the chapel. The original was dedicated to the patron saint of the Bourbons and consecrated in 1710. This pristine Chinese copy maintained the neo-classic Corinthian colonnade as well as its salon, where what was left of the child abductor awaited atop a small granite altar.

"I suppose he was able to hold on until you awoke since Mahasona had infected him just enough," Lancaster told him quietly. "But he has been eroding steadily since his attack on you, and your destruction of her."

Dr. Helen's acupuncture needles were gone, as were most of his legs. Only one shriveled stump remained, and even that was seemingly deflating as Key stepped into the polychromatic marble and white stone vestibule.

Encircling them was an amazing attempt to recreate the original's bas relief sculpture—*Louis XIV Crossing the Rhine*—only here reflecting the Chinese artistic vision of complex patterned decorations as well, with Louis's entourage reminiscent of terracotta warriors and Louis himself depicted as Buddha.

Key kneeled beside the creature who had started the whole thing and waited for the weak, watery eyes to focus on him. When they did, the erosion seemed to increase exponentially. As Key watched, Craven's hips and waist seemed to foam away, like the retreating wake of an ocean wave on the beach.

Craven tried to raise his arm, but it was already dissolving like ash at the end of a burning cigarette. So, instead, the sides of his lips twitched, as if attempting a final smile.

"*Maa Durga*," they heard him whisper. "*Dhanyavaad.*"

He had called Key by the name of the most venerated Hindu deity that mixed the Royal Bengal Tiger and the Great Lion. But he had saved his last breath to gasp, "thank you."

Then Lancaster and Key watched as the tormented tormenter turned to dust before their eyes.

About the Author

Richard Jeffries holds a degree in Creative Writing, obtained before he went to work for American intelligence. He has seen the world—and things in it—which inspired the writing of these novels. Now retired from covert ops, Jeffries divides his time between rural Connecticut and London. In his spare time he pursues his lifelong interest in Kung Fu and classical piano.

Printed in the United States
by Baker & Taylor Publisher Services